Dedication

*To all Sister Witches, wherever they may be,
whether they be sisters by blood or sisters of the
heart. . . .
Because the Sister Witches aren't always
connected by blood.
They're connected by power, shared and used
wisely.*

~Mother Shipton~

Mother Shipton and the Sister Witches

Jude Pittman and Gail Roughton

BWL Print 9780228615187
B&N Print 9780228615200
LSI Print 9780228615194
Amazon Print 9780228615156

BWL Publishing Inc.

Books we love to write ...
Authors around the world.

http://bwlpublishing.ca

2nd Ed. Copyright Jude Pittman and Gail Roughton 2020
Cover Art Michelle Lee

Chapter One

Lillian

Lillian Shipton surveyed the wind beaten garden with solemn brown eyes and muttered to herself as she shook her head. She picked up a bent vine heavy with pods and frowned at the broken stem. Another week and the pods would have been fat and round, but last night's windstorm had torn the vines from the network of rope supports that held them off the ground and piled them into broken heaps in the dirt. *I guess there's nothing for it, these peas must be picked.*

She shouted towards the barnyard. "Billy! Grab a couple of pails and bring Nell. We're going to have to pick all these peas so I can get them canned this afternoon."

A tall skinny boy sporting a crop of brown hair and an Alfalfa topknot, poked his head around the corner of the barn. "Nell's over gathering eggs. I'll help her get them inside and we'll be right over."

Lillian nodded and smiled at her younger brother. Bill was a good kid and a big help. He'd be along as quick as he tended to Nell and the eggs.

While she waited, Lillian's thoughts drifted back to last night at the Lindale dance and young Ben O'Sullivan. A smile softened her face and her eyes sparkled. She'd tell Mom this afternoon, before Ben showed up at supper time, but just for a little while longer she hugged the knowledge to herself. That very special understanding that Ben was going to ask Dad for her hand. Oh, the excitement of it all! She loved Ben with a passion few, except her mom, realized the serious young girl possessed. A middle child, between three older sisters and a younger brother and sister, Lillian had assumed the role of family cook almost from the day she was able to reach the kitchen table. Neither her mom nor her elder sisters had cared much for kitchen duty – as they referred to it – and they'd happily surrendered that domain to Lillian.

* * *

Ben O'Sullivan sat on the front porch of the old log house where he'd lived with his mom and dad and two younger brothers for the entire 20 years of his life.

In his hand he held a letter he'd just picked up from the shiny aluminum mailbox that stood like a sentry at the front of the driveway leading into the O'Sullivan farm.

Well, if that ain't a helluva thing. Ben read the message one more time just to make sure he hadn't misunderstood. He knew full well he hadn't but just in case.

Mr. Benjamin O'Sullivan, we have reviewed your medical records and our previous disqualification has been overturned. You are hereby ordered to report to the Canadian Forces Leadership and Recruit School in Saint-Jean-sur-Richelieu, Quebec on 29 May 2001.

Back in December Ben had made up his mind that with two younger brothers fully capable of taking on his share of the farm work, it was time to set aside personal ambitions. Several of his school friends were already in Afghanistan on Canada's latest peacekeeping mission and Ben figured it was time he stepped up to serve his country. He'd caught a ride into Edmonton with Frank Miller the following Monday and while Frank took care of business Ben took care of all the paperwork required at the recruitment office. The rejection letter, citing his less than perfect eyesight, had arrived two weeks later and had been a major blow to Ben's ego and his morale. Eventually though, he'd made peace with the decision. That had been over a year ago, and just last night, on the 30th of April, at the dance where he'd taken Lillian Shipton to celebrate her 18th birthday, Ben had asked her to be his wife and she'd accepted.

Now what was he supposed to do?

* * *

Lillian fairly danced through the front door of the Shipton farmhouse when Ben dropped her off after the dance. Finally, after all the years of waiting, the fairy godmother's wand had waved in her direction.

She'd met Ben O'Sullivan in first grade and from the day he grabbed onto the braids her mother had woven out of her thick brown hair, there'd never been anyone else for Lillian. Oh, it had taken several years of scrapping and competing at everything from fishing to baseball, but Ben had finally realized that his first grade nemesis was in fact the love of his life and Lillian had been waiting ever since her 16th birthday for him to finally declare himself.

Last night, on her 18th birthday, when their parents' arguments of "you're much too young" would at least be partially appeased by the fact that everyone expected Ben and Lillian to marry one day, Lillian's dreams had come true when Ben popped the question.

* * *

Three weeks. She and her Ben had had three weeks together after their marriage before he shipped out to Afghanistan. Two months later an IED took his life. and Lillian never remarried. She'd never had the desire or the need, and as for children of her own, well, if she'd never physically given birth to any, she'd helped raise a large family of them and besides, all her nieces and nephews were the children of her heart, because she'd known tragedy even before fate had taken Ben away from her. Maybe the steel forged in her soul by the earlier tragedy was the reason she even survived the second and the echoing sounds of the IED blasts that were all she could hear for days—no, weeks—after his death.

The third oldest of five sisters and three brothers, fate had decreed that she'd taken an even more active role in their sibling's lives than did most big sisters in large families. When Lillian's older brother Edward had died with his wife Alice in an auto accident leaving their three-month-old daughter Katherine, Lillian's parents had come closer to breaking than Lillian would ever have thought it possible for humans to come and still recover. No parents should ever have to bury a child and even at seventeen, Lillian understood that as much as her own heart ached, her parents' grief was distinctly different from hers. She'd stood outside her parents' door and heard her mother's sobs in the darkness of the night after the funerals.

She'd known instinctively that her parents would never truly heal; they'd simply find a way to make peace with this new reality that had so brutally torn her family in two— eventually. She could think of no way to help, other than to take as much off her mother's shoulders as she possibly could. Katherine was barely past newborn. Irene, the family youngest, was only three. A holding baby and a toddler were more than enough for any woman to handle, especially one who'd just buried her oldest child. So it was that Lillian came to be her younger siblings' self-appointed substitute mother. The bonds between herself and her younger brothers and sisters were tied with double knots. Family was her *raison d'etre*.

Still, she had no wish at all to remain at home, the old maid daughter, sister, aunt, dependent on family for the roof over her head and the clothes on her back. Ben would be ashamed of her. So when the grief of his passing dulled enough such that she could actually hear voices and follow conversations again, she took the widows' military benefits she was entitled to as Ben's wife and invested them in the best business education she could obtain. The concentration necessary to graduate from Wharton School of Business *summa cum laude* further helped reduce the echoing blasts of the IED she couldn't stop hearing. As a professional woman, and because hearing Ben's name stabbed her heart anew every time someone called her O'Sullivan, reminding her she was a Mrs. without her Mr., she'd kept the Shipton name, and after a successful career in the stock market—so successful she'd retired at forty—she'd spent the next seven years as a roaming family trouble-shooter. How she always knew which family member needed her and when remained a mystery to all, especially since the Shiptons were a large and far-flung clan, spread over a large geographical area. Sometimes she wasn't sure herself, but she'd learned long ago not to argue when that inner voice told her, *you're needed. Go.*

Chapter Two

Katherine

Semi-tropical breezes and swaying palms danced with the moonbeams bouncing off white caps. Katherine Shipton tilted her head and the scent of salt water tickled her nostrils.

"I could stay out here forever." She shook her head and a mass of dark brown hair tumbled over her shoulders.

A pair of tanned arms tightened around her waist.

"I hope I'm invited."

"This place is like an ad copy for Paradise."

"Paradise is anywhere as long as you're there."

"Hey, that's *my* linc!"

He pulled her closer.

Funny how life could change in the space of a heartbeat. Six months ago, she'd been in Tallahassee, engaged to another man. Now here she was on the balcony of a Tampa Bay beach house in the arms of her dream lover—jet black hair, smoky blue eyes and a smile that would melt ice.

"Care to share the thoughts that are giving you that glow?"

Her eyes sparkled. "Let me show you."

* * *

"If this is a dream, please let me sleep forever." Parker wrapped his arms around Katherine's back and rolled her on top of him. Her dark hair fell forward, framing her face and flowing across his white pillowcase. Her breasts heaved from their exertions and her brown eyes glinted golden.

"Mmmm!" She licked her lips.

Parker laughed. "I've got to leave early in the morning and we both need some sleep."

She shivered.

"You can't be cold."

"No. Just—I hate you being gone
for two weeks."

"You could come with me, you know."

"You're going on a business trip. You and your dad are cramming meetings on top of meetings. You don't need me along to worry about. Besides, I've got work to do myself."

Katherine's reputation as an up-and-coming artist had skyrocketed since her move to Tampa Bay, another sign she'd made the right decision. As if running straight into Parker Drayton's arms wasn't enough. Because that's what she'd done, literally. They'd collided in the sliding glass doorway of Macy's a month after her move, shopping bags flying everywhere. And the rest, as they say, was history and just went to prove the ironies of life. One of Katherine's niggling concerns during her engagement to Tallahassee attorney Quentin Ashland was the horror of being thought a gold-digger—a starving artist marrying a successful lawyer from an old southern family for money. Maybe because in the back of her mind, she'd been afraid it was true.

So what did she do? Without caring a damn what anyone thought, she'd tumbled head-over-heels in love with Parker Drayton, heir to Drayton International, a three generation Texas oil family.

"It's not like you'd be in a hotel room or anything. It's the family home in Houston. You could come out with me and set up a studio just the way you wanted it, God knows that house has plenty of unused rooms. So you'd have one here and one there."

Parker ran the Tampa Bay operations for Drayton International, specializing in the company's Gulf oil projects. Justin Drayton, Parker's father, and patriarch of the family stayed in Houston and ran central operations from there. A lot of their deals were the complicated kind, ones that required both of them to put it through. Parker traveled a great deal, Katherine knew that. It was a small price to pay for the gift of her perfect man. She'd go with him when she could, stay in place without complaint when she couldn't.

"I'll do that. But later. Right now I've got a couple of canvases already in progress, one with a really tight deadline I'll never meet if I let you whisk me off to Houston."

"Maybe you could surprise me when I got back. Like maybe finish that painting you've kept under wraps ever since you set up your studio here and show it to me."

"Or not."

"Or not. Artistic temperament and all that, yeah, I get it. Let's go to sleep."

"Let's."

* * *

Katherine flew through darkness. Dream darkness. Toward something. Sound barely audible coalesced and rose in volume, forming words. *Beneath these gray stone walls I stand, an ancient gypsy king...* The darkness lightened into shades of gray and a tower loomed.

A boat approached the tower. Inside, a woman, in Katherine's likeness. Not her, but near enough to be of her lineage. Floating over the woman, Katherine watched. A man, dressed as an ancient workman, fixed the boat against the steps leading up to the looming tower. Reaching down, he helped the woman from the boat, and pulled her toward a dark stairwell.

Another, in uniform, nodded to the oarsman, and took the woman's hand. His flickering torch gave barely enough light for the woman to make her way up the stone steps as she groped along behind him. The steps crumbled, and twice the woman almost fell when her feet slipped on the damp stone.

A fierce roar sounded in the night and Katherine knew it as a lion. The guard stopped in front of a scarred wooden door and pushed it inward. The flicker from his torch revealed a small barren chamber, with scant furnishing and a stone floor. Against the wall stood a crude bed with a single bed covering. The guard motioned the woman inside. She stumbled across the room and sank onto the bed. The guard used his torch to light a single candle. Then without a word, turned and left the cell.

The woman curled into herself. Great sobs shook her body.

Katherine floated back out into the courtyard. Standing in the corner an old man, dressed in the garb of a medieval gypsy, chanted.

"With heavy heart I bear the words of cruelest Mary Queen…"

Mary Queen? Tower? The scene changed in an instant, dream-fashion. Now she floated back to the cell. The same rough cot and threadbare blanket covered a still figure.

"These words I take in sorrow drear unto a lady fair…"

On cue, the woman rose from the cot and entered her dreams. Nobility for certain, possibly even royalty. Her time in the cell had dulled her eyes and matted her hair but yes, the chant was right. She'd been a lady fair. She would be so again, given fresh air and sunshine.

A lady who from birth was blest with visions strange but rare…

The door of the cell opened, and the old gypsy entered the cell.

"Tarot! My dear, dear friend! How good it is to see you!" The lady ran into his arms, and he held her to his breast.

"Milady."

"My grandmother. My husband and son. Is there news?"

"Your grandmother is well and fights ceaselessly for your release. Your husband— there's been no news from Russia. Except that he pleads for intercession from the Russian Court."

She smiled sadly. "I can just imagine how much he pleads. He is afeard he'll be tainted with the same brush that's painted me."

"No, Milady! He is doing all he can."

"Tarot, dear friend, 'tis a very bad liar you are, but I love you for it. Prince Frederick makes no effort on my behalf. He has abandoned me. As have all, in the face of the Queen's disfavor. All but you and Grandmother. And I bear them no ill for such. 'Tis asking too much to expect them to stand with me and risk a charge of witchcraft." She shrugged. "And for the prince, a chance to rid himself of a disappointing wife who only bore him one son."

"Oh, Milady! It hurts me so to hear you speak as though resigned to fate."

"Dear friend. Do not despair. My heart has always belonged to another, that fate sealed from childhood. If only I'd been stronger, surer! If only I'd followed my heart and run away with my Toby when—"

She broke off, her face losing all expression.

"Milady? What—a vision! 'Tis a vision you're seeing. Cease fighting them! Use them! Use the power!"

"I—Tarot, someone's watching us."

"Watching? I bribed the guards well. They have no cause to—"

"No, not the guards! Someone from— someone not here. Someone who sees us, who knows me. Knows me in her soul. Someone who can—dare I say it? Someone who can help me! Help me change the start of this disastrous path!"

In her dream, Katherine tried to leave, to get away. Enough of this misery that wasn't hers. Except it was. Somehow it was hers.

"Oh, please! Please don't leave! Help me! Help us!"

"How?" The dream Katherine spoke. *"How do I help you?"*

"I cannot tell you!"

"Then what am I supposed to do?"

"The portrait! Yes, I see it. There's a painting, a painting yet unfinished! 'Twill show

you the way! It must show you the way, or you will never be."

"Milady? Your vision speaks to you?"

"The portrait! The portrait will know!"

The portrait will know...the portrait will know...the portrait will know...

The words followed Katherine back through the depths of the dream and echoed in her ears when she woke, gasping into wakefulness.

* * *

"Kati?"

"I'm okay. Just give me a minute."

"You're shaking." Parker wrapped his arms around her and pulled her close. "Bad dream?"

"Horrible."

"What about?"

"I don't know. A lady in a tower. That painting I've never shown you. An old gypsy and a chant." She shuddered.

"It's just a dream. Try to relax, let yourself fall back to sleep. I'm sorry I ever mentioned that damn painting. Must have been what triggered this."

Parker adjusted the cover over them and slept again within minutes. She didn't. This dream…. She'd never had one like it. Except once. Not the same dream, but the same sense of urgency, of hidden messages of great import. The dream that sent her flying from Tallahassee and Quentin Ashland. Well, not the dream itself;

18

that wasn't quite right. The dream coupled with the painting under the canvas Parker had never seen. The painting that seemed to—*move*. The painting that spoke.

* * *

Katherine stared at the wrapped canvas on the easel. She'd been staring at it for two hours, ever since Parker had left for the airport and Houston. It hadn't moved, it hadn't spoken. It was an abandoned work in progress and nothing to be scared of, just the painting she'd started as a special gift to Mimi, the grandmother who'd raised her. An artist's recreation of the family legend passed down in her large and uniquely intertwined family. Mimi loved the story and repeated it at every opportunity.

Katherine had cut her teeth on that legend. Probably literally. She didn't even remember the first time she'd heard it; that's how long ago it had been.

Kitty-Kat, there's a very special lady back in your family tree. A lady with the gift of prophecy. Her name was Ursula, but people called her Mother Shipton. She helped sick people and sad people. Legend says she foretold great wonders, lots of things that've come true.

Was she your grandmamma, Mimi?

Lord, no, child, she lived generations ago. Four hundred years ago, in a time when kings and queens ruled. And she's actually on Poppy's side of the family, not mine, but I've always loved the stories and I've always felt very close to her. And that gift of prophecy… it's passed down through the years in the Shipton family, usually to the women, though not always. A gift from her, a legacy. A connection.

Katherine smiled at the memory. She'd never believed the stories, but she'd loved them. Katherine had researched her infamous ancestor just as soon as she'd been old enough to work her way around the internet, and it had been easy to confirm that though it might be debatable whether Mother Shipton and her prophecies had ever existed, the legend sure did. She'd waited for years to have the proper skill to do Mother Shipton justice and planned this portrait for her grandmother's sixty-fifth birthday. As frequently happened though, plans changed. Sometimes for the damnedest reasons. Hers certainly had, and that portrait never made it to Mimi's sixty-fifth birthday bash. She'd gotten the rough outline charcoaled in, Mother Shipton by her famous well, in front of her famous cave. Then she'd picked up the paintbrush. And Quentin had chosen that exact moment to come up behind and put his arms around her.

"Damn, honey, what the hell made you think of that for a painting? Who's going to want an ugly, wrinkled, old crone?"

First faint tingle of dislike.

"Excuse me? Some of the most beautiful women I've ever known are old and wrinkled.

There's great beauty in age. Wisdom. Life well lived."

"Well, you're an artist, after all. Beauty's in the eye of the beholder and all that."

"You won't want me when I'm old and wrinkled?"

"Hell, no. Goin' to trade you in for a newer model." He laughed. "Just jokin'. Of course I'll want you when you're old and wrinkled."

In that instant, she'd known. Known the truth. *Liar. No, you're not joking and yes, you'd trade me in. In a heartbeat.* His touch suddenly felt slimy. Unclean. She'd shrugged off his arms.

"Don't you have a trial to get ready for?"

"I don't get ready for trials, sugar, I just make deals. It's not how much law you know, it's *who* you know. And what you know about the jury pool."

"Well, I have a painting to work on. Mimi's present, remember?"

"Who?"

He really doesn't remember. Because he really doesn't give a damn. About me or anything about me.

"My *grandmother's* present. For her sixty-fifth birthday celebration back in Calgary. The one you can't go to with me because of your *trial* schedule."

"Oh. Right. Yeah, sorry about that sugar, but trials do pay the bills."

"And painting pays my bills, so I need to finish this while I'm waiting for last session's water color to dry on the Taylor commission."

"And that's called 'go away and leave me alone for a while', huh?"

"Yeah. It is."

"Okay, okay, no need to get bitchy about it."

"And close the door, please."

"Yes, *ma'am!*"

She'd stood for a moment after the click of the closing door, trying to re-center herself, to get rid of the sudden, intense dislike she felt for the man she was planning to marry, the man she'd lived with for the past year. And how? *How* had she been living with him for a year if his chance comment could trigger such a feeling of revulsion?

She squared her shoulders. Nobody liked everybody all the time. Of course he hadn't meant those cruel comments and certainly he hadn't forgotten about Mimi and her birthday party; he'd just been so focused on the trial he hadn't been thinking. And of course he was a good lawyer who knew the law, he didn't just rely on who he *knew*. Or what he knew about the prospective jurors. Did he?

She turned her attention back to the portrait. Mother Shipton's hand moved and she wagged her finger at Katherine.

Well, my lassie, it's a fine churl ye've taken into your bed this time, it is! Don't you have even a wee bit of the sight in those eyes of yours? Ye've got not a drop from me at all?

Katherine dropped the brush and backed away from the canvas. Slowly. Very slowly. She walked over to her canvas coverings and grabbed one, never taking her eyes off the portrait. She approached the painting once again. Then she ducked around behind the easel and threw the draping over the portrait, pulled it tight, grabbed the butcher's string she kept handy, and tied it up.

That night images from a Tarot deck flashed through her dreams. A rider on horseback who was Death. A woman on a throne, The High Priestess. An upside-down man suspended from a tree branch, The Hanged Man. And with every other card the same symbol appeared and re-appeared. The horned goat man. The Devil.

Memories of Quentin's touch filled her with revulsion. She'd awakened the next morning knowing she had to get out of there. She'd boxed up all her paintings and supplies, packed her suitcases and borrowed a friend's van. She rented a storage unit and made trip after trip to the unit until all her belongings and all her work was out of Quentin's house. Then she'd made a visit to Quentin's office. She couldn't tell him by phone or note that she was leaving him. It had to be face to face. It hadn't been pleasant, but she'd never regretted what she'd done those last two days in Tallahassee.

That had been six months ago. She'd accepted an offer she'd been mulling over from a well-respected Tampa Bay Gallery and fled Tallahassee and everything Quentin represented the minute she'd tied up details with her former Gallery.

She'd packed the portrait of Mother Shipton away in a closet of the Tampa Bay beach house. It was her home now. Any house was home with Parker.

She hadn't thought about the portrait since she'd moved in, not until last night—that dream. So real, the lady in the tower. *The portrait knows...the portrait knows.....* Right after Parker mentioned it, she'd changed the subject, but it must have stuck in her subconscious.

What was it about these dreams? The same theme. Danger. She knew that, somewhere deep in her soul. Mother Shipton's blood? *Oh, please.* Of course not. Just primal instinct. But the first time the warning had been specific. Danger. From Quentin? She hadn't understood it, but she'd known. What else would have made her bolt and run? This time, though—*help us! You must, or you will never be...* What was that all about? Would Mother Shipton tell her? She sure hadn't been shy about telling her last time. Even though it hadn't really been Mother Shipton at all, of course, just her subconscious beginning to knit together bits and pieces of this and that, weaving a pattern of reality into the pretty fantasies of Quentin and the man she pretended he was, when in fact, he wasn't.

Well, only one way to find out.

She approached the portrait and reached for the scissors to cut the string. Her phone rang. And her heart clenched. Quentin's ringtone. The one for his office number. She'd changed her number when she left Tallahassee, but she hadn't taken him off her contact list, not his cell, not his office. Not because she hoped he'd call—no, that good-bye scene hadn't been pretty at all—but because she wanted to know if he did call. If, in fact, he'd actually go to the trouble to find her new number. Which wouldn't take a lot, of course. She was an artist, she had business cards and she had to distribute her contact number. Still, Tampa Bay was a good distance from Tallahassee.

Answer it? Don't answer it? Hell, this was Quentin. Might as well get it over with. Because if he wanted to talk to her, he wouldn't stop calling until he did.

"Hello?"

"Well, well, she lives and breathes. Even if she hates the thought of talkin' to me so bad she changed her number."

"Didn't take much for you to find it, though."

"No, it didn't, did it? The new little darlin' of the avant art-fart circle."

"You phoned to call me names?"

"No, I called to congratulate you. Nice move. A Drayton. You must've had him waiting in the wings. Why settle for a lawyer's lifestyle when you can jet-set? Great pictures of you, by the way. The elegant artist and the rugged good-looking cowboy. The *paparazzi* have been busy. You two've been keeping them real happy."

Damn. Of course he knew. The Draytons were movers and shakers, no way news of her engagement hadn't hit the social circles all over Florida and Texas and probably quite a few other places, too.

"I didn't even know him when I left Tallahassee, Quentin, I'd never met him."

"You are such a good liar. Always were."

"Actually, I'm a very bad liar. Which is why I broke it off as soon as I realized we were making a mistake. So if there's nothing else, let's say good-bye, okay?"

"Oh, darlin'. We'll say good-bye for now. But I'm sure we'll be running into each other. Frequently. I might not be in Drayton's league but I ain't bush league. I'm sure we'll end up at some of the same parties. And don't worry. I won't tell anybody you've got a radar for money. Won't tell Parker what a hot little whore you can be in bed either.' Cause I'm sure you don't cut loose with him the way you did with me. Be too afraid of ruinin' that image I'm sure you're trying to maintain."

"How very considerate of you. And don't worry. I won't tell any of your clients your secrets of practicing law. As in it doesn't matter if a lawyer knows the law, just as long as he knows the right people. And some dirt on the jurors, of course. Good-bye, Quentin. Don't call me again."

Her finger was moving to the end button when his laughter chilled her bones. "That wouldn't bother my clients much, darlin'. Not at all. Because a good lawyer also knows where the bodies are buried. You take care now, you hear?"

Katherine pocketed her phone and cut the string on the portrait. She yanked off the coverings.

"Okay, Mother Shipton. If you *really* talked to me before—now's the time to talk again."

Chapter Three

Mother Shipton

Quentin Ashland slammed the receiver back down onto its cradle. Damn good thing he hadn't used his cell phone, or he'd have broken it. Again. He had a lot of anger management issues and they took one hell of a toll on his cell phones. They used to be sturdier in the days before the supermodels of the pocketsize mini computers came into vogue. And you just couldn't do without one anymore, either.

Little bitch! No, not just a bitch. A witch-bitch. Something about her—that quality of *otherworldliness* she wore so naturally she didn't even know she had it. That cloud of dark hair that floated around the slender shoulders, those dark eyes that lured a man into their depths, whispering of hidden passions, hidden secrets. He'd waited six months. Figured he'd let her get the independence out of her system. She'd be back. No way she'd want to give up everything they'd had together. Lifestyle, travel, parties, not to mention damn good sex. Then he'd turned on the news and there she was, his woman. And all he could see was Parker Drayton's smarmy looking face as the announcer babbled on about the impending nuptials.

No damn way that bitch was going to shake him off like so much dirt and move on up to royalty. He'd gone completely nuts. Then he'd calmed down. If she thought he believed that bullshit about not meeting Drayton till she left Tallahassee—what kind of fool did she take him for? Of course she left him because she smelled more money. Well, he wasn't from the Drayton definition of money, but he was an Ashland of Savannah, by God. Southern gentility. The type of background money couldn't buy, especially not lucky oil strikes back in the booming days of the Texas oil fields. Hell, they'd probably been sharecroppers. Probably why they'd struck out for Texas in the first place.

She wasn't going to get away with this. No way, no how. He wasn't just an Ashland. And he wasn't just any attorney. He laughed and reached for the phone. No, he wasn't just any attorney. He was an attorney who knew where bodies were buried. Lots of them. Time to remind some folks of that.

He punched in a number and waited for voice mail to wind down.

"We need to talk. Sandler's Oyster Bar. Tonight. Nine o'clock."

* * *

Katherine bit her lip. Moment of truth. Time to stop stalling. Of course it had just been coincidence that the picture talked to her— scratch that. She'd *thought* the picture talked to her at the precise time she'd seen Quentin for who and what he really was. And it was just coincidence she'd had that damn dream again the night before Quentin's surprise call out of the blue. Because that hadn't been a real surprise; she'd always known deep down he'd call. He couldn't just let go. It wasn't in him. Still and all, her Quentin epiphany came right after the portrait's ventriloquist act. The lady in the tower said the portrait had more to tell her. She had to give it a try.

She jerked the tarp off the portrait. And waited. Nothing. Of course nothing. She picked up a brush and loaded the bristles with cobalt blue.

With the first stroke, roaring filled the studio. Katherine dropped her paintbrush, slapped both hands to her ears. Well, she'd asked for it. And she'd gotten it.

"And about time it is, my girl. 'Tis stubborn you are." The same old crone she remembered stood in front of Katherine's easel.

"Why are you here? Why did I see you before? And why am I seeing you now?"

"You know why, child. In your heart, you know."

"What did you do to me last time? To make me cringe when Quentin touched me?"

"'Twas nothing I did. You did it yourself. You opened yourself to what you already knew was true. 'Tis in your blood, ye canna escape it. I just helped a wee bit with the seeing of it."

"That had nothing to do with blood. I just finally started putting things together about Quentin."

Mother Shipton shook her head. "Stubborn. But then all young folk be stubborn, can't complain, I was meself. And that stubbornness almost cost this family its very existence. Still might, do ye not listen to me with your head *and* your heart."

"Well, I'm not you. I'm me. And all I want to do is paint my pictures and marry the man I love."

"That might be all you want, m' dear, but 'tis not likely to happen unless ye listen to your dreams."

"My dreams haven't been exactly instruction manuals. I have no idea what they're telling me!"

"No, 'tis not that ye don't know what they're telling ye, it's that ye don't want to listen. Ye know full well there's something ye have to do, and now I'll tell ye more. If ye fail to answer the call or fulfill the task then ye will neither marry the man ye love nor paint yer paintings. 'Tis doubtful ye'll live a'tall. There's things need doin' in the past, or ye'll ne'er be born. Dreamed of a lady in a tower asking for help, did ye? And if ye pay no heed, the lives of all between me and thee will be forfeit."

"I don't understand."

"The lady in the tower. What's her name?"

"I don't know. I only heard her called Milady."

"True enough. Well, I'll give a bit of help with that. She was born Ursula Sontheil. And what's your name, child?"

"Katherine Shipton."

"Your *whole* name."

"Ursula Katherine Shipton."

"And why be that, do ye ken?"

"Because both those names have been in the family since the beginning of time and the back of beyond and—oh, *shit!*"

"Ah, so finally ye see a hint of sun over the horizon, do ye?"

"That's the reason? The connection? She's an ancestor?"

"Can't be telling ye that. Ye must see it for yourself. Time for a journey, child. A journey t'will help you understand. "

"I can't go anywhere. I have commitments, deadlines."

Mother Shipton cackled. "This journey— t'won't be like any ye've taken before. None will miss ye nor know you're gone."

"I'm having a mental breakdown. That's it, isn't it? I'm going crazy and you're a figment of my imagination."

"Kitty-Kat, please. Trust me, child. If I don't exist, I can't be after hurting ye, now can I?"

"Why'd you call me that? Nobody calls me that but Mimi!"

"Now what else would I be calling a girl named Katherine?" Mother Shipton moved to the sofa on the far wall. "Lie down, sweet girl. Let me soothe that wrinkled brow. And show ye—*wonders.* Wonders of the past."

Katherine backed up to the couch and sat down slowly, eyes fixed on the solid apparition.

Mother Shipton cackled again. "Well, 'tis a start. Ye don't trust easily and I can't be after expecting miracles. And a wee bit of caution and common sense bred into the bones over the years, that's a good thing. Ye think for yourself, don't take well to being told what to do. That lady in the tower, she could have done with a bit of it herself much sooner in her life, long afore she learned that lesson."

Mother Shipton laid her wrinkled hand on Katherine's forehead and rubbed lightly. "Close your eyes, girl. Lean back. And go visiting. To another time. Another place. Long ago. Very long ago. Float, Katherine. Float. None will see ye. None will know ye're there."

* * *

Katherine opened her eyes in an old barn, ripe with the good smell of animals. A girl, the mirror image of herself, lay sobbing into a pile of hay.

"How can I bear it?" the girl wailed. "How can I bear it?"

"Milady? What's wrong?" A young man stepped into view.

"Oh Toby, Toby." The girl flung herself off the hay and into the man's arms.

"What is it, Lady Ursula, what is it?" An unruly lock of straw-colored hair flopped into his eyes.

"King Henry! He's wedding me to Prince Frederick of Russia. I'm ordered to court. And I'm to wed the prince as soon as he returns!"

She gripped the man's neck and wept harder. "I must leave Gresham Manor in a fortnight and live at court."

Frozen into silence, Toby stroked her hair.

Long moments later, she moved from his arms and straightened her skirts. "I'm sorry. 'Tis wrong of me to burden you with my troubles."

"Milady, I'd give my life to see you happy. And I've no right to be saying what I'm about to say, but I know you! You'll wither and die at court. My family has a farm just across the border into Scotland. 'Tis not what you're used to but—"

She laid a finger across his lips. "Oh, Toby. Never could I do that. 'T'would disgrace Papa and break his heart. I've no right to speak this way, but I want you to now that I will always keep you in my heart and I'll never forget you."

* * *

Katherine jerked upright on the sofa and glared at the canvas lying face up on the floor.

No way that just happened! Schizophrenia? Multiple personality? Just crazy as bat-shit?

She picked up the portrait and placed it back on the easel. What time was it? She pulled out her phone and checked the time. Parker'd be calling from the airport when he landed in Texas. No missed call, though. And she'd only lost a few minutes in that psychotic break she'd just had.

At that moment Tibbins twined around her ankles, mewing. Katherine snatched the big white cat into her arms, hugging him so hard he growled. She laughed and loosened her grip. "Sorry, kitty. Getting hungry? Let's head to the kitchen." Tibbins didn't need another invitation. He bounded down the stairs toward the kitchen.

Katherine picked up his bowl and opened a can of tuna. "How about it, Tibbs, do you ever feel like you're going crazy?"

The cat kept his yellow gaze glued to the can in her hand. A cat on a mission.

"Guess not," Katherine said. "When would you have time to go crazy, between eating six meals a day and sleeping the rest of the time? Lucky you. Sleep." She paused with the spoon lodged in the can of tuna. Tibbs mewed impatiently. "Sleep, Tibbs. Is that it? I was asleep, you think. Narcolepsy? Could that be it?"

She emptied the can into Tibbins's bowl and set it down. Then she sprinted into the living room and switched on her computer for a quick Google search.

The most prevalent symptom of narcolepsy is suddenly and unexpectedly falling asleep during the day. In fact, narcoleptic attacks often occur at inappropriate times with significant consequences for those who experience them. For example, patients with narcolepsy may fall asleep while driving, during a meeting, and even during sex.

Well, she hadn't done that so far, but maybe it was a progressive disease.

Her cell phone vibrated in her pocket. Parker.

"Hello?"

"Hi! Is everything okay?"

"Of course. Why do you ask?"

"You sounded strange when you answered. Scared even. Must be the connection. Just wanted to check in and say I love you."

"I love you, too. And Parker?"

"Yes?"

"Oh, nothing. It'll wait till you get home. Be careful and think about me."

"How could I not? Bye."

Katherine leaned back in the chair and bit at her nail, wondering how to tell him she was either bat-shit crazy or likely to start falling asleep while having sex.

Tibbins marched past her and sat down at the front door.

"I suppose you want to go out there and chase birds," Katherine grumbled. "Let me get my shoes on, then. I definitely need a run this morning."

* * *

The run helped. Not enough to send her back to the studio and the portrait, but it helped. Besides, she had six weeks' worth of waiting correspondence and email. And wedding invitations. They'd arrived from the printer last week and nagged at her from the corner of her desk ever since.

Formal weddings were such a pain. And she'd had to fall in love with probably the only man she'd ever known who didn't think an elopement was a Godsend. He was right, though. A formal wedding was a great public relations opportunity for the Drayton Oil conglomerate.

Katherine sighed and shrugged. Might as well get to it.

She'd barely gotten settled when her cell phone rang. She'd have been grateful for any excuse not to address wedding invitations, but this call was welcome for other reasons. Katherine's relationship with her grandparents was two-fold, they were both her grandparents and to all intents and purposes, her parents. Bill and Mina Shipton had married young and gotten an early start on raising a large family. Katherine's father Ed had been the oldest of the Shipton kids, and Katherine had been three months old when he and her mother had been killed in an auto accident. Bill and Mina's little girl, Irene had been three. Since it would have been impossible to explain to a toddler why they weren't her Mommy and Daddy, but the baby's Grandma and Grandpa, they'd reinvented themselves and become Mimi and Poppy to both little girls, who were basically sisters rather than aunt and niece. The four of them were a very specially blended family within the framework of a larger family. Irene's ringtone delighted Katherine's ears. Exactly the person she needed to talk to now, even though she hadn't known it until right that second.

"Irene! I'm so glad—"

"Are you alright?"

"Well, hello to you, too!"

"Don't get smart with me, little girl! I had the weirdest dream last night, you were all curled up in a ball and tarot cards—*tarot cards,* of all things—were just *raining* down all over you!"

Katherine winced, the memory of a dream six months in the past washing over her again. Sure, the Shiptons joked about reading each other's minds, and Mimi always laughed and said Mother was at work, but this? Tarot cards? It had to be coincidence. She forced herself to laugh. "You and your dreams! They're just dreams, you know. Of course I'm fine, why wouldn't I be?"

"Then why'd you hesitate before you answered?"

Damn it! "Because it was just such an off-the-wall dream! Even for you! Shouldn't you be dreaming of wedding cakes and wedding gowns and bride's maid dresses? I'm not the only one getting married this year, now am I?" Irene's wedding was set for the month after her own.

"*My* wedding's under control, you're the procrastinator."

"So true, I'm staring at a big pile of wedding invitations right now."

"Stop staring and start doing. I've got to run or I'll be late for work."

"You're still home? But it's 11:00—oh. I always forget the time difference."

"Well, don't forget those invitations! Start addressing!" Katherine's cell clicked, indicating Irene had ended the call.

Katherine looked over at Tibbins. "Well, that was a nice reprieve while it lasted. But I guess I don't have any excuses left—" The doorbell chimed. "Wow! Saved by another bell, and aren't we the popular pair this morning? But I'm not expecting anybody, are you?" The cat yawned.

"I'll take that as a no, then." She pushed back the chair and peered through the peephole at her best friend and New York roommate during the starving artist years.

"Oh, my God! Carrie!" She threw the door open and flung her arms around the elegant blonde on the doorstep.

"Hey! Watch the hair! We international models have an image to maintain! Now let's get inside and you can tell me all about it."

"About what?"

"About whatever the hell's going on with you. 'Cause something damn sure is."

* * *

Parker Drayton frowned as he pocketed his phone. Something was up with Katherine. He didn't know what but whatever it was, she was on edge. Unnerved. One thing was certain, though. No way she'd tell him about it till she was ready.

"Parker!"

He turned his head to the left and smiled. It never failed. His father had radar where his children were concerned. He'd never yet not spotted one of them in a crowd in under ten seconds flat, not even in a crowd as big as the one at Houston's George Bush Intercontinental Airport.

"Dad! Hi!"

His father threw his arm around Parker's shoulders and hugged him. Justin Drayton was big enough to fit Texas. Tall, big boned, unabashedly unashamed to show affection in public.

"Glad you're here, son. Opportunity's waiting. Have I got a deal to tell you about!"

Chapter Four

Carrie

Back in Tallahassee, Quentin Ashland pulled out a private file. He had lots of private files. Like he'd told Katherine, he knew where lots of bodies were buried. This file though, this file wasn't one of those. This file was all about a body he'd *like* to see buried. Let's see now, where to start, what could he use?

He flipped through the news clippings reporting on the social comings and goings of the Draytons. A man should always know his enemies better than he knew his friends. He should know when they came and went and with who. Or was that whom and who gave a damn? What he cared about was the fact Parker'd just left Tampa headed for Houston on a long business trip. He needed to know where and when on that trip Parker would be most vulnerable. He could get the muscle for this, that was no problem, but he sure as hell wasn't just turning muscle loose without direction and tight hands on the reins. His hands.

He pulled out the folder holding the latest prospectus of Drayton International and flipped through the pages. He almost passed it, until the light bulb in his head exploded and shouted "Eureka!" Oh, it was disguised and shrouded under business rhetoric like "most cost-efficient", "highest and best use of existing resources" and "least possible adverse effects to the environment", but to anybody reading between the lines it was damn clear. Drayton Oil intended to renovate abandoned oil rigs off the Gulf Shore and put them back in operation. Which they wouldn't do without a hell of a lot of research and first-hand inspection. Parker Drayton was the company specialist in development. He'd be doing that first-hand inspection himself.

Quentin reached for the phone. Time to call in another individual with some bodies buried.

"I need some surveillance. In Houston."

* * *

"Damn, Dad!" Parker laughed and yanked hard on the door handle of his father's 1989 truck. He didn't have a choice about yanking hard, not if he wanted it open, damn thing had been sticking since 1997. The old workhorse of a truck wasn't even a fancy one, just a plain Ford F-150. "Real nice of you to bring the fancy ride to pick me up. How many miles on this thing now?"

"Heading toward 300,000." Justin Drayton threw the truck in reverse, backed out carefully, and began maneuvering out of the airport parking lot. "And I don't put it out on the road for just anybody. You should feel honored. I love this truck."

"Yeah, I know you do. But sooner or later, you're gonna have to bury it, you know."

"That's gonna be as later as I can make it. Best truck I ever had. And the only two things a man really needs in life is a good truck and—"

"And a good woman. I know, Dad."

"Yeah, I'm a lucky man. Man couldn't have had a better woman than your mother or a better truck than this one."

Parker smiled. His Dad didn't fool him a bit. His mother had ridden many miles in this truck with his Dad over the Drayton oil fields. For Justin Drayton, she still rode shotgun in the passenger seat, always would. And when this engine died, a new engine would go under the hood. His Dad would never let this truck go.

"I miss her, too, Dad."

"I know you do, son. But now you've found your good woman. We just must find you a good truck. You couldn't talk Katherine into flying out with you?"

"I tried, but she said she had deadlines on a couple of commissions. So what's this new deal you're all excited about?"

"Well, not so new. More *renewed*. You remember Bowman Oil went into bankruptcy a few years ago?"

"Sure."

"They had some Gulf oil rigs been sorta hanging in limbo, the trustees not knowing whether to sell 'em or try and put 'em back in operation. Bowman never was real good at picking drilling sites, you know. Those rigs never put out enough oil to be worth drilling."

"And something's changed now?"

Justin smiled. "You could say so. That new geologist you hired last year. The one with the real thick glasses?"

"Harrison. Sean Harrison. Wonder boy from Texas A&M. He scares me, he's so damn smart."

"Yeah, well. Those oil rigs. They're sitting on hidden black gold. Okay, not really. They're sitting *near* hidden black gold. And they'd save us a fortune if they're in good enough shape to move, I mean they're not a mile away from a really big field."

"You already got the leases to that field, I'm thinking?"

"Son! You really need to ask me that?"

Parker laughed. "No, of course not. But we'll need to check those platforms out with a fine-tooth comb. A year or two out there in the Gulf with no maintenance could've taken a real toll on 'em."

"That's your department, son. Got the company chopper standing by to fly you out for your preliminary. Whenever you're ready."

* * *

44

Neither Parker nor his father noticed anyone following them. Nobody was. GPS was a great thing, the best thing to happen to the surveillance industry since dark glasses. Well, maybe those electronic listening devices you could hook up anyplace and buy for twenty bucks on eBay gave the GPS trackers a close run for their money. Limited range, of course, but you couldn't have everything.

The man smiled as he listened to this father and son conversation while watching the truck move through traffic on his phone screen. This job was so damn easy he almost hated to take any money for it. Almost. Especially considering that old truck of Justin Drayton's was a legend itself within the Houston oil community. No problem to find it, no problem to plant the tracker. And no problem to unlock it to install the bug. Not with those 1989 locks.

He hit a number on his cell phone screen.

"Okay, I think this might be what you're looking for. Seems Parker Drayton's going to be taking a chopper ride out to the Gulf sometime this week."

* * *

Carrie lounged back against the sofa cushions and sipped from the tall glass of iced tea in her hand.

"Don't just lie there all languid and southern and keep me in suspense." Katherine frowned at her best friend. "And don't think I'm not glad to see you, but what are you doing here right *now*? Aren't you supposed to be in Paris getting ready for season debut?"

Carrie Bennington waved a manicured hand in dismissal. "I'm skipping the season this year."

"Excuse me?"

"Skipping. The. Season. That means I'm not going to be starving or busting my ass in a frantic tizzy backstage changing clothes and getting poked and prodded and yelled at in French and Italian and Spanish by egotistical little dictators."

"Oh, my God! Who are you? And what have you done with my best friend Carrie Bennington? The international model who lives and breathes for fashion? Where is she?"

"She's turned back into Sally *Benton*. The girl from the wrong side of the tracks in Plumnelly, Georgia. Which doesn't even *have* any tracks, now that I think about it, but you get my drift."

"Plumnelly? You did break down once and tell me you were from North Georgia, but you never told me exactly where. There's a town named *Plumnelly*?"

"Sho' nuff, darlin', cause it is *plum* outta Tennessee and *nelly* outta Georgia." Carrie rolled her eyes in rhythm to the exaggerated roll of vowels.

"You've lost your mind. That's the only explanation! After all you went through to get where you are? Have you forgotten our ratty New York apartment, all those Ramen Noodle and frozen pizza suppers? The only ones we could *afford?*"

Katherine and Carrie went way back. Back to their late teens, and a chance meeting in the lobby of a fashion magazine in that Mecca of all Meccas for starving artists and aspiring models.

"Carrie, you worked for years to get where you are! How often have you told me a high fashion modeling career has a set and non-extendable timeline and you intended to stretch yours as far out as it would go? If you miss a season, you're *done*, Carrie, you know that! So stop with the country girl routine and tell me what's really going on, why don't you?"

"Okay." Carrie leaned forward and dropped the exaggerated southern accent. "I'll tell you. I *have* busted my ass to get where I am. Which is on top and that's how I want to go out. I've made all the money I'll ever need, and one thing I've learned in this business is there's more important things than money. And two things are *way* more important to me right now than money. One is the only best friend I ever had, the sister I always wanted, and I've had the feeling for the last couple of weeks of something—okay, don't freak on me now—but of something *stalking* you. And last night I woke up and it wasn't a feeling anymore, it was a sure thing. Something's going on with you and I want you to stop side-tracking and tell me what it is. Right now."

Katherine felt an icy finger tracing a line up and down her spine. *Just damn. First Irene and now Carrie? Am I broadcasting?* She gave herself a mental shake. "On one condition."

"Which is?"

"You tell me the other thing more important to you right now than money."

"My baby. I'm not starving myself and putting my baby at risk to fit in a size zero for a couple of extra days. I mean, that's a losing battle to begin with. Besides, suppose a round of morning sickness hits me and I toss my cookies all over an eighty-thousand-dollar dress in a walk down the runway? Oh, yeah, that'd be a glorious end to a glorious career."

"You're *pregnant?!*"

"Yep. And no, you don't know the father. And *no,* I'm not ready to talk about it yet. I just need to be with you a little while first. Can we just leave it at that for right now? Pretty please?"

"That's always been one of our biggest bonds, Carr', that we can just be with each other and leave each other alone until we're ready to talk. But can you at least tell me—are you happy about it or upset?"

"I'm happy. Really. About the baby. Biological clock ticking and all that. I've had a great career, a fairy-tale career, even. But not one that lends itself real easy to family life and motherhood. So I'm kinda glad it just happened, and I didn't have to decide to have a baby. It's not like I've been stupid with my money, I can open a high-end boutique in one of the big cities, Atlanta probably, back to the home roots, don't you know, and that'll keep me as involved in fashion as I'd ever need to be. And give me plenty of time for this little boy or little girl, whichever it turns out to be."

"So—I take it that means Daddy's not going to have any part in this? By choice or does he even know?"

"Not now, Kat. Really. Not now. Later."

"Sure. Sister-hug!"

Carrie laughed and hugged back fiercely. "Definitely needed that. But watch the hair. And now back to business. Your business. What the hell's going on?"

* * *

"No wonder I woke up in the middle of the night. Talking portraits, trips to the Sixteenth Century, Quentin Slimeball Ashland calling out of the blue. Any one of them by themselves is cause for a trip to Tampa. Though Quentin's the one that really gives me the heebie-jeebies. You know I never liked him. Give me a refill, sugar." Carrie held out her tea glass. "I can't seem to get enough to drink lately."

"I thought this story would have you calling the men in the white coats." Katherine got up and took Carrie's glass. "And all it's making you call for is more tea. Be right back." She headed for the kitchen. Carrie got up and followed her.

49

"Now tell me again exactly *what* it is this Mother Shipton ancestor of yours wants you to actually do?"

"Hell if I know. She never got that far. That little side-trip seemed to be more a tease than anything. A promise of things to come. A threat of what *won't* come if I don't help."

"And those prophecies of hers you've told me about before, they've been right on the money on a *lot* of things, as I recall."

"Prophecies in general always use phrasing that can be interpreted to mean pretty much anything you want it to, Carrie. Don't go reading a lot into that."

"Well, I don't think it's doing us any good sitting here trying to figure out what she wants. Shortest distance between any two points is a straight line. Let's go ask her."

* * *

"Okay, you asked for it, you got it." Katherine took a deep breath and yanked the tarp off the portrait in progress.

"Uh, honey? Nothing's happening."

"Thanks for that astute observation." Katherine picked up her palette and brush. "This seems to be the trigger." She touched the brush to the canvas.

Mother Shipton materialized in front of the easel. Her head moved up and down as she inspected Carrie.

"'Tis a giant you've brought to visit, my girl! Rail-thin and six feet tall! Wherever did you find such a creature?"

"*Excuse me? Creature?*"

"This is my best friend, Carrie. She's a model, a very famous one. All high-fashion models are tall and thin."

"And what be this 'model'?"

"They—well, that's something in my time, not yours. And not important, even, not right now. What's important is she's my best friend. We're like sisters."

Mother Shipton leaned forward and crooked a finger at Carrie.

"Bend down, child, and look into me eyes."

The two locked eyes. Katherine couldn't have said whether it went on for a few moments or a few minutes. Or longer. Mother Shipton straightened. As much as her bent shoulders allowed, anyway.

"'Tis the gift you have, for certain sure, my girl. The gift of prophecy. You came because me Kitty-Kat needs you. And you knew it."

"Yes."

"Tell her. She has to believe."

Carrie looked at Katherine. "This is bigger'n both of us, girlfriend. I think we're about to take a little vacation. To someplace jets don't go."

Mother Shipton threw up a hand. "There's no *we* here, young seer. This is Katherine's journey. And you be with child. You can't be about junketing around through time—"

51

"I'm not going to be junketing around through time. Not my body. And how'd you know I'm pregnant, anyway?"

"It's looking like I fell off the turnip cart yesterday I be, is it, lassie? And it's a bit of a seer meself I be, ye be forgetting."

"Whatever. We're a package deal, lady. Consider it a two-for-one bargain. 'Cause I'm not about to let her go without me."

"Twoferone?"

"Think about it. You'll figure it out."

"There be no blood tie, no blood *connection*—"

"Let it be a challenge to you."

"'Tis a fine friend ye have, Kitty-Kat, giant or no. And love's a better connection than blood, for certain sure. Join hands with me, my beauties. And let's be seeing if 'tis enough. Be ye ready for your travels?"

"Ready as we'll ever be. But how do we get back? When we're ready to come back?"

"Girl! You just come back. The power's in ye. In both of ye."

Chapter Five

Time Travelers

[Hampton Court, England, 1534]

"Damn, the stench of this place!" Nicholas, Earl of Gresham, cursed as he rode through the gates of King Henry's Palace at Hampton Court. Hooves, heads and entrails of deer and cattle in various stages of decay lay in fetid piles, and packs of royal dogs snarled over the reeking portions. Rugs fouled by the dogs and thrown haphazardly over posts and pillars exuded noxious fumes. Nicholas's home lay in the North of England where the fragrance of heather and pine scented the air. He was unaccustomed to the squalor and filth that attended the court.

Two disincorporated essences floated above him, unseen and unheard.

"Damn! You smell that? Good thing my stomach's back in the twenty-first century or I'd barf all over that dude's head. Whoever he is."

"So would I and I'm not even pregnant."

In the courtyard of the palace, Nicholas dropped his reins and slid off the back of his black stallion, Thunder. "Here lad," he hailed a young page. "Take my mount to the stables. See that a groomsman has him properly cooled and brushed before he's given aught to drink." He tossed the boy a shilling and strolled towards the great hall. Here he pressed through swarms of clamoring petitioners as he moved towards the Presence Chamber.

"Greetings, Lord Steward." Nicholas stopped at the doorway and addressed the steward. "I've received a summons from His Majesty."

The steward passed his eyes over the scroll and motioned him to a seat.

Knowing the king, Nicholas prepared for a lengthy wait. It had been years since he'd visited the Royal Chambers, and he scanned the furnishings with critical interest. Sparkling jewels and finely woven murals lined the walls. Nicholas shuddered at the sight of imported sculptures and fine brass stacked on piles of fouled rugs. The combination of elegance and filth was the hallmark of the Tudor Court.

"His Majesty will see you now, My Lord." The Steward interrupted Nicholas' inspection and led him into the Presence Chamber.

King Henry, resplendent in a crimson robe trimmed with gold ropes and flashing gems, nodded in response to Nicholas's bow.

"Oh, my God! That's Henry the Eighth!" Katherine reached over and tried to grab

Carrie's arm before she remembered they really didn't have arms to grab.

"How do you know?"

"The 'Your Majesty' sort of gave it away."

"Yeah, but there've been lots of 'majesties'."

"Hans Holbein painted this one. And the basic image is there, but old Hans must've been a brown-noser. The portrait sure looks a lot better than the real thing."

"Yeah, glad he's got the king thing going for him. He'd have a hard time finding a date otherwise. Got piggy eyes, don't you think? Which fits because the inside of this place smells about as bad as the outside!"

"You grow ever more like your revered father, My Lord Gresham. It's been a good many years since God's messengers called him homeward, but his foul murder still plagues my soul. As do thoughts of the murdering Turks who killed him. Come. We'll sit and talk as old friends do."

A cold chill shot down Nicholas's spine, but he took a seat facing the king.

"I've no use for the Turks," the king continued. "They're a bloodthirsty bunch of barbarians, and it'd be a fine Christian act to rout them from the kingdom they stole from you."

The chill from Nicholas's spine crept out into his veins. Born Moldavian, he was the rightful heir to Moldavia's throne. Something he didn't want. Years ago the gypsy King, Tarot, had rescued him and raised him as his own. Tarot had always warned Nicholas his duty lay with Moldavia, but until recently he'd all but forgotten. He was English now. He had no wish to claim a foreign throne.

"I'm afraid I've had no opportunity to look into the plight of my countrymen these past years, Your Majesty."

King Henry nodded. "I've long cursed the fates that I've been unable to help restore your throne, but at last I'm happy to say there might be a way."

"I'm grateful for Your Majesty's concern." Nicholas chose his words carefully. It wasn't wise to anger a king, especially not one as volatile as Henry. "Truth to tell though, I've never felt much like a king, and my life in England has been happy and fulfilling."

"That's good to hear, My Lord Gresham." The king's tone held a mild rebuke. "Still, as I myself have often found, duties have a way of intruding on a man's pleasure."

"Oh, that's rich!" Katherine snorted.

"Why?"

"Carrie! Don't you know anything about Henry the Eighth?"

"Never had much impact on the way I buttered my bread, no."

"He made a career out of ensuring his own pleasure! The damn hypocrite!"

"Most men don't?"

"Don't what?"

56

"Make a career out of ensuring their own pleasure?"

"Got a point there."

Nicholas steeled himself to hear what the king had to say. He was unprepared for the king's next words.

"I'm told you have a comely daughter."

Nicholas's face lit up "She's a beauty, our Ursula. She has the grace and charm of her mother, but she gets her flaming tresses from my father. With her sapphire eyes and auburn hair she could almost pass for a pagan goddess."

King Henry lifted his brows. Catching the danger in his response to the king's inquiry, Nicholas hurriedly added. "Oh, there's no mistaking the noble British blood that runs through her veins. I like to think her beauty is a compliment to the mingling of bloodlines."

"I'd heard she pleased the eye." The king nodded approval. "That's why I know you'll be glad I've arranged an excellent marriage."

Nicholas's mouth dropped. "But Your M-m-majesty – Lady Kathleen and I planned to have her grandmother, Lady Margaret, present her at court next spring."

King Henry shook his head. "Lady Ursula's royal birth requires consideration. You'll find the match quite suitable. The husband I've chosen is Prince Frederick of Russia, a cousin to the tsar's own betrothed." The king's voice and eyes hardened. "There are many advantages to this match, and since the tsar won't rule without his guardian for another six years, Prince

Frederick and Lady Ursula will remain in England for the duration."

Nicholas forced a smile. Even in Gresham, Nicholas and Lady Kathleen were privy to court gossip. Only last year Prince Frederick's affair with Lady Millicent was the talk of the court. The affair ended abruptly when Prince Frederick returned to Russia. King Henry appeased the lady's angry father by betrothing her to a disfavored duke. Nicholas shuddered to think what sorrow that careless young man might bring his daughter.

The king however was well satisfied. "Frederick will arrive in early fall. It would be well for Lady Ursula to be presented to the court at once. You have my leave to depart and begin preparations."

"As you wish, Your Majesty. I shall return to Gresham Manor at once, Your Majesty." Nicholas bowed and left the Chamber.

The girls floated back out over his head.

"You get the idea this Lord Gresham dude's not real happy with any of this?"

"Sure do. And Lady Ursula's going to be a lot less happy than him."

"How do you know that?"

"She's the girl. She must be. The girl I saw in my first trip back. Crying her eyes out in the arms of a guy named Toby. A very good-looking guy but there's no way he's Prince Anything. Or even Sir Anything. He's a commoner."

"Oh. Shit."

"Yep."

* * *

Thunder crested a hill. The lush green meadows of Gresham manor spread out below. Stately birches bowed in the wind, their leaves glistening silver in the sunlight. Nicholas breathed the fragrance of new mown hay. He flicked the reins to give Thunder his head, and the black stallion, anxious for home and pasture, flew down the hill and across the meadow, following the gray granite wall that circled the manor and stretched from its southern boundary to the Northern cliffs and sea.

As they galloped onto the green pasture, Nicholas spotted Lady Ursula streaking towards them. Her auburn hair glinted like burnished copper in the sunlight. Moments later Thunder skidded to a stop and Nicholas gathered his daughter into his arms.

"Welcome, Papa." Her ladyship hugged him tight. "I thought you'd never come home."

"It's been a difficult trip," Nicholas brushed his daughter's hair back from her forehead and kissed her cheek. "How's your mother?"

Her eyes clouded. "The babe's getting so big. She's very tired, but she'll be better now you're home."

Nicholas smiled. He hadn't wanted his wife to risk this pregnancy, but she'd insisted, knowing it was her last chance at another child. "I'm anxious to see her. First though, you and I need some words. I have news from the king.

Walk with me." He handed Thunder's reins to a groomsman and took Lady Ursula's hand. "We'll stop a few moments in the rose garden."

On the side of the manor, Lady Kathleen's roses bloomed in a garden. Blossoms of every hue and fragrance climbed the rock fence and clung to the curving arches of the gateway. Pots of blooms hung from trellises and spilled in perfumed splendor over the sides of containers.

Nicholas took a seat on a stone bench and patted the space beside him with his hand, inviting her to sit. He draped his arm over her shoulder and pulled her close.

"My business with the king is going to have a grave effect on your life." He tightened his arm around her. "I know I've told you little about my family," he continued. "I hoped to wait until you were older before we talked this way, but unfortunately the king has changed all that."

"I'm not a child, Papa." Her eyes flashed with indignation and Nicholas smiled and squeezed her hand.

"Please forgive a father's wish to keep his daughter close as long as possible."

"Oh, Papa." She pressed her face against his chest. "Is it something terrible?"

"Or something wonderful. You will have to decide which for yourself. First let me tell you about my father. He was a member of the Moldavian Court. You've always known that. What you don't know is that he was King of

Moldavia. He and everyone in my family were murdered when the Turks invaded Moldavia."

"Oh!" She covered her mouth with her hand.

"I had no wish to tell you this until you were older. King Henry's father and my father were cousins, making you the king's cousin as well. When my father realized Moldavia was about to be attacked, he sought help from his English cousin to smuggle me out of Moldavia and bring me to England."

"How awful to be sent away from your family!"

"It was long ago, and I was a child. I barely remember my family. My foster father Tarot has always been enough family for me. Until I met your mother, of course."

"The gypsy? I always wondered where you and he met, how you became such fast friends. Why he always seemed to be—your guardian."

"Yes, Tarot the Gypsy. And yes, he's always been my guardian. And yours, whether you've known of it or not. King Henry, our king's father, enlisted his aid to smuggle me out of Moldavia in the hope no one would search for Moldavian royal blood in a gypsy caravan. That hope was fulfilled. He and King Henry feared for my safety and never told me of my birthright until I prepared to marry your mother. That's when I first learned I was heir to the throne of Moldavia."

"When I was a little girl, I used to pretend you were a king and one day we would live in a grand castle. But I never meant it." Her voice broke and she swiped at her eyes. "You haven't told me what King Henry wanted."

Nicholas frowned. "Because you are a Moldavian Princess, King Henry has decided you must wed a prince. He has chosen Prince Frederick of Russia to be your husband. Your mother and I have been ordered to send you to your grandmother, Lady Margaret, to be presented at court."

"Prince Frederick? The prince who disgraced Lady Millicent at court. Word of that even reached us here at Gresham Manor! How can King Henry expect me to wed such a rogue?"

"He's the brother of Princess Anastasia. She is betrothed to Tsar Ivan and the king is anxious for an alliance. He sees this match as a way to bring Russia and England closer. It is my belief the king intends to challenge the Turks for the throne of Moldavia. And put me on it as his proxy king."

"You can do nothing to stop this?"

Nicholas placed his arm around Lady Ursula's shoulder. "My heart is heavy, knowing you must pay the price for my refuge. Because should the king restore Moldavia, I must tell you that I do not intend to accept the monarchy."

"Will you have a choice?"

"Yes. There is one. I cannot rip your mother away from England and I am certain the king knows this. 'Tis for sure he doesn't understand it but know it he must. I will abdicate in your favor, which is basically abdicating in favor of your husband. This I believe to be the king's goal and thus his choice for your husband. No fool is our King Henry."

"But what if I don't want to leave Gresham Manor?"

Nicholas tightened his arm around her shoulders. "We are bound to obey the king. To disobey would be treason. You are young. You will enjoy the adventure, whether you think so now or not, whereas it would kill your mother to take her from her birthplace."

Lady Ursula bowed her head. Father and daughter embraced in silence.

Finally she lifted her chin and stiffened her shoulders. "Don't be sad, Papa. If I had my choice, I'd wed someone kind and gentle, like our steward Toby. But that can't be, so the king's choice is no more burden than any other loveless match."

Toby? The steward? Nicholas noted the color in her cheeks and wondered as to the direction of his daughter's heart. He had not been vigilant. A princess of Moldavia could not marry a mere common steward, no matter whether she'd known of her royal blood or no. Perhaps King Henry's plan was a wise one after all. It seemed sometimes the fates knew best.

"Don't worry, Papa." Lady Ursula noted her father's frown. "I mean nothing untoward, only that in my heart I longed for a kind and gentle man who would share my life right here at Gresham Manor."

Nicholas's frown darkened. More reassurances seemed necessary. "I'll wed Prince Frederick, and I'll work hard to be a good and obedient wife."

Nicolas sighed. "I wish I could make things different." He drew Lady Ursula against his chest.

"We must make the best of what the fates deal us. 'Tis what you've always said. 'Tis what Tarot's always said." She rose and crossed to the stables.

Nicholas watched her walk away. Then he squared his shoulders and turned towards the manor. It was his duty to tell his wife of coming events, much as he disliked bearing news bound to upset her, especially with her so close to term.

Carrie sighed. "Well, that's the original 'it is what it is'. Poor kid. That sucks."

"Big time."

"Where's she going?"

"Carrie! To Toby, of course! That's the part I've already seen. Right now we're further back in time than my first trip."

"But we still don't know exactly what's the connection between all this and you. And Mother Shipton."

"We're going to. Time to have a talk with our resident seer. Don't you think?"

"I think."

* * *

"Okay, where the hell is she?" Carrie glanced around the room. The only Mother Shipton in sight was the sketch of an old woman on the half-finished portrait.

"In the portrait again, maybe?" Katherine picked up her palate and brush, ready to call Mother Shipton back.

A loud blast of rock-n-roll roared into the room, followed by a high-pitched shriek.

"What the—" The girls raced down the hall, following the sound. Mother Shipton stood in front of the television, hands clasped over her ears.

Katherine grabbed the remote and clicked the TV off.

Mother Shipton turned to face them. "What—what manner of sorcery is *that?*" She pointed at the screen. "And that *noise!* Surely 'tis from Lucifer himself."

"Lots of folks say that about hard rock, and that's a fact, but more about Ozzie Ozborne than Metallica." Carrie laughed. "Welcome to *our* century, Mother Shipton. That's a television. Tuned to MTV."

"'Tis a devil box!"

"Don't throw stones, Mother. Your century smells like hell. Guess we all got our little sack of rocks to tote around."

Katherine held up both hands. "Hey, let's not get into century bashing. You two sit down. I'll get us something to drink. And then we're

65

going to have a talk. That means you're going to talk, Mother Shipton—oh hell, what do we call you?" Katherine headed into the kitchen.

"Grandmother would be quite seemly. I've been around a few centuries; your language patterns are not completely unfamiliar."

"Do I detect a trace of sarcasm there? Okay, Grandmother. If you two will call a truce and sit down, I'll get some things from the kitchen and we'll have our chat."

"Bring something carbonated. My stomach's still lurching from King Henry's Court! And some Ritz crackers and peanut butter!"

"Some international model you are. Don't you want caviar and canapés?"

"I'm *pregnant*, remember? I want soft drinks and salt! And besides—you can take the girl out of the country but—"

Katherine laughed. "Nobody's *ever* going to take the country out of you, girl! Part of the charm that got you to the top. Back in a minute."

* * *

Katherine set a tray on the coffee table and handed a glass of tea to Mother Shipton. "You'd better stick to this, Grandmother. That soft drink's going to send bubbles up your nose and make you choke."

Mother Shipton clinked the ice back and forth against the glass. "'Tis too warm for ice. More sorcery?"

"I guess you haven't spent too much time hanging around this century." Katherine chuckled. "So have a little more sympathy for how we felt when we found ourselves floating over Henry the Eighth's stinky smelly court."

Mother Shipton ducked her head but not before Katherine spotted a smile flitting across her wrinkled face.

"For sure he smells. He's only been *dead* a mere 500 years."

"Okay. Very funny. Now, why? What's he got to do with me? And why am I watching Lady Ursula? I get that she's my great, great, great something or other, but what does that mean to me? And the part we saw—she's a teenage girl getting her world knocked off its center! I know that's how it was back then. You married who you were told when you were told but seeing it—really makes me appreciate being a modern woman, I can tell you that. And she's a *baby!* How old is she, anyway? Fourteen?"

"She's a full-grown woman!"

"Yeah, right. In your world. Sure as heck not in mine. But the point is what has that got to do with me and my life?"

"She's your link. The reason ye *be*. But only because you helped her."

"Excuse me?"

"Things are coming to Lady Ursula. Some she wants, some she don't. Her blood survives.

67

But *only* because you helped her. There's a crossroad up ahead. Or back in the past. Depends on how ye think on it. If she takes one, well, then her fate—and yours—is sealed. If she takes another, her fate—and yours—is changed. And it's here I be to make certain sure that happens."

"You know you're not making any sense at all, right?"

Mother Shipton shrugged. "And ye've found in your young life that all things make sense, have ye?"

"She's gotcha there, hon." Carrie laughed.

"And what makes no sense to others, they seek to destroy," Mother Shipton continued. "'Always have, always will. 'Tis the way of the world. And it almost destroyed—us. All of us. Whether we be connected by blood or only by spirit. The sisters of prophecy. Those of us with the gift."

Mother Shipton waved her hand toward the television screen. It flickered and came to life.

On the screen guards in medieval garb rode behind a horse drawn cart. Inside a woman bound in chains kept her head down and her eyes averted from the crowds lining the streets of Knaresborough. Lady Ursula. Older now, with signs of strain marking her face, but it was her ladyship. Lady Ursula of the tower dream.

The sounds of laughing, jeering voices followed the cart and the girls knew, just as Lady Ursula herself did, that many of the faces in the crowd belonged to those her ladyship considered friends.

The peasants, electrified by the spectacle of nobility paraded through the streets like a common prisoner, worked themselves into a frenzy, calling out as she passed:

"Witch, witch, witch! Burn the bloody witch!"

"Oh. My. God." Katherine's face turned white. "Bloody Mary's witch hunts. That's why she was in the tower. Not just any tower. The Tower of London."

"Aye."

"How do you know that?" Carrie asked.

"I had a thing for English history as a teenager."

"Okay, so you were a nerd. I get it. What about this Bloody Mary?"

"King Henry's heir was Edward. A very sickly, short-lived king never married. He was succeeded by his sister, Henry's daughter. Mary. She was a fanatical Catholic. Known to history as Bloody Mary. Because she burned pretty much anybody she didn't like the looks of—Protestants, supposed witches, accused traitors. Whoever displeased her fancy."

"And she didn't like Lady Ursula, I'm assumin'."

"Obviously not. Okay, Grandmother." Katherine turned to face Mother Shipton, who had just smothered a large yawn.

"You want us to stop this, don't you?"

"Welllll—mayhap I do and mayhap I don't. Mayhap this is what *will* happen if Lady Ursula picks the wrong path when she gets to the crossroad. And will never happen if she picks the right one."

"So where the hell is that damn crossroad? And how will we know it when we get there?"

"Ye'll know it. The power will tell you. The power was *born* in you, girl! Born in both of you. Because the Sisters of Prophecy aren't always connected by blood. They're connected by *power*, shared and used wisely. "

"Some damn, Grandmother." Carrie slammed her glass down on the table. "Pep talks like that, you could be an NFL coach. So send us back already. We got a crossroad to find!"

Mother Shipton laughed. "An adventuress, this one. Ready, my girls?"

"Ready."

Mother Shipton waved her hand. "Then let go of the ties of the present. And journey back—to the past."

* * *

"Okay, where the hell are we now?"
"Someplace dark."
"No kidding?"
"And cold."

Katherine and Carrie hovered together, getting their bearings, adjusting to night vision. A bedchamber. A massive four poster bed draped with curtains of some heavy material.

They peered between the cracks of the bed draping.

"It's her. Lady Ursula."

"Thank God. Don't think I coulda taken Henry Ocho again. For sure not in his nightgown. Or even worse, not in his nightgown."

A scream shattered the silence. Lady Ursula bolted upright and threw the covers back. She raced out the door.

A young woman urged an older woman in front of her down the hall.

"Hannah? Is it Mother?"

"Lady Ursula! Yes, 'tis time. I've just summoned the midwife. Matilda, will you *hurry,* for the love of God?"

Lady Ursula followed them into her mother's room. Lady Kathleen lay on the bed and writhed in pain.

"Mother!"

The old woman bent over the bed and lifted the covers, her hands working out of sight. When she stepped back, she motioned Lady Ursula and Hannah to her side.

"'Tis not well, I fear. 'Tis the Lord's own foolishness, bearing a babe at her age."

"'Tis not your place to judge my mother, Matilda! She's buried two babes and lost three more since she bore me. She well knew the time was near when there could be no more."

"Aye, that's all the truth, Lady. And it's much afeard I am that this will truly be the end."

"Where's father?" Lady Ursula asked Hannah.

"He's sleeping in another room."

"Why haven't you called him?"

"Her Ladyship asked me to leave him sleep. Besides, there's little he could do except worry."

"He didn't hear that scream. My God, he could just be here holding her hand!"

"This is a man's world, Carrie, not our world. Women didn't think of childbirth the way we do. They didn't even want the men there."

Through the night the pains continued and still the child would not be born. The midwife bathed Lady Kathleen with wet cloths and rubbed her stomach through the contractions.

"That woman Matilda's worse than useless, Kat! She needs a doctor!"

"She needs a C-section and she needed nine months of good prenatal care before that, but honey, none of that was really available back then. We're not in our own time, Carrie."

"Can't we do something?"

"Like what? We're not even physically here."

After a particularly long and agonizing contraction, the midwife drew Lady Ursula aside.

"I know nothing else to do. That babe has no wish to be born. Her Ladyship's strength is almost gone. There'll be a bad end to this I'm much afraid, and like as not, it's me who'll be held to blame."

Lady Ursula blinked back tears and turned to Hannah. "Please, go call my father."

She dropped to her knees beside her mother. "I've sent for Father," she whispered in Lady Kathleen's ear. "He'll be here soon."

Lady Kathleen opened her eyes and reached for her daughter's hand. The hours of pain had drained her strength and she could barely squeeze Lady Ursula's fingers.

"You shouldn't be here," she whispered. "Shouldn't have watched this. Selfish of me not to send you out."

"Mother don't say that! And 'tis well you know I wouldn't have gone."

"Stubborn girl," Lady Kathleen whispered. She squeezed her daughter's fingers again.

Nicholas rushed into the room. His hair was sleep-tousled, his eyes wide with fear. He grasped his wife's hand and pressed it to his lips. Kathleen opened her eyes and a ghostly smile flickered across her face.

"I'm sorry, my love," she whispered. "Sorry I could never give you your son."

A half-sob escaped Nicholas's lips. "All I ever wanted was you, my love."

"Oh, shit! I'm going to cry! Or I would if I was really here and could."

"Should we go back? This can't be good for you to watch—"

"We'd feel like we were deserting! And this is so not happening to me! My baby's goin' to just jump right out!"

73

"Yes, it will. With you as its mother, it'll probably walk out and twirl on the runway."

Lady Kathleen's breathing turned slow and shallow. Nicholas's lips moved in prayer, and still the ordeal continued. Her temperature rose, her body turned hot to the touch. Lady Ursula bathed her mother in cold cloths but any respite they offered was short-lived.

Just before dawn Lady Kathleen raised her hand and pulled Nicholas's head to her breast. "I love you." And she breathed no more.

Lady Ursula fell across the bed and sobbed. Nicholas lay with his head on his wife's breast, adding his tears to the sweat-soaked linens.

Finally Lady Ursula pulled herself up and spoke. "Hannah, you must send for the vicar."

* * *

Time seemed to fast forward. Katherine and Carrie hovered above a small crowd. Lady Kathleen's funeral.

They buried Her Ladyship in the rose garden. When the other mourners left, Nicholas pulled his daughter over to a bench among the roses. "Sit with me, my child. We must talk." He focused his eyes on Lady Ursula's face. "I'm so sorry. Your mother was my life. Now she's gone. And you, my child—you must also leave me."

"I'm not going to leave you," She shook her head and set her chin. "King Henry will just have to understand. After such a loss, you need me here."

Nicholas gripped her hands. "You must not even think such. The king has decreed. To lose my darling Kathleen is bad enough, but to defy the king. You cannot. It would mean your death. You cannot ask me to stand by and watch. You will leave tomorrow for Hampton Court."

Lady Ursula sobbed and swiped at her eyes. "I only want to please you, Father. If it is your wish that I wed Prince Frederick, then wed him I shall."

"My poor child," Nicholas pulled her into his arms and rocked her like a baby. "All this is so unfair to you. And I've thought of nothing but my own grief. Please forgive me."

For long moments father and daughter clung together.

"She'll like it here," Lady Ursula said finally. "Surrounded by her roses."

Carrie flounced passed the stone bench and attempted to stomp her foot.

"I don't like this century. At all."

"I'm not very fond of it either."

"Where's she going now?"

"Where do you think? Her mother's dead, her father's walking around like a zombie, and they're getting ready to ship her off to this Prince Frederick, wherever the hell he is. She's going to the man she loves."

* * *

Lady Ursula hadn't seen much of Toby. If she was to leave tomorrow, this was her last chance. And he was going to promise her he'd look after her father. Besides, she'd loved him since he'd taught her to ride. Since she'd been a little girl and he little more than a lad himself. Before she left, she needed to tell him that, make sure he knew. Even if there wasn't a thing to be done about it.

She found him in the birthing barn, rubbing salve into a mare's distended belly.

"Toby," she whispered, stepping up beside him. "It's almost time for me to leave and I would speak with you."

"Yes, Milady." He dropped the salve and stood to face her. "I wanted to offer my respects for your mother, but I didn't want to intrude."

"Thank you. I know you cared for her, and I'm sure you grieve her loss. But I'm worried about my father. He insists I honor the king's marriage arrangement, and that means he'll be all alone here. I leave tomorrow." Tears sprang up in Lady Ursula's eyes, and Toby touched her arm.

"Don't cry, Milady. I'll be here for your papa as long as he has use of my services."

"Thank you." She placed her hand over his. "I want your promise that if anything happens to him, you'll come for me at Fairhaven."

"Of course I promise, but nothing's going to happen. I'll see to that."

"And there's something else I would say to you while I'm still here to say such." A deep flush covered Toby's suntanned face. "Oh Toby," she whispered. "Please don't treat me like a stranger. I can't bear to go away without at least telling you what's in my heart."

His voice choked with grief. "Milady, as much as I'm yearning to hear what's in your heart, much as I hope it's the same as in mine, I'm begging you not to say further. I'm a plain man, and the trust your father has given me here at the manor is more than I'd ever hoped. Master Nicholas has been uncommon kind to me. There's few Englishmen that'd give even a lowly job to a Scotsman, but your father raised me up and trained me as a proper Steward. He's always treated me with kindness and respect, and I'd never betray that trust."

"But Toby, you've earned his respect. You've worked hard for us from the first day you came here."

"Yes Milady but speaking to his daughter in a way I've no right to would be just that kind of betrayal. Fact is, I've grieved over what I've already said to you, and I'm hoping you forgive me. Seeing you crying that day in the barn—I said things I shouldn't."

Tears trickled down Lady Ursula's cheeks. "Please Toby, never say you're sorry. I know you'd never betray father. Maybe it's wrong for me to want to tell you my feelings, but I can't bear to go away without a word. If only my life were different! If only I were just a simple farm girl, I'd make a set at you t'would shock your senses."

Toby smiled despite himself. "I'm not much for words. 'Tis the best I can do to tell you how it was the first day I laid eyes on you. So beautiful, 'twas as if the angels themselves had fixed up one of their own and set her down before me. I was lost from the very moment I laid eyes on you, I swear I was, and if'n you were that simple farm girl, I'd take you for my wife and that'd be the end of it."

"Why Toby, that's beautifully spoken. I know you don't want me to say this, but it's the truth and I need you to know." Ursula moved in front of him and placed her hands on his shoulders.

She reached her hand behind his neck and gently pulled him forward. Mesmerized, Toby locked eyes with hers and surrendered.

"I love you, Toby Shipton. I've loved you from the day you lifted me up and set me down on Gypsy's back."

Toby opened his mouth to object, but Ursula placed her fingers on his lips.

"Shhh. Don't stop me now. I need you to know. I may never have another chance to tell you. My course is set by the king, and I am powerless to stop what will come. But believe this, my love. My heart belongs to you now and ever will."

With that she raised her lips to his and drawn by a magnet far more powerful than he could resist Toby's lips came down on hers and they sealed their love in the kind of kiss that endures through the ages.

Finally Ursula drew away. "I'll never forget you, Toby."

Carrie stamped her foot and grabbed through Katherine's ethereal arm.

"Okay, this really sucks!"

"Big-time."

"Isn't there anything we can do?"

Tears glistened on Katherine's eyes. "I don't see what. And I feel so helpless. I can't believe Ursula is my, I don't know, tenth great grandmother and I must sit here and listen to her lose the man she loves. I hate this century."

"Do you think this is what Mother Shipton wants you to fix?"

"I don't know. She keeps saying I'll know what I'm supposed to do, but I don't, I don't know anything."

"It's okay. Don't cry." Carrie soothed her friend. "Look, she's going back to the manor. We need to go with her and see what happens next."

Chapter Six

Betrayal

Sarah wakened her mistress before dawn. "Come, Milady. The men are ready to leave. You've just time for a bite to eat, and then we must dress you and be on our way."

Lady Ursula's heart broke as she said goodbye to her father, but she kept her tears firmly bottled up and solemnly extracted a promise from him that he'd look after himself.

"Looks like we're going back to the castle." Katherine and Carrie perched on top of the coach and waited for Lady Ursula's party to settle inside.

"Oh, joy! Back to the House of a Thousand Stinks." Carrie leaned over the side and looked inside. *"Can't say they didn't travel in style, but those robes smell a little too much like bunny rabbits for my taste."*

"Get back up here before you break your neck." Katherine laughed and tried to pull on Carrie's weightless arm.

"We're not really here, remember? And if we stay up here on top, we're going to miss all the conversation. C'mon down!" Carrie settled on the seat beside Sarah.

"Got a point." Katherine slipped through the coach door as the footman closed it and sat beside Lady Ursula.

The coach pulled slowly down the long drive. Lady Ursula's eyes lingered on the stables, but there was no sign of Toby. Her father stood alone in the courtyard. How different his life would be now, with his daughter far away and his wife sleeping in the Rose Garden. How empty the halls of Gresham Manor? Tears came unbidden as home faded into the distance.

Enough! Especially enough of tears. The resilience of youth and her mother's training rebelled. She was a grown woman. She had a new life. She couldn't control that. She could control whether she looked for happiness or remained burdened by past grief. This day would be full of new adventures. She sat up straighter in the seat.

"'Tis glad I am you're with me, Sarah."

"I'd never leave you willingly, Milady."

"You've always been such a friend to me, Sarah. Tell me of this place we'll stay the night. The Market Inn? I've never been in such a place, we must explore."

Sarah gasped. "Oh, Milady, you mustn't think such! We'll go to your room and it's staying there we'll be doing! Ladies don't mingle with the commoners in the tavern, t'wouldn't be seemly!"

"Hmmm. We'll have to see about that."

"Rebel in the making," said Katherine.

"Oh, yeah. Reminds me of us in New York."

* * *

Lady Ursula grabbed her chance when Sarah went down to the tavern's kitchen to check on their supper trays. She peeked into the main room, raucous with male laughter and the slosh of ale. Sarah might be right. This might not be the best place for her. Quietly she withdrew and stepped into a small side room, thankfully empty. She warmed her hands over the cheerful fire burning on the hearth. For a moment, she gave herself the luxury of pretending she was in front of the big fireplace at Gresham Manor.

"Oh shit! Ursula, look out!"

"She can't hear you, Carrie!"

Katherine scanned the room, looking for a weapon. She tried to pick up the fireplace poker and failed miserably.

"Damn, this no physical body thing sucks!"

A hairy arm encircled Lady Ursula's waist.

"Well, well, what have we here? A right comely wench and make no mistake!"

Lady Ursula swung around and gasped at the hairy beast of a man with glittering black eyes. His face was hideous. A scar ran from the corner of one eye down to his mouth, pulling his upper lip into a perpetual snarl. She fought her way out of his embrace.

"How dare you touch me with your filthy hands! I'm Lady Ursula Sontheil, daughter of Nicholas, Earl of Gresham! Step away or I'll shout for my guardsmen."

"You tell him, girl!"

The monster laughed so hard he choked. "Well, pardon me, *Milady!* But then, we don't expect to find a lady in a public room, now do we?"

"I don't see where it's any concern of yours, but I was on my way to my own chamber. Now move out of my way so I can leave."

"Of course, *Milady.*" He stepped back and gave an exaggerated bow. His black eyes glittered as he glared insolently at her bodice. "I bid you goodnight," he sneered. "But perhaps we'll meet again."

Lady Ursula raced from the parlor back to the bed chamber and careened into Sarah in the doorway.

"Milady, you gave me such a fright! I got back with our supper and you're nowhere to be found! I was on my way to look for you. Wherever did you go?"

"Oh, Sarah! You were right. Downstairs is no place for me!"

Sarah cringed as she heard the story. "Milady, you must never do such a thing again. Oh, and what would your poor mum say if she ever knew!"

"I know Sarah, I'm sorry, truly I am. I really won't ever do it again. That creature was more beast than human. But his eyes—that's what scared me the most. His eyes were evil. Will you sleep in my bed tonight?"

"Of course I will. Now don't think about that monster anymore or you'll have nightmares. We'll eat our supper and go right to bed. We have a long journey tomorrow."

"Okay, she's back safe in her room. But that was one mean-looking dude. You think we ought to do some reconnaissance?"

"I do. Let's flit back down and see where Monster Man went. Though what we'll do if he heads up the stairs, I don't have a clue."

* * *

In a secluded corner of the Inn, three men gathered around a pitcher of rich, dark ale.

"It's her all right, there's no doubt." The black bearded beast smiled lasciviously at his partners. "I thought her a common wench when I came across her in the parlor." He stopped speaking, giving a snort of laughter and swigging from the jug his mates passed to him.

"I'd figured to have a bit of sport with the wench when I found her in the parlor, but I no sooner put me arm around her waist then she rounded on me like a wild cat. 'I'm Lady Ursula, daughter to the Earl of Gresham.' She fairly spit on me. Of course I'd of had my way if the name hadn't hit me like a brick."

A man with pointed nose and beady eyes nodded and smacked his hand on the table. "Allah be praised. Suleiman will be well pleased, Kahib. Now we can dispose of her quickly and get our reward."

"Kahib? What kind of name is that for an Englishman? And who the hell is Suleiman and why would he have a reward out to dispose of Lady Ursula? Dispose how?"

"Wake up and smell the roses, Kat! Whoever this Suleiman is, he's got a hit out on her. And they're not English. But neither is her father, remember? He's the freaking King of Something—oh, yeah, Moldavia! And Henry Ocho wants him to reclaim the throne, that's what all this marrying Lady Ursula off to whathisname of whichaway is about!"

"Of course! That explains the Kahib and the Suleiman! The Turks took Moldavia, that whole region was part of the Ottoman Empire for centuries."

"Never underestimate the value of a BFF who's a history nerd!"

Kahib licked his lips and lifted the jug for another swallow of ale. "I tell you, Achmed, I was tempted to grab her right then. But the public rooms didn't seem the place. You know her maid is with her. She went missing before she was safely tucked away for the night. The maid would have the guardsmen out looking."

"Smart man." Achmed nodded agreement.

"I scolded her up about young ladies not being found in the public rooms, then bid her good night."

"So you let her get away?" Hasheim, the youngest of the three, scowled over his ale?).

"She's not got away, fool. Didn't I follow her right back to her bedchamber?" Kahib grinned. "Far better to slip in when the inn's asleep and make away with her then, and don't be forgetting, since I'm the one that found her, I get first sport outta her. And 'tis for certain her maidservant will be right there with her. More sport."

"Ah!" Achmed's eyes gleamed. "That farmhouse we stopped at should suit our purpose. Hasheim, you ride in and get rid of the old man. We'll keep the old woman till we leave. She might be useful. Be ready for us. We'll take a bit of pleasure with the wenches before we finish them."

"What about her guards?"

"We have till dawn before they'll know she's missing. We'll leave the farmhouse before daybreak. That gives us time to reach Gresham Manor before the guards finish searching for the lady and return to alert the Manor. Suleiman wants them all dead, and our ship sails in four days, so we've no time to waste."

"Oh, my God! They're going after her father, too!"

"Of course they are! She's just the heir, he's the real king! At least until he abdicates!"

"When do we start?" Hasheim rubbed his hands in anticipation.

"We'll sup and give them time to be asleep. Have the horses ready at the back door."

"What the hell do we do?"

"Hell if I know."

"We're beginning to sound like a broken record, you know that?"

* * *

Achmed and Kahib crept silently up the stairs. "It's the door at the end of the hall," Kahib whispered. "Once we're in the room, don't waste time. I'm after the lady. You gag the maid, wrap her in bedclothes and head for the door. I'll be right behind you."

Kahib put his ear to the door and listened. He opened it and stepped aside for Achmed to follow.

"That one," he whispered pointing to the far side. Silently they approached the bed. Working as one, they thrust thick scarves into the mouths of the sleeping women. They stripped two coverlets from the bed and rolled the women inside. Tossing the wrapped bundles over their shoulders they raced down the steps and out the back door to Hasheim and the waiting horses.

They slung their bundles in front of the saddles like feed sacks, mounted and spurred the horses into a gallop.

Lady Ursula struggled to breathe inside the heavy coverlet. Was Sarah all right? Who were their captors, and what did they want with them?

Katherine and Carrie raced through the air above the pounding hooves.

"There's got to be something we can do! Is this what we're supposed to change? To stop?"

"I don't think so. It doesn't feel right. Grandmother said we'd know. What do you think?"

"I think your grandmother's a damn sadist who knows exactly where that freaking crossroad is! She just won't tell us!"

Finally, just when Lady Ursula was sure she would suffocate, the horses halted and the man behind her dismounted. Someone dragged her off the horse's back and dumped her onto the hard ground.

"Help!"

A hand yanked the coverlet back and the black-haired monster leered at her.

"Well, *Milady*, things have changed a mite." He grasped her hair and turned her head to face him.

"Where is Sarah? Have you killed her?"

"Oh no, Milady. We won't kill the wench— not before we've had our fun with her."

Lady Ursula's face contorted, and a sob escaped her lips.

"Girlfriend!" Carrie's hands moved toward Lady Ursula's shoulders before she remembered she couldn't touch anything. *"This is so not the time to just give up and cry! Show some backbone!"*

"She can't hear you, remember?"

Lady Ursula's shoulders straightened, and her eyes narrowed. She glared hate at Kahib and he put his foot on her head and shoved her into the ground.

"Hey! Did you see that? See her straighten up and glare at the bastard right after I said that?"

"Yes! Yes, I did! Coincidence?"

"Maybe. Maybe not. Maybe we can't do anything big, but we might at least give her some nudges."

"Hell of a time to figure that out. We could've told her to leave the damn inn before this happened!"

"They'da just come after her coach and killed the guardsmen. Wouldn't have changed anything. But maybe we can help her through this, at least a little."

"I'll take whatever we can get right now."

"Hasheim. Take her ladyship to the barn and put her in the manger. And keep your hands off her. All this has whelped some hunger. Have the old woman make herself useful and feed us. Give us some strength to have our sport."

Hasheim lifted Lady Ursula off the ground. Kahib turned his back and strode over to the horses. "Where the devil are you, Achmed?"

"I'm here, Kahib," a rough voice answered. "This one's been fighting like a tiger."

"Well, dump her in with the other. They can fight and kick together. You come with me and get some ale out of the cellar."

Hasheim dumped Lady Ursula into the manger and moments later Achmed tossed Sarah on top of her. The girls wrapped their arms around each other and crawled to the farthest corner of the manger.

"Keep your eyes on those two," Achmed ordered Hasheim. "If they try to get out of the manger, cut the maid's throat."

With Kahib gone, Hasheim took a stand in the doorway.

Sarah put her mouth to Lady Ursula's ear. "We've got to get you out of here, Milady, before the mean one comes back. I've an idea. That Hasheim. I can distract him, and you slip out that back door.

"Distract him how?"

"I've some experience with what men want from a woman. My Davy and I did a sight more than just walk out on those nights when you let me meet him. Now please! We haven't much time, and the only way you can save us is to get away from here and get help."

"No, Sarah!" Lady Ursula whispered back. "I can't leave you. We'll escape together."

"Milady, you must do as I say. 'Tis our only chance! There's a horse inside a small pasture just beyond this barn. I saw it when they took off the blanket. As soon as I get Hasheim distracted, slip out the back door and grab the horse! Ride for help."

"You know what that man will do to you?"

"Milady, if we both stay, we both die and that's the short of it! This is our only chance!"

"Listen to her, girlfriend!"

Lady Ursula shuddered. But she nodded. Sarah loosened the ties of her nightdress and stood up.

"You look like a man who knows what a woman wants. Why don't you and I have some fun while we're waiting on them others?"

Hasheim whirled and brandished his knife. Sarah pulled her nightgown open, offering a view of creamy bosom. Hasheim gaped and stuttered. "K-k-k-ahib said for you to stay put."

"You always do what you're told?" Sarah shook her shoulders and grinned when Hasheim fixed his eyes on her bouncing breasts.

"But I can't—Kahib will slit my throat if the lady gets loose!"

"Her?" Sarah pointed to Lady Ursula. "She's a spineless thing and I think she's gone off her head. She'll give no trouble."

Taking Sarah's cue, Ursula mumbled and thrashed her arms.

Sarah climbed out of the hay and held her nightgown high. Hasheim's eyes focused on the black triangle at the apex of her legs.

"Surely there's no harm in a little fun," she coaxed. She moved up beside Hasheim and stroked her hand across the hard knot in the front of his pants.

In minutes, the barn echoed with moans and gasps as the couple thrashed around on the floor. Lady Ursula climbed out of the stall and raced across the barn. She reached the back door, lifted her hand, and grasped the handle.

Sarah tracked her progress and groaned and squealed to cover the noise, as Ursula yanked on the door to slip outside.

Just as Sarah said, a little mare grazed in the pasture. Lady Ursula sidled along the side of the barn and grabbed a halter rope from a fence post.

"Move it, girl! Don't stop now!"

Lady Ursula didn't stop. She slipped the rope around the mare's neck and used a fallen log to boost herself onto the horse's back and headed directly into the forest.

The moonlight faded inside the thick forest. Lady Ursula had no idea what direction to take but driven by fear and desperate to get help back to Sarah, she urged her mount into a gallop.

"Ursula, no!" Katherine shouted. *"That's too fast in the dark, dammit!"*

The mare broke out of a tangle of bushes right into a rushing creek, swollen with the last week's rain. Her hooves slipped on wet mud and rock and she stumbled clumsily. Lady Ursula spilled from her back and down onto the rocky banks. The *crack* of her head connecting with rock sounded even above the rushing water.

"Too late," said Carrie.

* * *

Kahib flung the barn doors open and roared. "You son of a dog! The girl! *Where is she?!*"

Hasheim rolled off Sarah and scrambled to his feet. "I—I—she—"

"*She's gone! That's where she is!* You've let this whore play you by the cock and she's *gone!*"

Kahib grabbed Hasheim by the throat and pulled his dagger.

"No! No! We'll find her! You need me!" Hasheim struggled to croak out the words.

"Pull your breeches up and fasten your codpiece, you worthless son of a whore! We don't need *her!*" He pointed to Sarah, crawling toward the door. He turned Hasheim loose and swooped down on Sarah. The dagger flashed a straight line across her throat. Blood gushed, and Sarah slumped boneless onto the barn floor.

"Achmed! Where are you? I'm surrounded by fools! Get the horses ready! We ride for Gresham Manor before the girl reaches help and sounds the alarm!"

"But 'twill take us hours to reach the Manor!'

"By the road. Not as the hawk flies!"

"We cannot ride that fast through woods at night! We risk the horses! Our necks!"

Kahib's hands flashed out and fastened around his cohorts' necks.

"I care not for your *necks*. I'd slit your throats myself for a farthing. For nothing if you cost me my fee for this task. We ride. And pray to Allah we get there before break of day!"

* * *

"So what the hell do we do now?" Katherine and Carrie flitted back and forth over Lady Ursula's unconscious body.

"We got through to Lady Ursula. We think, anyhow. I mean, she did seem to listen to us back in the barn. Maybe we can get through to somebody else. Grandmother said we had the gift. Whatever the hell that is."

"And who do you think we can get through to out here in the damn woods?"

"Nobody. That's why you're staying here with her and I'm going back to the inn. Let's see if I can get through to the guards."

"Oh, no! No offense, honey, you're just too damn polite. And Lady Ursula's your freaking ancestor anyway, not mine! Let me go back to the inn. I guaran-damn-tee you I'll get the guards' attention!"

"You sure?"

"Positive."

"Okay. But hurry. And what about Sarah?"

"We can't do anything for Sarah, Kat. We can't get any help back to her in time. She's on her own. And she knew that when she planned the diversion. All we can do is make sure she didn't do it for nothing."

* * *

The three riders approached the dark walls of Gresham Manor just before dawn glowed over the edges of darkness. Kahib's eyes moved over the shadowed landscape, assessing. Planning. He motioned his companions toward the left with his hand, routing them close to the encroaching woods and toward the back wall.

Kahib dismounted and handed his reins to Achmed. "You two fools stay here with the horses."

"Why?"

"Because you have not the sense of a mule between you! The only chance for success is finding a back way into the Manor. Over the back wall if needs must. But most English manors have a hidden back gate. And in these past years of peace, it might be unguarded. And I swear to Allah the two of you would make more noise than a company of armed knights! Wait with the horses."

Kahib unsheathed his dagger and dropped into a crouch. He moved toward and along the wall. There. The shadows jarred, oddly asymmetrical, seemingly out of line with the shadows of the wall. He moved closer and groped carefully, feeling his way, finding his reward. A small barred gate sat recessed into the wall at the rear. Kahib pushed lightly, testing for the strength of its lock, the sound of a guard pacing at his post. By Allah, these English were stupid. Not only unlocked, but unguarded. An arbor, heavy with roses, painted black by darkness, covered the path. Kahib ignored the stabbing thorns. Quiet was important; a bit of pain was not. He cleared the vines aside and peered into the grounds. His eyes scanned the garden and settled on the long shadow hugging the ground. His eyes moved upward.

He could not be so lucky. But yes. He was. Nicholas, unable to find solace in sleep, sat beside Lady Kathleen's grave with bowed head and slumped shoulders. If he heard any sound from Kahib's passage across the garden, he gave no sign.

Kahib pulled his dagger. The blade glowed faintly in the first streamers of dawn. Nicholas looked up. A momentary spark lit the blank depths of his eyes. As if realizing that death would join him with his beloved Kathleen, he closed his eyes. Kahib lifted the knife and plunged it into Nicholas's heart.

* * *

Lady Kathleen's maid Hannah missed her mistress. She could still start the day by speaking with her, though. She visited her grave every morning and found comfort in their conversations. Milady was still with her in those visits; she could feel her. This morning, though, this morning was different. And what was that mound by the grave? She came closer. And ran shrieking back toward the courtyard.

"The Death Hound! The Death Hound stalks us! He stalks Gresham Manor!"

Toby raced from the barn toward her shrieks.

"Hannah! Hannah! What's amiss?!"

She crumpled into his arms.

"The Master! The Manor's been cursed and the master's with the mistress now! And what's to become of us all?"

* * *

Toby summoned the magistrate and set a stableman to dig His Lordship's grave. He'd promised Ursula he'd bring her word if anything happened to her father. He had to keep that promise. It wasn't a promise he could delegate to another, no matter how his heart would break, watching her face as she learned of her father's death. And besides, Lady Ursula was the heir of Gresham Manor. It was her place to determine what best to do for the manor now, not his. At least until the king learned of Nicholas's death and sent his emissary roaring in to rule. But who'd look after the manor and its people while he was gone?

Of course. The Shipton's had a small farm across the border in Scotland. He sent the widow Graham to fetch his father, Matthew, and saddled Sybil, Ursula's favorite mare. His father was the only man Toby trusted to watch over Gresham Manor until he could return with Lady Ursula's instructions.

Toby galloped across the countryside and allowed his own grief to wash over him. What would become of the manor now, with its master and mistress gone and Lady Ursula promised to a foreign Prince? Momentarily hope flared for Ursula's return, but it quickly died.

The manor would pass to Lady Ursula, the same as saying it would pass to her husband. And with that husband being a foreign Prince, a regent—approved if not hand-picked by the king, of course—would take over the estate. Like as not, Lady Ursula would never set foot on the grounds again.

* * *

Snores filled the darkened room, just beginning to lighten with the first hint of dawn.

Carrie flitted above the three sleeping guards.

"Rise and shine, sleeping beauties! Rise and shine!"

Nothing. Time for more forceful tactics. She braced and pictured herself reeling in energy from the gathering light. Then she threw it straight at the sleeping guards.

"Okay, soldiers! Get your asses up! Move it, move it, move it! Do you hear me?!"

As one, the snores cut off in mid-stream. One of the men sat straight up. And one was all she needed, he'd wake the others.

"Oh, way cool!"

"Ned! Jamie! 'Tis dawn. Travel time's a'wasting, it's on the road we should be getting!"

The other two guards stirred and groaned.

"Stop your groaning and get up. Ned, go see about getting some food, and Jamie, go check the horses. I'll go rouse Milady and her maid."

* * *

Ursula's head guardsman barreled down the stairs, bellowing for his men.

"Ned! Jamie! Ned! Jamie!"

Ned emerged from the kitchen with the innkeeper. "Yell louder, John, why don't you? 'Tis possible someone in the inn might still be sleeping! What's amiss?"

"She's gone! Milady's gone!"

"Gone? Gone where? What do ye mean gone?"

"He means gone, Einstein!" Carrie popped Ned on the back of his head, not that he felt it since her hand passed straight through. Still, it made her feel better.

"'Tis gone I said and gone I meant! Don't ye speak the King's English, man? She's not in her room!"

"Did ye ask the maid?"

John popped Ned on the back of his head. Carrie winced. No way ol' Ned didn't feel that meaty hand connect with his skull.

"Ye dunderhead! The maid's gone right along with her!" The guard turned to the innkeeper. "Check all the rooms! Who was here last night? And who's not here now?"

"Oh, my God! I don't have time for this! None of you big strong guards noticed the freaky dudes with the so-not English names last

99

night!?" Carrie concentrated and pounded the thought into John's brain with the force of a hammer.

John's eyes widened.

"There were three men here last night! *Furriners!* Check their room!"

* * *

Toby rode through the peacefulness of early morning with shattered heart. Lady Kathleen lay beneath the dark and healing earth, surrounded by the roses she loved, voice silenced, graceful movements ceased. He'd miss Lady Kathleen. And Lady Ursula—Toby slammed the door on the mental image of her lithe figure running in and out of the barn, sneaking apples to the horses, laughing in delight as they nuzzled her face. Aye, she'd powered more than the manor. She'd powered his world. But she'd never been his, never would have been, not in the eyes of the world. Only in his heart. And now she was gone. Oh, she might be back for an occasional visit. And she might not. Many young girls, having once left, never came home again. It depended on their husbands. And now the master, too, was gone, his blood spilled on the land he loved and his body waiting burial beside his beloved Kathleen.

"Ah, Sybil!" He leaned forward and rubbed his hand under the mane of Lady Ursula's favorite mare. "Reckon 'tis only me and thee now. 'Tis for sure some hard and lonely days ahead of us, my girl."

Sybil gave a soft whicker. Toby leaned forward and hugged her neck. A good thing. Without her support, he'd have fallen to the ground under the onslaught of the scream vibrating in his brain.

"Toby! Toby, where are you? Why do you not come to me? I need you, my love! I need you…I need you…I need you… ."

"Milady? Milady, where *are* you?! What's happened?"

"I   need   you…I   need you…follow…follow…follow…"

Toby flicked the reins and set himself into the saddle.

"Fly, my beauty! Fly like the wind! I understand no more than you do, but Milady needs us!"

* * *

Katherine flitted restlessly over Ursula's body. What was going on in that unconscious brain? Something was. She could feel it, feel a subliminal hum, like voices through phone wires, like electricity through power lines. Not that any such things would exist for four hundred or so years.

"Who are you talking to, Ursula? Carrie, hurry!"

No answer. Not directly. Only the echo of Mother Shipton's words.

There's a crossroad up ahead. Or back in the past. Depends on how you think on it. If she takes one, well, then her fate—and yours—is sealed. If she takes another, her fate—and yours—is changed.

The crossroad! Was this it? The crossroad? Katherine concentrated, and power hurled across the years, out of the past and into the future.

"Grandmother! Can you hear me? This is it, isn't it? The place in time where destiny can change. But what do I do? What can I do?"

"You know what to do. Like calls to like and blood to blood. Show her! Show her where following her heart will lead her, the treasures she'll reap! And show her what mindless obedience to the king will bring her!"

"But I don't know any of that!"

"I do, child. And the visions of those two paths will flow from me to thee to her."

"How the hell do you know? And if you do know, why not just show her yourself?"

"Child! What's my name? What's her name? What's your name?"

"Would you please stop talking in those damn riddles of yours and just tell me what to do?"

"Child! The names! Remember the names!"

"You're Ursula. Ursula Shipton. She's Ursula. Ursula Sontheil—oh my God! Shipton! Toby Shipton! You're her and she's you and she's Ursula Sontheil now but she's got to become Ursula Shipton! Or I'll—I'll never—"

"You'll never be born, child. Ursula Katherine Shipton will never be born. Nor any of the line before you from whence you sprang."

"I still don't understand! If she's you—if you're her—why can't you just show her yourself?"

"I do! Through you! At this moment! Because you exist, I exist. Because I exist, you exist. If this moment passes, that chance is lost, and I become that woman in the Tower, the one you saw in your dream. The one who'll never live to be an old woman!"

"Oh, God, my head hurts!"

Mother Shipton's soft laughter echoed over the years.

"Sure and it's a tangled coil, my girl! Now open that mind of yours to the wondrous power you own and show her!"

Katherine drifted closer to Ursula's unconscious body, her outstretched hand hovering over her forehead. She took a deep breath. What to say, how to start? What had Mother Shipton said to her?

"Close your eyes, Ursula. And go visiting. To another time. Another place. Float, Ursula. Float. None will see you. None will know you're there."

* * *

Ursula floated in a warm cocoon of silent darkness. Except it wasn't silent. Not completely. A voice intruded into the quiet, growing louder. A familiar voice. A voice that sounded like—her mother's? No one ever really heard their own voice, certainly not in Ursula's time when nothing existed remotely resembling even the earliest recorders. Toby could have told her why the voice was familiar, had he been there. But he wasn't. It was familiar because it sounded eerily like her own.

"Follow me, Ursula! Follow my voice! See what waits for you! If you're strong enough...strong enough...strong enough..."

The air outside her warm cocoon grew colder. Cold as winter. She didn't feel it, but she did. She looked down and saw herself, seated on a stool in front of a blazing fire. A little girl with long golden hair and beautiful blue eyes stood in front of her as she brushed out the child's curls. Ursula caught her breath. The child was a perfect miniature of her mother, Lady Kathleen. A blast of frigid air blew into the room with a slamming door.

"Brrrrrrrr." A man hung a heavy coat up on a rack and turned to face the fire. "Colder'n icicles out for sure! It's some warming hugs from my best girls I could be using right now!"

"Da, you're home! You took such a *long* time, Da!" The beautiful little girl ran into his arms and smothered his face with kisses. The man turned to the laughing Ursula sitting on her stool.

"What? My big girl's got no hugs for me this fine e'en?"

Ursula watched herself as she stood and moved into the circle of embracing arms. "Perchance I do."

"Toby?" whispered the Ursula who floated just outside the physical boundaries of the room.

"Toby," the voice confirmed.

"It cannot be. T'would ne'r happen, no matter how I wished for it!"

"It can happen. If you're strong enough to follow your heart."

"I'm betrothed. Promised to Prince Frederick of Russia! 'Twould dishonor my family to refuse."

"Then move along, Ursula. Move along and see the outcome of your blind obedience."

* * *

Ursula floated in her warm cocoon, away from the happy vision of the little family, the family the strange voice insisted could be her own. The cocoon wasn't warm and cozy this time. This time it was different. Cold. Stark. Howling winds tossed her high and pushed her across a stormy sky. When she descended, she hovered over a dark castle encircled by a deep, dark moat. *That's the Tower of London. Why are we here?* As she watched, a boat rowed up to an iron gate. The oarsman jumped out and cranked open the portal.

Ursula spotted a woman huddled inside the boat. The cloud drifted lower and she gasped in horror when she recognized the woman. *That's me. They're imprisoning me in the Tower of London.*

"*No,*" whispered floating Ursula.

"*Yes.*"

"*How? How could simply obeying my king and my father lead me to—this?*"

"*Watch.*"

* * *

Ursula felt her cocoon shift. It veered and changed direction, moving slowly at first and then accelerating. Pressure tightened around her chest and just when she feared she'd suffocate, the vision cocoon stopped again and hovered over a coach, pulling to a stop at a roadside inn, somewhere in the countryside. The coachman jumped down to the ground and moved to the horses. The two guards riding behind the carriage dismounted and approached the door. Ursula recognized the woman leaning out the window. The image stared back at her every morning from her polished brass mirror. The woman was a little older, though, and not just in years. Her eyes no longer looked out at the world with innocence. They viewed the world with knowledge the younger Ursula didn't possess. Somehow, younger Ursula knew she didn't want to possess that knowledge. She'd been much happier without it.

The woman in the coach spoke to the guards.

"Have the kitchen prepare a basket while you tend the horses. We'll stop to eat along the way. I'm tired of stuffy old buildings. 'Twill be a rare treat to enjoy a meal in clean, open air."

"Where am I now?"

"Good question. Wish I knew."

"You jest with me?"

Katherine gave herself a mental kick. She was supposed to be the guide here. But she didn't have a clue where or when this scene was occurring. She concentrated and reached for the connection, the memory link, that bound her with Mother Shipton on one end of the long chain of prophesy and Ursula Sontheil on the other.

"Child! It's trying too hard you are! Ease your mind and let the memories flow, from me to you, to her!"

"You're married to your Russian prince. And it hasn't been a fairy tale. He's a two-timing jerk and—"

"What means this 'two-timing'? And ' jerk'? Does it mean rake?"

"Rake! Thank you, yes, that's what your time calls it!"

"Then he's not a faithful husband? Most husbands aren't, I ne'r expected such!"

"And your Toby? What would you expect of him?"

No answer. Katherine hadn't expected one. The two watched the coach and its dust trails move beneath them.

"Let's float lower. So you can see better. Hear better."

"This is foolishness! 'Twill change nothing! I want to go back. I don't want to see!"

Katherine's patience snapped. Carrie was off trying to collect Ursula's guards, but Katherine knew what Carrie *would* say if she was here. No reason she couldn't say it herself.

"Girlfriend, I'm just about sick of this woe-is-me-my-fate-is-sealed thing you got going on! Grow a backbone, why don't you? There's a lot more at stake here than just your life!"

"Like what?"

"Like mine! Now get your butt down there close enough to see the show!"

* * *

The Ursula riding in the coach spotted a small river and signaled the coachman to stop.

"Spread our basket under those trees." She pointed to the deep shade of a group of oaks. "Stay back," she ordered the guards. "I needs wash away some of this journey's dust before we sup. 'Twill only take me a bit."

"My Lady should anything befall you, the Prince will—"

"I *said* stay back with the coach."

"Wow!" Floating Katherine whistled low in admiration. *"That tone'd freeze ice cubes. Guess you have grown some backbone by now, girl. Congratulations."*

"Ice cubes?"

"Never mind."

"My maid. The one with me—her—now. She's not Sarah. Where's Sarah?"

"Honey, you know damn well where Sarah is. Or rather, isn't. You know your kidnappers killed her. And don't go into hysterics on me about it. If you hadn't run, you'd both be dead. Not just Sarah. She knew that when she gave you the chance to run. There was never a chance for both of you. Only the certainty that it was her or both of you."

Ursula headed into the woods alone. She sank to her knees gratefully beside the water and splashed her face. She looked around. Good. The guards hadn't followed her. Impatiently, she stripped out of her clothes and threw them over some nearby limbs. She was so hot, so tired, so dirty. So heartily sick of court and the ever-crowding press of people. Of duty. She could take these few minutes to wash all that away, to float in the soothing river water, to pretend she was a child again, playing in the streams of the manor. Pretend her father was still alive, guarding her childhood while she played in the water.

Floating Ursula's eyes widened as she read physical Ursula's thoughts.

"My father—he's dead! The monster that took me—he killed him! Within hours of my escape! Why? Why? Because I escaped? I caused his death?"

"No! Use your head here. Not because you escaped! Because that was his job. To kill not just you. Your whole family. And if you hadn't escaped if they'd killed you—your father would still have been dead. Within hours."

The slight swelling of physical Ursula's belly, the fullness of her breasts, gave away her secret.

"She is—I am—with child?"

"So it seems."

"Then—whichever path I take, I deny life to one child or the other?"

"Maybe you should watch the whole show before you go into moral spasms over that."

But the invisible floating entities weren't the only ones watching this show.

"Oh, my God!" Floating Katherine clutched floating Ursula's arm, or tried to. *"You had to pick now to grow a backbone?"* She pointed to the riverbank's bushes.

"That's—that's the monster! The one who took us! The one who killed Sarah! And my father! He's followed me ever since. For how many years?"

"Several, that's for sure. Not a man who gives up easy. Probably scared to go back to his own country without his assignment completed. You've got a stalker on your trail, that's certain."

Kahib smiled in satisfaction. So many hours of stealth and hiding, watching and following. Finally, finally, he would prove his value and finish his task. Alone she would be an easy target. He felt his loins tighten as he watched her in the water. Her thick, auburn hair glistened in the sunlight as she swung her head to dry her hair. Her breasts gleamed white in the sun. Lust raged in Kahib's body. She'd denied him his play when she'd escaped, thanks to that whore of a maid of hers. By Allah, she'd not deny him now. The sounds of the river would mask any noise of approach. Moving as quietly as possible, he reached the low branch where Ursula's clothes hung and pulled them down. He rolled them into a ball and crouched behind the tree. And waited.

Ursula stepped out of the pool and started towards the tree where she'd hung her clothes. Her face puckered into a perplexed frown. *I know I hung them on this branch*. Behind her the branches rustled and a hand covered her mouth.

She struggled against the restraining arm and managed to turn. *The monster! The monster who'd kidnapped her and killed Sarah. And her father*. Her legs collapsed, and she slipped to ground. Kahib flashed a dagger in front of her eyes. "If you squeal, I'll run you through. Do you understand?"

Ursula nodded. He removed his hand from her mouth and moved it to her breasts. She gasped and tried to cover herself with her arms.

"You didn't think I'd forgotten you, did you?" He laughed and squeezed the soft flesh so hard her eyes teared in pain. "You'll beg me to stroke these before I'm finished with you. But now we need to get out of here before your guards come looking." He held out her gown. "Get dressed. For now. It'll come off again soon enough. You owe me for all the extra time and trouble you've caused."

Ursula stood and yanked the gown over her head. Kahib grabbed her around the waist and tucked her under his arm. "Remember! One sound and I'll run you through!"

Kahib hurried her through the trees to his waiting horse. He tossed her onto its back and mounted behind her. The horse began to pick its way through the thick underbrush, taking them farther and farther away from Ursula's party while Kahib's filthy fingers moved over her body.

"What should we do?" The invisible entities floated above them.

"There's nothing we can do. We're just watching. You need to see this. I don't know why, I just know if we're seeing it, there's a reason."

Physical Ursula forced herself to think rationally. She had to do something before Kahib reached his destination. This ride was her last chance. She forced herself to ignore his roving hands and watched the landscape around them.

The first few miles took them through dense forest. Gradually the trail grew wider and the undergrowth sparser. Ursula picked out the markings of a ravine stretching out beside them. Willing herself to wait, she prayed Kahib would ride close enough to the edge to fling herself off the horse and take her chances on rolling down the cliff. If that killed her—well, that death was preferable to her certain end if she didn't take the chance.

The trail narrowed. Kahib guided his horse along the edge of the ravine. Finally! The terrain roughened and required both his hands on the reins. She ducked her head beneath his arm and flung herself sideways off the horse.

She struck the ground hard. For a heart stopping moment, she teetered on the edge of the embankment.

Kahib reined in his horse.

"Worthless *bitch!*" He jumped down and came after her. "Not *again!* Allah's sword, you will die screaming for this!"

Desperately she positioned herself and timed her move. Moments before Kahib reached her, she crouched and jumped over the edge.

She half-rolled, half-skidded, down the embankment until she hit a patch of bracken and lodged up against a rock, half-hidden in undergrowth. She lay motionless, her breath coming in uneven gasps. Time was a luxury she didn't have. She forced herself to sit. Blood seeped from a jagged cut on her leg. Her shoulders and back burned from scrapes and bruises, but otherwise she seemed unhurt. Spears of dried grass stabbed into her back.

She looked up to the top of the ravine. Kahib slid downwards toward her, bracing himself by crawling on all four limbs as he

113

followed the path of her own descent, clearly visible up to the point where she'd hit the bracken and skewed off into the partial shelter of underbrush and rock.

Ursula searched the ground for something she could use as a weapon. Her fingers closed around a jagged edged rock, half-buried in the dirt. Her fingers dug desperately in the dirt around it, loosening it from the ground. She yanked it out of the ground and clutched it tightly in her hands. And waited.

She flattened herself behind the bracken and watched as he lowered himself, legs first, to within a couple of feet from the rock that stopped her fall.

Ursula held her breath and lifted the rock high in the air. When the top of his head peeked over the boulder, she brought her arms down as hard as she could. For one horrifying moment, Kahib's face loomed inches from Ursula's. One of his huge arms reached out to her. The gaping wound in his head gushed blood, painting his face scarlet. For an eternity they hung suspended, clinging to the steep face of the cliff. Then the ground beneath Kahib's body gave way and he crashed to the bottom of the ravine.

"Oh, you go, girl! You rock! Pun intended."

"Go? Go where?"

"Nowhere! Damn this language thing! I meant—you did good!"

Physical Ursula lay back panting, relief leaving her limp. But resting wasn't a luxury she could give herself. She forced herself to move and crawled doggedly up the face of the cliff. In the distance, she heard shouts.

"Milady! Milady! Where are you?"

Her guards. Thank the dear God Almighty.

"Here! Here! Help!" She shouted back at the top of her lungs.

Her guards rode toward her.

"Milady! We feared you were lost to us!"

"I feared so myself! And would have been had I not been able to strike the man who took me with a rock and make him fall from the cliff. I think the fall killed him, but I'm not sure."

"We must make sure."

"I'll go down," the youngest of her guardsman volunteered. They watched him wind his way down the cliff. He stood over the body a moment and started back up toward them.

"He's dead, right enough. The predators will make short work of him. Just what the filthy dog deserves. 'Tis a fine day's work you've done, Milady!"

"He's got that right. Damn, girl, wouldn't have thought you had that in you."

"'Twould not have thought so myself. But don't you see? If I don't follow this path, I deny life to the child I now carry in it. And if not me, if not now, on this path—who will avenge my father and Sarah?"

"Got no answers for you, honey. All I can tell you is if you do follow this path, you deny yourself the happiness that glowed all around

you in that first scene we visited. Which I got to tell you—this Ursula, she doesn't look very happy, does she? And you deny life to that beautiful little girl you saw in it. And just incidentally—to me."

"You speak in riddles."

"Tell me about it. I've been in the middle of a riddle for the last damn twenty-four hours. At least."

"But my father and Sarah—"

"Oh, I see. Both loved you so little they'd deny you a lifetime of happiness just, so you could personally kill the bastard who killed them. And for all you know, Kahib will still get his just reward without you if you choose your alternate path. I mean, the Bible hasn't changed so much between our times that it doesn't say 'Vengeance is mine, sayeth the Lord', has it?"

"No....."

"And besides, I don't think we're done yet. Feel that? Feel the wind? It's about to blow us to the next thing you're supposed to see. I can feel it. Feel it coming...."

* * *

"Well, this is quite a change." The invisible entities hovered in a grand chamber. This Ursula was obviously older. A beautiful woman still, but faint lines of stress had begun carving the youthful lines of her face. She sat in an ornate chair, facing a handsome man.

"We must be at court."

"I'd say. And I'm guessing this is your Russian Prince. He's a hunk, I'll give him that."

"I know not your meaning."

"Of course you don't. He's a good-looking—I mean, he's a very handsome man."

"I've never actually seen him. Until now. But all the stories I heard spoke of his comeliness."

"And his come-on to the ladies, I'll bet."

"I do not—"

"Know my meaning. I know, I know. He liked the women. And they liked him."

"Yes. There were stories of such."

"I'll bet. He's talking. We need to listen."

"Russia is rife with turmoil. The Regent Helena has been poisoned at her own table. Even you must know Helena has been England's strongest ally in Russia. King Henry is very much afraid for the young Tsar Ivan. Rumor has it that the Council of Boyars is behind the poisoning of the Regent. This is fearful news because the tsar and his brother are helpless in their hands. King Henry's ambassador believes there is a plot to murder both the boys."

"How horrible." Ursula gripped the arms of her ornate chair.

"There are those among the Boyars who have long been anxious to overthrow the Tsarist Court. King Henry is gravely concerned for the tsar's safety. He has asked me to return to Russia and look after the boy."

"Then of course you must go."

"Stephen is to come with me. King Henry wishes him to become friends with the tsar. The tsar will need allies in the days to come. Allies he can trust. Allies bound by blood. Stephen is, after all the tsar's cousin."

"My son? The babe she—I—carried in the vision past?"

"I'd bet the bank on it."

Ursula stiffened in the chair. "No. You cannot take my son. He's just a babe."

"He is not a babe. He is seven, almost the age of the tsar himself. He is, through you, the heir to the throne of Moldavia. And the tsar's own cousin. This is his destiny, his duty."

"He is English. I am English. Moldavia's given me nothing but my father's death. *This* is his place, his country."

"And if this is his place and his country, he is of the age for fostering. You know that. So he will leave you in any event. You cannot be so selfish as to try and keep him with you. What noble boy does not foster at seven? And why should he foster with an English noble when his blood ties are with Russian royalty?"

Ursula's teeth clenched. "Then I will come with you. I will not lose my son."

"Would that you could, dear wife, but I have already broached that possibility with the king. It is his wish you stay in England. Your grandmother is not in health or years able to properly direct Fairhaven herself. She depends on you. Certainly she could not steward Gresham Manor, too. You do not want the king to appoint an unknown regent for Gresham Manor, who would likely try to take it for his own, surely? Or at the least, divert its bounty into his own coffers. It is Stephen's English birthright, after all. And your responsibility to hold it for him."

"Son-of-a-bitch!" Floating Katherine swore. *"He's really covered his bases. And I think that's called checkmate."*

"Even I catch your meaning. And he is lying. He has tricked the king into ordering exactly as he wishes. He does not want her— me—with him. I can feel the truth. It rushes from him like a storm. I have been a disappointment. One child in all these years. Nor do I bow down and worship him as he feels is his due. So he will take my son. Though it is true. At seven, I would lose him to his foster family. It is how things are, how they will always be."

"Not always. But Grandmother was right. You needed this. You're growing up fast."

"I do not know your grandmother."

"Doesn't matter. She sure knows you."

Physical Ursula sat, carved in stone, unable to stop the whisper hissing from her lips. And her heart. "I hate you. And I hate the king."

"You said something, my dear wife? You must speak louder if you wish me to hear you."

Ursula stood. She had to get out of this room. "I shall go begin arrangements for your journey."

Chapter Seven

Treachery

"And we're done here." Floating Katherine raised her head and turned it into the rising psychic winds.

"Yes." Floating Ursula moved in front of her. *"'Tis coming for us again. To blow us—we know not where."*

"But wherever it is, you're ready for it, aren't you? No more woe-is-me?"

"Whatever it is—the worst that can be done to me has already been done."

"Welllll—I don't want to scare you, honey, but uh—no. I don't think it has."

"My child is gone. They took my child from me. My husband and my king. The two men sworn to protect me, guard me. But not to love me. Never did they swear that. There is no worse. The wind dallies this time. I wish it would hurry. I wish to finish this."

The psychic winds rushed, pushed, and deposited them at their destination.

Floating Ursula's face softened. Her lips curved in a small smile.

"You know where you are?"

" 'Tis an ill wind that blows no good. I'm home. At Gresham Manor. In my sewing room. I've been here for a time. Several years. Long enough for England's crown to pass. To a woman. Neither Henry nor poor little Edward sit upon the English throne."

Floating Katherine smiled. *"And how do you know that, Ursula?*

"I know because she knows." She pointed down below them.

Physical Ursula sat before a blazing fire, a warm fur throw across her lap as she worked her embroidery stiches. She glanced toward the window, gauging time by the sun.

"What are you doing, honey?"

"Waiting. Timmy—one of the farmer's sons. Of an age with my son. He visits me. And I—this is secret. Should the Church or his father know, they would be angry."

"Because he visits you?"

"Because I give him reading lessons when he visits. They would be angry. Because I teach him. And because I can. 'Tis unseemly for a woman to read. No one now living knows I can. Papa taught me."

Physical Ursula's face turned parchment white. The pupils of her eyes enlarged, turning them black as night with no hint of blue. Her sewing fell from her hands onto the rushes of the floor. She sat, frozen in time, for only the space of seconds. She flung the fur off her legs and sprang to her feet, the sound of her footfalls echoing down the hall as she raced for the front door.

"What the hell is that all about?"

"Timmy. I think. I cannot catch it all but—I think he's in trouble. And she—I—know."

"Because she—you—saw it."

"No! Such is sorcery. I do not really see things. I never have, never! 'Tis dreams they are, merely dreams."

"Methinks the lady doth protest too much. How long have you seen things, honey? Not through me, not like this. Yourself. How long have you seen things, these mere dreams of yours?"

Floating Ursula wrung her hands and turned away. Katherine gave no quarter.

"How long?"

Floating Ursula swung back around to face her.

"Always. For as long as I can remember."

"Figures. Well, now it all makes sense. Sorta."

"What does?"

"You'll see. As you said. Let's finish this."

Physical Ursula grabbed her heavy fur cloak from the chair by the heavy doorway, kept there for convenience by her own orders over Hannah's protests. She flung it over her shoulders and ran across the courtyard toward the stable.

"A horse! Saddle a horse! Not Bella, I need a stallion. Saddle Thor! Quickly, quickly!"

"Milady! Your dress, your shoes! You cannot ride in this cold in those clothes. 'Tis your death you'll catch! And Thor's a handful, you've no—"

Usually Ursula loved the solicitous care her staff extended in seeing to her needs. Their love, freely given as the natural result of hers for them, provided balm for her aching, lonely heart. Not this time, though. Not this time.

"Obey me! Thor! Now!"

* * *

Ursula pushed her horse like a woman possessed, galloping across the fields to Timmy's father.

"Ralf!" She started shouting as soon as soon as the farmhouse came into view.

Timmy's father ran from the barn.

"Milady? What's amiss? Is something wrong with my boy to send you out in the cold alone? Why did he not come back with you?"

"So he did set out for the manor this morning?"

"Aye, Milady. Did he not get there?"

"Ralf, you must listen to me! Ask me no questions, just trust me! Timmy tried to cross a creek over a log. The log rolled, his foot is wedged underneath, and there's a deep drop-off in the water right beside the log. He cannot regain his footing. The creek is swift, 'tis one of the creeks fed by the northern mountains, but I do not know which one. He struggles to keep his head above water. He's tiring quickly! We must get to him. Do you know such a place?"

Ralf stepped back. He stared at Ursula and made the sign of the cross, safe enough now that Mary wore the English crown.

"Ralf! Timmy tires quickly, we must get to him! Do you know such a place?"

"I've told him and told him not to go there alone, but he often plays near where I set my fishing nets. The deep spot, the trout like it. Likely he went by to check the nets 'afore he headed to the manor."

"Mount behind me, Thor will carry us both!"

* * *

"There, Milady! There!" Ralf pointed past Ursula and the sound of the rushing water. "Let me down here!"

Ralf tore through the undergrowth and into the icy water to his son. When Ursula reached them, Timmy's arms circled his father's neck in a vice grip. Ursula pulled an extra blanket from the back of Thor's saddle. "Wrap him in this, Ralf."

"'Tis a rare fright you gave us, lad!" Ralf scolded as he wrapped the boy tightly in the blanket. "And you can thank Her Ladyship we got to you in time!" He pulled his son close and hugged fiercely. "Milady, might I ask if you could see your way clear to—"

"Of course, Ralf. Lift Timmy up to me, I'll get him straight home to his mother and in front of the fire. I'll come back for you."

Ralf's face beamed. "No surprise Your Ladyship knew just what I was about to say, not what with you knowing my Timmy was in trouble and all. But you just get him back to the farm and his mum and that fire, Milady, no need to come back for me, 'tis lickety-split I'll be there myself."

"'Twould be no trouble to come back to fetch you, Ralf."

"No, Milady. 'Tis the boy that's important, not me. Get him back to his mum and he'll be right as rain between the two of you."

* * *

"Well, Milady, 'tis a good day's work you've done for sure."

"You mock me again."

"No, I really don't. It's just—I'm afraid we haven't seen the last effect of that vision that sent her—you—to Timmy."

"'Tis certain we haven't. And 'tis almost certain I am what we'll see next."

"So have you seen enough? Enough to choose?"

"I started this journey. I will see it through."

The floating entities looked down as scenes rushed past them. This time the journey was short.

"Are we still at Gresham Manor?"

"Aye. 'Tis the parlor where guests are received."

The floating entities looked and watched as Ursula served cider to her visitor.

"'Tis good of you to visit, Lady Grenville."

"'Tis grateful I am for your welcome, Princess Ursula. Though I fear you may think it garnered through false pretense."

"How so?"

"I beg a favor of you. I want—I need—to ask you something."

"Ask."

"'Tis said—I've heard—well, 'tis said you can command the future to reveal itself." Lady Grenville took a sip of cider and fixed her gaze on Ursula.

Ursula sat back. Timmy's rescue. She'd known, somehow she'd known. There would come a day when that day's work would return to her and weight her down. But no matter. Timmy was safe. She'd do it all again.

"As you know, my husband and I are childless. I beg of you, Princess. I beg you to tell me. Will I ever bear my own child?"

Ursula reached over and took her hand. "Dear Lady Grenville, it grieves me I cannot help you, but I have no power to command the future. 'Tis true, sometimes I'm given glimpses into things to come, but never have I been able to call them to me at will."

"But you saved the farmer's son. And you knew before he spoke, he was going to ask you to get Timmy home on the stallion! "

"'Tis a blessing I was granted that chance to save young Timmy, and I thank God for it. But I could no more have called upon that vision than I can fly. And as to knowing his father would ask me to take Timmy home— Milady, that was nothing more than having a bit of a brain in my head. Of course he wanted his son home as quickly as possible. He was soaking wet on a frigid day. I was on a horse, and he was not. 'Twas merely what anyone would ask."

"But you knew!"

"Milady, so would you have known."

"So you will not help me?"

"Lady Grenville, I cannot help you. I would if I could. But I cannot call forth the future."

"Wrong answer, I'm afraid. Honey, you've just made an enemy."

"An enemy who has connections at court. Yes. 'Tis possible I've just signed my death warrant."

"So—can you choose now? Or do we keep going?"

"I began this journey. I will see it through." She turned her head into the rising winds that blew only for them. *"Come, my winds of prophecy! Blow me to my end!"*

* * *

The winds heard. And obeyed. Ursula and Katherine soared high in their grip, pushed forward in ever-increasing momentum, and then rushed downward, the view beneath them coming into focus as they descended.

Guards in medieval garb rode behind a horse drawn cart. Inside a woman bound in chains kept her head down and her eyes averted from the crowds lining the streets of Knaresborough.

Laughing, jeering voices followed the cart as the spectators, electrified by the spectacle of nobility paraded through the streets like a common prisoner, worked themselves into a frenzy, calling out as she passed.

"Witch! Witch! Burn the bloody witch!"

"I've been here before," floating Katherine whispered. *"Grandmother's shown me this. I didn't know why but—"*

"But now you do. Aye. The beginning of my end."

The Ursula in the cart raised her head proudly. She was, by God, a Sontheil of Gresham Manor, and legitimate Queen of Moldavia by birth, not that she'd ever cared a fig about that. A Princess of the Russian royal house by marriage. She would be damned if this mishmash crowd of nobility and common folk would see her break. Not now. Not ever. Her lips curved in a faint smile when she saw Lady

Grenville back in the crowd. An accused witch had no friends.

The winds pushed the floating entities forward, but gently.

"We're fast-forwarding a bit," said Katherine. *"And thank God. I don't know how much of this I can watch, and I don't see how you're watching it. Are you—do you want to stop now?"*

Floating Ursula smiled. *"Fast forward? 'Tis strange but I do understand the meaning of your strange phrases now."* She shrugged. *"Or at least that one."*

"Do you want to stop here?"

"No. We go until I know the fate of the child of this path. Unless you can tell me that?"

"I'm sorry. I don't know."

"Then we go until we do." She shrugged again. *"Or until I'm put to death. Whichever event should first occur."*

The winds stopped. They hovered in darkness, watching as the cart neared the looming darkness of a stone tower and stopped at a gate by the River Thames. The guards dismounted and took Ursula from the cart, placing her in a barge. The oarsman pushed off and rowed towards the dark Tower.

"The Tower of London."

"Yes."

Tower guards waited at the landing and took her up the steps. Flickering torches gave barely enough light for safe traverse. The steps were crumbling and much disused, and twice the Ursula they watched almost fell as her feet slipped on the damp and slippery stone.

Darkness hung around her like a cloak. Haunting cries floated through the air and lingered in the stairwell. A fierce, desperate roar echoed through the darkness.

"What the hell was that?"

"A lion. Doubtless from the royal menagerie. A fitting salute, is it not? From one captive to another."

The guards came to a halt in front of a heavy wooden door. One guard lifted a latch and pushed the door inward. He motioned Ursula to step within. The flicker from his torch lit the small barren chamber. A crude bed stood against the wall. The floor was devoid of covering rushes.

The guard lit a tiny candle from his flickering torch. He turned without a word and left her alone. She dropped to the bed, her vow fulfilled. No one had seen her break. She broke now. Great gulping sobs racked her body. Fear clawed her throat and rose like bile to choke and gag her, and finally, all emotion drained from her body. She fell sideways on the filthy bed covers and slipped into exhausted slumber.

* * *

The winds pushed gently, and the hovering entities floated off, descending back into the same dank cell.

"Same channel, different time," said Katherine. "I wonder how long she's—you've—been here."

"'Tis difficult to say. Do I look older? Or is the haunted look on my face merely the etching of desolation?"

"I'd guess—desolation. Honey, truly—don't you think it's time to leave?"

The Ursula lying on the bed sat up. Rather, she bolted up. Her face went even whiter and her pupils expanded, turning her eyes to pure blackness with no hint of blue.

"Oh, damn, I know that look! She's—you're—seeing something! But what? What good does it do you to see her have a vision if you're not seeing it yourself?!"

Floating Ursula moved downward and hovered directly over the immobile figure.

"I am her and she is me. And if I make a mighty enough effort—I shall see! I must see! As must you! Come. Float closer and take my hand." Floating Ursula stretched her arm up to floating Katherine.

"We've tried that! We can't actually touch anything, we're not physically here!"

"Believe!" Floating Ursula shook the hand upstretched to Katherine. "Believe and it will happen! I need you with me! I need your strength to help me bear what I will see!"

Katherine reached down. Nothing. She concentrated harder. Still nothing.

"Believe!"

"Grandmother, damn it! A little help here!"

Katherine clutched down hard. And felt it. The solid flesh of floating Ursula's physical hand. And entered the vision within a vision. Entered Hell.

* * *

Battle raged. Screams of agony, roaring fire. Giant flames leapt and glowed in vivid patterns, crackling and popping as one building after another ignited into a fierce inferno.

Everywhere they looked, blood crazed soldiers hacked and stabbed at bleeding, screaming, yielding flesh.

The scene shifted, moved inside an ornate hall, spiraling down, and focusing on the figure defending a back corner. Prince Frederick. His sword parried and thrust in his desperate attempt to protect the small figure behind him.

Too many. He sank to his knees, staring at the blade protruding from his heart. Hands yanked him forward, away from the small figure he guarded. Blades flashed downward. A child screamed, the echo bouncing off the stone walls and dying away into silence. The silence of death.

"Enough!" Floating Ursula pulled her hand out of Katherine's, catapulting them back into the dank cell. The rigid Ursula sitting on the bed wailed and collapsed back into the filthy blanket. *'Tis done!"* Floating Ursula's eyes streamed tears. *"I know the fate of the child who*

will never be. Take me back! Back to my Toby!
He and our beautiful little girl wait for me!"

* * *

Toby pushed himself and Sybil, moving through the trees as the crow flies, praying he was still on the right path. It had been a long time since he'd heard the calling echoes audible only to him. Too long? Had he heard anything at all? Or were the calls imagined, born of his own need to hear her voice?

"Follow my love! Follow....follow..."

Finally, and thank God for it! This call sounded much closer. They started down sloping ground. From the sound of it, a creek in full spate roared down below. Sybil didn't care. His arms strained with the effort to hold her back. Had he given her the okay, she'd have rushed down in a gallop.

Down below, against the gray-green-brown of the creek bed....Was that a flash of white? He reined Sybil in and jumped down. The white of a nightdress! The gleam of ivory skin, deadly white. Auburn hair spread like a sunrise over the gray of a rocky pillow.

"Milady!" He gathered her close and cradled her in his arms. "Milady!"

"Thank God!" Katherine hovered above, as exhausted as she ever remembered being. *"Ursula, he's here! Your Toby's here!"*

"'Tis not blind I am, only senseless. For the moment."

"But you're not going to be senseless when you wake up, are you?"

"I misdoubt we give the word the same meaning. But yes. When I wake, I wake to a new life. I know what I must do. Duty no longer has high import with me. At least—not duty to the king."

"And you won't backslide?"

"Backslide?"

"Change your mind?"

"Not if the sun ceases to circle the earth."

"Bad choice there, girl, be a while before anybody figures that out, though. But I understand what you mean."

"My thanks to you. Whoever you are, wherever you came from. Though never will I see you again, will I?"

"I wouldn't be so sure of that, Milady. You'll see me again. In the future. Since I actually have one now."

"I do not know your meaning."

"Doesn't matter. You will. Be happy."

Toby shook unconscious Ursula slightly; a faint moan his only reward. Where was Sarah? And where in Lucifer's hell were the guards? But for now it didn't matter how and why she'd ended up in the middle of the woods, unconscious and in her nightdress. All that mattered was getting her home. Back to Gresham Manor. He laid her back down and stripped off his cloak. He wrapped her in its folds and carried her back to Sybil.

"You have to help me, Sybil. Stand very still, my beauty. I hope you paid more heed to our journey's path than I did. Take us home, beautiful girl. Back to the manor."

* * *

Katherine stayed in place and watched Toby ride off with his lady fair. A good day's work. Night's work. Year's work. Whatever. Damn, she was tired. And where was Carrie and those guards? They were sure taking their sweet time getting back.

On cue, Carrie flitted back down the slope.

"Jeeezzz Louise, I never thought I'd get them here! Damn stubborn idiots! I pull 'em one direction, they go in another just outta pure spite, I swear to God, thought I was watching re-runs of The Three Stooges! And—holy shit! She's gone! What the hell?"

"Long story. Long, long story. This was it. The crossroad Grandmother talked about. Her Toby came and found her. Mostly because she called him. And all is now well with the world. Mine, anyway. I mean, I'm here, after all, and I wouldn't be if everything wasn't. All right, I mean."

"You're not making a lick of sense, you know that?"

"I know. Tell you about it when we get back. 'Cause I am beat up. Absolutely

exhausted. You lose your guards again? Where'd they go?"

"Hell, I don't know! They're as bad as herding cats, but they were right behind me! And who cares now? She's not here for 'em to find. So we can go home now?"

"Hell to the yeah. Let's go home."

Chapter Eight

Lillian – Present Time

Lillian Shipton glanced at the GPS on the dashboard of her rental car and checked the turn. Yep, right street. Now just a few curves down to the proper street address and she'd be at her niece's house. Well, technically, her niece's fiancé's house, at least at present. Lillian had no doubt from Katherine's phone conversations, some of which had been speaker-phone conversations with Parker in attendance, that what belonged to him belonged to Katherine and vice-versa. True soul mates, those two, and Lillian couldn't be happier.

Such a relief that was, Katherine ending that farce with Quentin Ashland. Even the man's name left a bad taste on Lillian's tongue. No good would've ever come out of that relationship, and she'd known it. But she'd also known Katherine had to realize that for herself and hadn't even tried to talk her out of it. And she thanked all the powers of the universe for whatever happened that sent Katherine running so abruptly.

And at least this time, there was no mystery as to why her inner voice was telling her—no, yelling at her—to go to Katherine. Like *yesterday*. The entire family knew Katherine hated formal functions, especially Mina and Lillian, who'd conferred at length about the logistics of keeping both Irene's and Katherine's weddings on track. They especially worried about Katherine's wedding, since in the Drayton world, social functions had tremendous potential to impact big business, something Lillian understood completely and had used to her advantage in her own successful career. With Parker off for a two-week business trip, it had been a no-brainer. Mina would stay in Calgary and ride herd on Irene's wedding and Lillian would make sure Katherine's wedding stayed on track. If Lillian knew her niece, and she did, those invitations were sitting on a desk or counter somewhere and would stay there until cobwebs covered them. She hadn't even given Katherine any advance notice of her impending arrival. She'd just come. And she wasn't leaving until the invitations were mailed, the flowers selected, the menu set, the wedding gown fitted, and Katherine's last name was Drayton.

At least with Katherine's impeccable artistic sense, she didn't have to worry about the bridesmaids' dresses being ugly. Katherine wouldn't do that to her friends and family. Katherine's sensitivity was a dominate personality trait and she had a true talent for diplomacy, as evidenced by her decision regarding her Maid of Honor, or rather, her Co-Maids of Honor, because of course it was unthinkable that Irene wouldn't be Katherine's Maid of Honor. However, the strong streak of Shipton independence that had sent Katherine off on her own to New York City at eighteen—and hadn't Bill Shipton nearly had a stroke over that—had given Katherine another sister, her roommate Carrie Bennington. Lillian had mitigated the hardships of those years as much as the girls had let her, which wasn't terribly often, with little treats and extra luxuries, but they'd worked hard to make it on their own. That shared bond of those years in New York as they fought their way up had made them true sisters of the heart. Of course Carrie had to be Katherine's Maid of Honor. Katherine's edict that she was having Co-Maids of Honor was the perfect solution.

She pulled into and down the curving drive and took the circle leading to the front. Katherine could tell her where she needed to park later. Lovely, lovely house. A happy house. She walked up to the door and rang the bell. No response. She'd caught a glimpse of Katherine's car when she'd negotiated the drive. Still, Katherine was a runner and might be out. Midafternoon was mighty hot for that, though, Katherine should have enough sense to run in the mornings or the evenings. Television was on, too. MTV? Odd. Katherine's tastes hadn't run to MTV in a long time.

Lillian rang the bell again and knocked. Nothing. She tried the door knob, just because, and laughed at herself as she did. Of course Katherine wouldn't have left the door unlocked. And if she had, she'd be hearing about it from Aunt Lillian. The knob turned. Oh yeah, Kat was going to hear about this!

* * *

Mother Shipton sat in the recliner next to the big curved sofa where the girls slumbered, one on each end. She stared in fascination at the big screen TV and punched the buttons on the magic box in her hand, watching the little world captured in the big window shift from one impossible image to another.

"Oh my God!" A whirlwind raced across the room toward the girls. "Katherine! Carrie! Who the *hell* are you and what have you done to my girls?"

The figure sitting in the chair rippled like a disrupted television transmittal. It smiled and disappeared.

"'Tis done! The line is safe! And into your hands do I leave the stewardship of the sisters. The sisters of prophecy, whether they be sisters by blood or sisters by heart."

The figure was gone, the girls still unconscious.

"Katherine! Carrie! Wake up, damn it! Talk to me!"

* * *

Katherine floated back to the surface of Reality River. It really wasn't hard, this time travel via mind thing; she was getting used to it. Though she didn't recall anybody'd been shouting in her ear before. The TV'd been blaring, yes, but nobody'd been calling her—or Carrie—by name. Certainly nobody who sounded like—

"Aunt Lillian?" Katherine opened her eyes and blinked. "What are you doing here?"

"Oh! Oh, thank God! And Carrie?" Aunt Lillian shook Carrie's shoulder. "Wake up, child, the two of you scared the *hell* out of me, what on earth is going on?! And there was an old woman here when I walked in! And now she's gone, she just disappeared!"

"Guess she had to leave, once she'd done what she came for."

"Too bad, too." Carrie stretched her arms over her head. "I kinda wish we could have shown her around a bit, I think we could have made a modern woman of her the way she loved to blare MTV."

Lillian stared down at her niece and adopted niece. "Should I call the gas company and have them check for leaks? Neither of you seem terribly grounded right now."

"House is total electric, can't blame it on that."

"Katherine! I come in, you and Carrie might as well have been in a coma, and there's a strange old woman sitting in the recliner watching MTV! Now explain yourselves *right this minute!*"

"That's going to take a lot more than a minute, Aunt Lillian. What time is it? And what are you doing here, anyway?"

"It's five thirty. In the afternoon. And *somebody's* got to make sure you get these wedding plans finished!"

"True. Sounds like a job for you, Aunt Lillian. Is it just me or is anybody else hungry?"

"Starving!" Carrie stood up and headed for the kitchen. "This psychic time-travel thing really works up an appetite."

"Girls, I'm losing patience here!"

Katherine laughed. "Let's go start some steaks on the grill. And then we'll tell you all about it."

"And I haven't heard the end of the story, either, remember, I was off trying to herd those stupid guards in the right direction."

"I got here just in time. Both of you have totally lost your minds."

"Yeah, well, trips down rabbit holes and through looking glasses tend to have that effect on people."

Chapter Nine

Dark Clouds

"You're late. I said nine o'clock. It's almost ten." Quentin Ashland glared at the figure settling into the shadows across from him in the back booth of Sandler's Oyster Bar. The restaurant was full of shadows. Nick Sandler knew what his customers wanted, and they didn't want oysters. They wanted shadows. Some business transactions required darkness.

Tony DeNitizi glared back. "Oh, quit your bitchin'. You don't own me, Ashland. I'm here. So talk."

"Yeah, you're here. I own enough of you to make it a *real* bad idea to cross me. Don't even think about forgetting that."

"So what the hell you want?" Tony's hand itched to pull his Glock out of his shoulder harness and unload every damn bullet into Quentin's head. That'd wipe the smug expression off Ashland's face. Permanently. That day would come. But it wasn't here yet.

Ashland had too many files stored in too many places. Files the DEA would love to get its hands on. Not to mention the ATF. And every state law enforcement agency in every state from Florida all the way up the coast to New York and New Jersey.

Quentin leaned forward. "What the hell you think I want? I called you, didn't I?"

"Who? And you got any idea of where and when?"

Quentin slid a picture across the table.

DeNitzi picked it up and threw it back down.

"Are you fucking crazy or just plain stupid?"

"You talk to all your customers that way?"

"You're not a customer. You're a blackmailer. And that's a Drayton. Of Drayton Oil."

"You actually read the papers?"

"I watch the news, too. Parker Drayton. Heir apparent of the oil company dedicated to making America independent of foreign oil. Not exactly anybody that's gonna just slip unnoticed from the radar. Why the hell would you want him dead?"

"None of your damn business why. Didn't think you'd be squeamish about it."

"I'm not squeamish. I'm a businessman. In a business involving calculated risks. This one's not a risk to take."

Quentin leaned forward. "What'll happen if you don't isn't a risk, my man. It's a certainty. I will take you down." He waited for that to sink in. "Besides, Drayton's not a risk. Just an unfortunate accident. He's going to be taking a chopper ride out in the Gulf in the next few days. To some old abandoned offshore oil rigs. His regular pilot's not going to be available. I'm sure you've got someone who can fill in for that pilot. And that chopper—well, it's going down. With no survivors. Not that anyone knows about anyway. Whether there actually are any—well, that's your call. Because if there aren't any survivors, nobody's ever going to know what happened, now are they?"

"And you guarantee when that chopper ride's gonna happen?"

"I'll know."

"Might work."

"You better hope it does."

* * *

"…and so they all lived happily ever after." Katherine finished the story and sipped her wine. "You believe us, Aunt Lillian? Or you want to call the men in the white coats to take us away?"

Lillian held out her wine glass. "A bit more, please, Kat. Of course I believe you. I'm a Shipton. Blood calls to blood and like to like. Besides, I never heard of two psychos having the exact same story. And I don't think you could have planned this as an elaborate joke to hit me with. You didn't know I was coming."

145

"That is just so not right," Carrie sighed. "Y'all sitting there drinkin' wine in front of me, knowing I can't have any."

"You aren't off the hook yet, young lady." Aunt Lillian pointed her finger. "You still haven't told us the story behind our impending little bundle of joy."

"I know. And I will. I just—I'm not ready to talk about it yet, Aunt Lillian. The mosquitos are really beginning to cut loose out here, I think patio time's over, let's go in."

Katherine's phone rang.

"That's Parker's ringtone. You two go on in, I'll be in in a few."

"We wouldn't eavesdrop if you came inside and stopped feeding the mosquitoes, you know."

"I know. But it's more romantic out here by the pool. I can pretend he's not a thousand miles away."

"Kat and Parker sittin' in a tree, k-i-s-s-i-n-g…"

Katherine laughed. "Carrie, quit it! I'll be in in a minute."

The sliding glass doors whispered shut.

"Hello, handsome!"

"Hi, beautiful! Have you had a good day?"

Katherine almost laughed out loud. "It's been an *amazing* day! Absolutely amazing. And guess what? Carrie flew in this morning to surprise me and Aunt Lillian flew in this afternoon!"

"Did they coordinate that?"

"Not on purpose, no."

"Well, I'm glad. Haven't met either of 'em yet, but from the speaker phone conversations I've heard, they're exactly what you need to get the wedding motivated and organized."

"Don't think I'm not going to take advantage either! I'm going to stay in my studio and paint and let them do the whole thing."

"Slacker."

"Smile when you say that, cowboy. Did *you* have a good day?"

"Sure did. Dad's got this new deal taking off. It involves recycling some older oil rigs out in the Gulf."

"Who says you can't be a businessman and an environmentalist at the same time?"

"Knew you'd like that. I'm going out to start inspecting them early tomorrow morning and I doubt phone reception's going to be great. Like leaving at the crack of dawn tomorrow morning early. Gotta be at the helipad at six a.m. So don't worry if you try to get me and can't."

"Don't know if you've noticed this yet, but I'm not the clingy type who's got to have hourly phone conversations. I never bother you when you're working."

She heard his smile through the phone. "I've noticed. I even worry if you'd call me in an emergency."

"Of course I would!"

"I guess what I really mean is, I worry about what you'd class as enough of an emergency to call me."

"I'll just avoid having any emergencies. Problem solved. Deal?"

"Deal."

"Now you."

"Me?"

"You avoid having any emergencies, too. Especially while inspecting offshore oilrigs. Helipad, huh? Helicopters scare me."

"We use a top of the line independent contractor for planes and choppers, you know that. We're oilmen, not air jockeys, and we know it. We let the professionals do the flying and the maintenance, much more cost efficient. Our only venture into flying is to keep helipads in strategic places. And I'll do my best to avoid emergencies, too. Promise."

Chapter Ten

Danger Above and Below

Quentin Ashland paced his study and looked at the clock above the mantle, not for the first time. He yanked his cell out of his pocket. It wasn't the first time he'd glared at it in the hours he'd returned from the Oyster Bar, either. This time proved the charm. "Unknown Caller" lit up the screen as the generic ringtone sounded.

"What have you got? And what the hell took you so long?"

"You called me at ten o'clock this morning. It's a fucking miracle I got anything for you at all. And I had to finish another job that went hot and heavy before I could get back with you."

"You stopped to finish another *job* before you bothered to call me?"

"Ashland, you're not my only client. Or even my most profitable one. Just my biggest pain in the ass one. You want to hear or not?"

"Okay, okay! So what you got?"

"That chopper ride to the Gulf's happening tomorrow morning. The chopper's set to lift off at six a.m."

"You sure?"

"Yeah, lucked out on that."

"Lucked out? I don't pay you this type of money to luck out on anything!"

"Look, hotshot. You didn't give me enough time to bug the house. The old man's a rich widower. The kind who has live-in staff. The best I could do in the time I had was slap a few outside bugs around the patio and pool. Rich boy came outside by the pool to call his fiancée and I was parked close enough to the house to pick it up. So yeah, I'm sure. Unless he's lying to his fiancée just for the hell of it."

"Which airport is the helipad at?"

"You're kidding, right? We're talking rich people here. The helipad's at Drayton Oil Corporate Headquarters. So what do you want me to do now?"

"Make sure you know about it if his plans change. And that I know it two seconds after you do."

* * *

Tony DiNitzi knocked over the glass of water he habitually kept on his nightstand and swore loudly into the darkness. He groped for his cell phone and snorted when he read the "Unknown Caller" designation. He should be so lucky. Quentin Ashland. He could feel the slime through the phone casing.

"Tony? Chrissakes, issa middle of the night, ain't anybody got manners anymore?" Tony's latest live-in mumbled the words through the pillow she'd rolled around her head.

"Sorry, baby, this asshole ain't never *had* any manners. Go back to sleep, I'm going in the living room."

Tony stubbed his toe on the couch while he fumbled for the lamp.

"*Sonofabitch!* Ashland, what the fuck?"

"Not the best greeting for the man who *owns* you, Tony. That *sonofabitch* could get you a visit from the DEA if I were the sensitive type."

Tony laughed shortly. "Even if you were the sensitive type, what you want from me's way too sensitive to call the DEA in on. You didn't call to say sweet dreams. What's up?"

"It's happenin' sooner than I expected. Tomorrow, six a.m. So look through your payroll and find somebody you can switch out for a chopper pilot."

* * *

Tony smiled as he hit the *End* button of his phone. Oh, yeah. He had just the guy for the job. Not the job Ashland wanted, of course. Ashland was thinking with his dick, not his brain. Musta been a hell of a woman to knock him so far out

151

of reality he thought he could order a hit on Parker Drayton just like *that*. Or that he didn't realize his threats were toothless as an old man without his dentures. After all, Ashland wasn't the only one who knew where the bodies were buried. If Ashland turned Tony over to the authorities, well, Tony had just as big a file on Ashland as Ashland had on him. Along with one big advantage. Of course the Feds watched Tony's organization. But Tony knew from his inside contacts the Feds were all over Ashland like white on rice. They kept track of a *lot* of cartels through Ashland. He was just too damn arrogant and stupid to know it. Tony hadn't enlightened him either. Because there was a big shipment in the immediate horizon Tony'd been beating his brains out to coordinate. Too big to trust to the usual pipelines. And praise the saints, this new potential pipeline dropped straight into his lap. Because what would Justin Drayton do to get his son back safely? *Shiittt.* He'd do anything. Most fathers would.

Tony ran down his contact list and dialed.

"What the hell, DeNitizi? It's the middle of the fuckin' night! Hell, it's damn near *morning!*"

"You keep banker's hours now? Got a job for you. And you got to set up quick."

* * *

At 5:45 a.m., Justin Drayton pulled his old truck up to the helipad installed in one of the

152

back lots of corporate headquarters. Parker pushed hard on the door with his body as he yanked at the door release.

"Dad, you have *got* to break down and start driving one of the newer trucks!"

"Not a damn thing wrong with this truck, lots of miles left on it. Now you be careful out there, son, you hear?" An unnecessary and completely worthless admonition to give a grown man and Justin knew it. But some things never changed, and no parent on earth ever managed to delete it from their repertoire, no matter how old their kids got.

"I will. And backatcha." The truck door slammed, and Parker headed for the chopper.

"Son!" Parker turned around at the sharp tone. His Dad's head rose over the truck cab, he'd opened the truck door and stood up. Parker knew exactly what he wanted, too. He gave a thumbs up and snapped off a quick salute.

"Yes, sir! Got it with me, sir! Following orders, Sir!"

"Don't get smart with me, boy! You sure you got it? You're bad about—"

"Dad! Really! I've got it. Won't need it, but I've got it!"

"Okay, then. See you tonight."

* * *

Parker tossed his backpack behind the passenger seat of the Bell 407 and turned back to his pilot, hand out-stretched.

153

"Hi, Parker Drayton. Where's Joe? He usually flies whenever I need a chopper."

The pilot shook Parker's hand. "Joe's had a stomach bug the last couple of days, Mr. Drayton. I'm Sam Carver, I'll be flying you out this morning."

"Parker. Even my dad's not Mr. Drayton. Well, let's get this thing in the air. You know where we're heading first."

"Yes, sir."

* * *

Parker looked out over the expanse of blue beneath them. Brilliant glints of sunlight bounced up off in the horizon, refracted off the massive metal frame of the first offshore rig. Parker turned to speak to the pilot and reached for the name. Sam, he'd said his name was Sam.

Before Parker got the name out, the pilot's hand flashed out toward Parker's arm. Parker felt a sharp sting. A bee sting? What the hell was a bee doing on the chopper? That was his last conscious thought before he slumped sideways in the seat.

The pilot adjusted the radio to a private frequency.

"Okay, got him. And he's just gone beddy-bye. I'm still headed to the first rig?"

"Yes, you definitely are."

"Seems kinda stupid, taking the chopper exactly where everybody expects it to be."

"That's the point, dumbass. To all outside eyes, the chopper's exactly where it's supposed to be. And through the day it'll keep going exactly where it's supposed to go. That way no eyebrows get raised about a missing chopper. Nobody but Justin Drayton needs to know we've got his baby boy. And he's not going to be telling."

"Whatever. Don't matter one way or the other to me. I just follow orders."

"That's why it's such a pleasure doing business with you. Keep him healthy. And keep him on this first rig till I tell you to move to the second one."

* * *

Justin Drayton glanced down at his phone screen. Parker. What the hell? No way Parker was getting cell reception, not where he was traveling. Not even on the rig. The rig hadn't been used in several years. Communications would have to be reconnected and upgraded before cell communication was going to work out there.

"Hey, son! Where are you? What's the problem?"

"No problem, Mr. Drayton, Parker's right here with me on the first rig to be inspected. Gonna get that straight 'cause no point in you wasting time trying to have my calls traced. We're right where we're supposed to be." The caller wanted that established up front, seeing as

155

how he was calling from a cloned phone and was nowhere near the vicinity of the first rig. Something Drayton surely didn't need to know. Not that he thought Drayton would risk calling in the authorities. His devotion to family was legendary.

"Who is this? Where's Parker?"

"Let's just say he's not able to talk right now."

"What the hell do you want?"

"Cooperation."

Justin snorted. "I already know that. You think a stupid man runs a company the size of this one?"

"No sir, I surely don't. And that's why I think you and me are gonna get along just fine and you're going to fall all over yourself cooperating."

"I want to talk to him."

"Not possible."

"Pretty damn stupid on your part, son, calling me from Parker's phone and not letting me talk to him. Makes a man worry if his boy's all right. And a worried man ain't good at cooperation."

"He's just taking a little nap. He'll be up real soon. I'll let you talk to him then. In the meantime, you can start putting some cooperation into action."

"What do you want?"

"The Drayton transport fleet. Not all of it, of course. Just the ones handy to a few ports."

"And just what are they going to be transporting?"

"Don't think I'd be worrying about that if I were you, sir. All you need to know is that little bit of extra cargo is going to get you your boy back. In the meantime, you might want to be checking on exactly where that cargo fleet's deployed right now. I'm not even going to insult your intelligence by warning you it'd be a real good idea to keep all this just between us. As in you and me. Nobody else. I'm sure you understand." The caller hung up.

* * *

Justin stared at the silent phone. *Think, Drayton, think!* The chopper pilot was a ringer. Obviously. The company they used sent Joe Arnett whenever he or Parker flew. By request, a request that had long been on the company records. Good man, Joe, and no way he was involved in this. So, somehow whoever was behind this had switched pilots and Justin hoped to hell Joe was all right and not an unidentified body waiting to be discovered. But the ringer pilot hadn't been Justin's caller. A stupid caller not to realize that any oilman knew nobody was calling via cell from a disused offshore oil rig not yet refurbished with an upgraded, reconnected and operating communications system. Justin might not have been raised in the high-technology generation but by necessity, he was a lot more comfortable with it than most men his age. Whoever'd called had cloned Parker's phone to make it seem as though they were right there with him when in fact they couldn't be. Not if he was on the rig. And since he hadn't gotten a call from the air service, they used that Parker's chopper was off course or off the radar, he was pretty sure Parker was, in fact, on the rig. What use that was now, he didn't know, but at least it was assurance Mr. Mastermind wasn't as smart as he thought he was.

What the caller wanted couldn't be clearer, not if he wanted use of the transport fleet. He wanted it for transport of highly illicit merchandise in a very large quantity of such value that his organization needed a previously unused and therefore non-suspect conduit. Drayton Oil. And needed it badly enough to risk kidnapping a Drayton to get it.

Now. On to more important things. Like who he knew. He needed some low friends in high places. Relatively speaking. He shrugged off the "just between you and me" warning. Mr. Mastermind claimed he didn't think Justin was a stupid man, but obviously he did. Doing nothing signed Parker's death warrant in permanent ink, and nobody but a damn fool wouldn't know it.

Justin reached into his right-hand desk drawer and pulled out an old flip-top address index, the kind with the little slide on the side to position over the alphabet letters. An antique now if ever there was one, he supposed, but some things he just didn't need or want to carry around programmed into his phone.

"Justin Drayton! Long time, buddy! Too long."

"You might ought to reserve judgment on that, Bob. 'Cause this ain't no pleasure call."

* * *

Fifteen hundred miles away, Senator Robert Whithers, Chairman of the Joint Drug Task Force, leaned back in his chair and chewed thoughtfully on his lower lip. "Well, the good news is—we're not dealing with a rocket scientist here. Not if he thinks we're dumb enough to think he's with Parker and calling you on a cell from that rig. Now, on the other hand, that chopper itself—you're sure it's on the actual oil rig?"

"Yep, I'm sure. Leastways, our air transport service ain't called me and told me it was off course. No way they wouldn't know if that chopper was somewhere it wasn't 'sposed to be, not unless they didn't know where it was at all. Guess that could be the case and they just haven't decided quite how to handle it yet."

"And you're sure Parker's on the chopper?"

"I'm sure he *got* on that chopper. Now, whether they've thrown his body out of it into the Gulf's another story altogether. Know what I'm saying?"

"No way, Justin. No way they'd dispose of their ace in the hole that quick, not right at the start."

"Hope to hell you're right. But like you said, we're not dealing with a rocket scientist here. And stupid men are quicker on the trigger. Parker's head's on the other end of that trigger."

"There's that. But don't worry. I know exactly who to talk to."

"I hope to hell you do. Can't they track that cloned phone? Even if it's not being used? Don't phones have that damn GPS thing now?"

"Depends on what kind of phone it is, I think. And I'm sure that'll be the first thing my buddies think of. But I'm sure as hell gonna mention it anyway. What's Parker's number?"

* * *

"Yes, sir. I understand, sir…Oh, of course, sir! I'll keep you informed every step of the way, sir!"

"Don't go off half-cocked, Johnson. If Quentin Ashland is behind this, he's got several layers between it and him. The Shipton woman may or may not be involved, and if she is, she's just one more link in the chain. That cloned phone's in Tallahassee. Not at Ashland's address, which is no surprise. We're setting up now. And coordinating with the Coast Guard. The chopper's GPS still has it on that first oil rig. First priority's getting Parker Drayton back safely."

"Yes, sir."

DEA Special Agent in Charge of the Miami Field Division, Derek Johnson, hung up the phone carefully and took a deep breath. It wasn't every day he got a call directly from the Administrator. Thank God. And it wasn't everyday a pet project he'd gone out on a limb for paid off like this. He'd known, though. The gut didn't lie. They'd been watching Quentin Ashland for years. No way that scumbag wasn't dirty, not with his clientele, not with his success record. Not with the mysterious way witnesses testifying against his clients suddenly developed memory problems. But they'd left him alone, because sometimes the devil you knew was more valuable than the devil you didn't. Some good busts had come from following Ashland's trails. Far enough up the trail from him such that he didn't know he was under observation, of course.

His internal radar dinged a bit when Ashland's fiancée suddenly flew the coop and relocated, but it hadn't gone off in a full alarm. There were two possibilities. Either she'd stumbled on something she didn't like and bolted like any half-way intelligent woman would, or she was working with Ashland to set up some operation. He wasn't sure which, but he'd put orders out to check in on her from time to time. Just in case. Because while he didn't understand how any half-way intelligent woman would have ever fallen for Ashland's bullshit in the first place, by most women's standards the man was a looker and a charmer. And for damn sure a manipulator.

And whatdaya know? That same woman had Parker Drayton's ring on her finger within three months. As in Parker-Drayton-heir-to-a-major-American-oil-company. A company with oil tankers that traveled everywhere and financial resources out the whazoo. Coincidence? Yeah, and he had some nice oceanfront property in Utah to sell, too. The fiancée hadn't broken it off with Ashland. She was helping him set the Draytons up. And now they'd made their move.

He pulled his cell and hit a number. His Special Agent in place in Tampa picked up on the first ring.

"Williams."

"They've made their move. Bring her in."

Chapter Eleven

Carrie's Baby Daddy

Special Agent Austin Williams pulled up in front of the circular drive of Parker Drayton's casually impressive beach house. He shook his head ruefully. He was in the wrong business.

He rang the bell and waited, his badge at the ready.

"Yes?"

"Katherine Shipton?" An unnecessary question from his perspective, of course, but she didn't need to know he knew her name, social security number and clothing sizes right down to lingerie. Not right now, anyway.

"Yes, can I help you?"

He flipped open the leather case holding his badge.

"Special Agent Austin Williams. I need to speak with you, Ms. Shipton."

"Special—Parker! Has something happened to Parker?!" Her face drained of color and she swayed on her feet. Concern? Or shock that the DEA was on her doorstep this quickly?

"If I could come in—"

"Oh! Oh, of course! Please!" She opened the door and motioned him inside. Feminine laughter floated out into the foyer.

"You have guests? This is rather private, Ms. Shipton—"

"My aunt and my best friend. We've been doing wedding prep stuff. We'll go in the office."

"Katherine? Are you all right, dear?"

"I'm fine, Aunt Lillian, I'll be back with you in a few minutes." She closed the double doors of the office behind them. "At least, I sure hope I'll be back with them in a few minutes. Please tell me what's wrong. Something's got to be for a Special Agent—I'm sorry, what agency are you with? I didn't even notice."

"DEA, ma'am. Let's sit down."

Katherine walked to the sofa. "DEA? But this just gets—if Parker was in an accident, shouldn't the police be here? No, that's crazy, he's in Houston. His father would call me! Unless—*oh, my God!* He's not dead, please tell me he's not dead?"

* * *

Carrie and Aunt Lillian huddled outside the office, ears pressed as close to the crack between the double doors as possible. Damn, this house was well-built. All Carrie could distinguish was the soothing sound of a masculine voice. A professional voice. Something, though. Something niggled.

Professional, yes, but a voice intentionally remaining in control of an underlying accent. A southern accent, but not the standard deep South drawl. Twangier southern. Damn! Mountain southern. Like the accent she'd grown up with. She pressed her ear closer, willing the murmurs to resolve themselves into words. There! Finally. Now that she had the underlying accent pegged, she was beginning to pick out a word or two.

* * *

"No, ma'am. And I never said Parker was in an accident. I never said why I was here at all. You just jumped to that conclusion. Might I ask why?"

"*Why*? Because I'm a woman whose fiancé is on an out-of-town trip, for God's sakes! You don't know accidents are the first thing women think of when anybody with a *badge* shows up on their doorstep? Even if you're not married, don't you have a mother?"

"Yes, ma'am, I do. I mean, I'm not married but yes, of course I have a mother. And you're right. Accidents are definitely the first thing women think of."

He gave himself a mental shake. He knew this woman. Knew she preferred beer to champagne, ranch dressing to vinaigrette, mixed greens to iceberg lettuce salads. Blue jean shorts to Prada. But he didn't *know* this woman. He'd observed from afar, compiling data. This was the first time he'd spoken to her, been near her. And for the first time, he wondered. Wondered why a woman who preferred blue jean shorts to Prada would be involved in any criminal activity calculated to make mega-money. Up close and personal, he could easily believe this woman would be just as happy in a modest subdivision home as in this specially designed beach house. Well, believing and proving were two different things. He had to get a grip.

"Then why are you here?"

"Ms. Shipton, what do you know about Quentin Ashland's business dealings?"

* * *

"I *knew* it!" Carrie hissed. "I *knew* Kat wasn't done with that slimeball!"

Aunt Lillian hissed back into Carrie's ear. "*Sssshhh!* You'll get us busted!"

"Sorry!" Carrie cupped her hand over Aunt Lillian's ear. "But why in the *hell* would they think Kat knew—even *wanted* to know— anything about that bastard?!"

Aunt Lillian cupped her hand over Carrie's ear. "Way the world works. But I don't like this. *At all.*"

* * *

"Business dealings? He's a lawyer. That's his business. How do you know I even know who Quentin Ashland is?"

166

"Mr. Ashland's come under observation by our agency on several occasions. Because of the clients he represents." Special Agent Williams chose his words with care. Entice. Don't entrap. And most important, get her out of this house, her safe ground, down to the Miami Field Office. Preferably voluntarily.

"Well, he's a criminal lawyer, yeah. I mean, this is America, somebody must represent them. Otherwise it'd be the Middle East. That's how he always explained it, anyway. And you still didn't answer my—oh. Yeah, I guess you did. Answer my question. Because if you've been 'observing' Quentin, you know I was engaged to him. Key word—*was*."

"Yes, ma'am. So if I might ask—why did you break your engagement?"

Katherine shuddered, so slightly another observer might not have noticed. Austin Williams did. "I don't suppose a response like 'personal reasons' would be considered satisfactory?"

"No, ma'am, I'm sorry, it wouldn't."

"Because I came to see him under the charming facade, he always shows the world. And I didn't like him."

"And exactly what caused that revelation?"

"You wouldn't believe me if I told you."

"Try me."

"A dream."

"A dream?"

"Told you, you wouldn't believe me."

"Ms. Shipton, dreams usually come from things we've seen, noticed, things we don't consciously know we know. It'd be a real help to us if you'd come down to our offices and talk to some people. See, we're certain Ashland's involved in something big that's going down right now. And we think maybe you know something about it that you might not even know you know." *Or that you might have helped mastermind.*

"Well, of course I'd be happy to help—"

"Oh, *hell, no!*"

The door burst open. Aunt Lillian and Carrie almost fell into the room in their haste to put a stop to this. "You hold it right there, young man! My niece is not going *anywhere* with you! Katherine, he doesn't want your help. He's trying to get you to an interrogation room! Well, not without a warrant, he's not! And not without a lawyer either! The Draytons must have legal power on retainer in Tampa Bay. Who is it? I'm calling them *right now!*"

"Aunt Lillian—"

"Ma'am, I assure you—"

Carrie stood stock still, carved of stone, staring at Special Agent Austin Williams. At least until she exploded into harpy mode and started toward him, hands flailing.

"You! You lyin' son-of-a-bitch!"

"Sally! *Why the hell did you run again?!* And what are you *doin'* here?!" Special Agent Austin Williams's careful, professional, modulated accent disappeared as though it had never been, dissolving into the twangy southern accent native to the North Georgia mountains.

"Sally?" Aunt Lillian asked of no one in particular.

Katherine grabbed Aunt Lillian's hand. "Her birth name's Sally Benton. We got to get her off him, c'mon!"

"Why? She's doing just fine."

"Aunt Lillian! You want her arrested for assaulting a law enforcement officer?!"

"But it's just getting good!"

"Aunt Lillian!"

"Okay, okay!"

Katherine and Aunt Lillian each grabbed one of Carrie's flailing arms and pulled her back. Special Agent Williams had managed to keep her hands from connecting with his face, but his crisp shirt and tie weren't crisp anymore.

"Sally, I'm goin' to ask you one more time! *Why the hell did you run from me this time?"*

"What do you care, you lyin' scumbag! You never said one damn word about being a DEA agent! You said you were there on *business!* That it was just pure luck runnin' into me!"

"I *was* there on business!"

"And you knew damn well I thought that meant *bank* business! That you'd taken over the bank for your daddy! You never said a *word*!"

"Sally, for God's sakes! Think, girl! You know there's no such thing as a small-town bank anymore. The conglomerates took 'em over years ago! And anyway, I never told you

169

what business, you just assumed it was something about the bank!"

"Yeah, and luck, too! If you're investigating Katherine, you knew full well I was her best friend! You acted like you were just so happy to see me! *Bullshit!* You were trying to *use* me! To get something on *her*!"

"You're—wait a minute! You're Katherine Shipton's best friend?"

"Yeah, have been for years, so if you didn't know that, just how good is that file you're building on her, *Mr. Secret Agent Man*?"

"It only goes back to Quentin Ashland. I didn't have a clue you and she were friends! Did I ever mention her name? Try to pump you about her? No, I surely did not! I was too busy thankin' God I'd run into you again! And prayin' you wouldn't turn tail and run this time! *But you did!*"

Katherine turned to Aunt Lillian. "Why do I have the feeling we just entered a private war zone?"

"Because, dear. We just did. Let's just sit back and enjoy the show. Because I don't think they even remember we're here."

"Well, you must not've looked for me real hard, *Mr. Secret Agent Man!* 'Cause for certain sure a big DEA agent coulda *found* me if he'd wanted to! I'm not lil' ol' Sally Benton from the poor side of town anymore, I have *press agents!*"

"I've followed you for *years*, you stubborn damn woman! Could I have looked for you when you ran in New York? Sure. Could I have found you? Damn straight! But why would I? If you don't want to be with me, what good would it do to find you? What's that old sayin'? 'If you love somebody, let 'em go 'cause if they don't come back, they were never yours to begin with.' And you sure as hell ain't never been mine, have you?"

"Don't give me that bullshit, Austin James Williams the *Third*. You just wanted to slum. You didn't want to embarrass your family! I heard your mother!"

"You heard my mother say what? Where? When?"

"In Miss Aline's dress shop! When I was payin' on the prom dress I had on lay-a-way, 'cause that's the only way I coulda had one! She was over at the real expensive racks. She didn't know me from Adam's housecat. And Miss Aline asked her who you were takin' to the Senior Prom and she said she didn't have the slightest idea. You hadn't told her, and she sure hoped you got outta that phase fast!"

"And from *that* you got that I was ashamed of you?!"

"Well, why the hell else wouldn't you have told your mother?"

"'Cause I was an eighteen-year-old asshole goin' through that phase of not tellin' his parents *anything!* About *anything!* And *that's* what she meant about hoping I got out of that phase fast! And over *that* you left town *before* the prom, *before* graduation, you just melted into the night and disappeared without a word to anybody?"

"Well, who was there to care? Just a foster kid the system didn't have to worry about anymore! Not that my foster parents ever worried. You remember them, Austin? Only thing they'da cared about was losing that monthly check!"

"I cared, damn it! Your teachers cared! And my mother cared! 'Cause when you disappeared, I was so damn scared something'd happened to you, I did tell her. All about you. And the fosters. I thought you were *dead*, Sally! Because if they'd done something God-awful to you, surely, *surely* you'd have come to me! And Mama personally went out and gave your fosters an interrogation from hell! I know, she took me with her. And she made the sheriff and DFACS actually *investigate*. And guess what? They took all the other foster kids outta there, and those lowlifes never worked the system again. But you were good, I'll give you that! Just disappeared off the face of the earth. Right up till the time your face just popped up on all the magazine covers! You got any idea what I felt like when I saw the first one?"

"Why didn't you tell me all that in New York?"

"I didn't know *what* the hell to say to you in New York! I was scared to say anything! I just followed your lead and you were like 'oh, how nice to see an old friend'. So I just played along."

"You really cared when I left town?"

"I went through hell from the time you left till the time Carrie Bennington hit the fashion world. But at least when you ran this time, I knew I didn't have to worry about you being hungry or cold or homeless. Or *worse!*"

"Oh, my God. I'm—I—I don't know what to say. I'm speechless."

"Well, that's a damn first."

They both jumped when Aunt Lillian spoke. She'd been right, of course. They didn't even remember they'd had an audience. "Personally, dear, I think I'd just hush and kiss the man."

"Good idea," Austin said.

"If I've put you through all that for this many years, why would you even want me to?"

"God only knows. Now get your ass over here and kiss me."

Chapter Twelve

Cold Dark Death

Sam Carver carried the unconscious Parker Drayton over his shoulder and through the closest door off the rig's helipad. An office of some sort, it looked like. A cheap vinyl sofa, mildewed and tattered, still sat over on the right. Smelled like hell, but it would do. Might damage the merchandise to just throw him down on the hard floor. He deposited the limp body and reached for the small backpack he'd slung over his free shoulder, the one holding a few pieces of equipment necessary in his line of work. Like handcuffs.

Parker moaned. Shit! Probably should've cuffed him on the chopper, but with that damn dose of happy juice, Drayton should be out a longer than this. He dropped the backpack open on the rusted metal desk and dug with one hand. He held a Glock steady in the other, pointed

174

straight at Parker, just in case he roused completely before he was properly secured.

Parker gasped, his hand going to his throat as he struggled to sit up.

"Lie down!"

"Can't…can't breathe…"

"Lie down, damn it!" What the hell? Drayton hadn't even looked at him, hadn't seen the Glock. And was gasping for breath like a fish out of water.

"Can't…gotta sit…can't breathe…"

"Lie down!"

Well, this was going to hell in a hand basket. Drayton's face turned pale. Beads of sweat popped up on his face. His lips were turning blue. Bad reaction to the happy juice?

"Asthma…gotta have…inhaler…"

"Oh, shit! Where is it? Where the hell's your inhaler? C'mon, man, if you know you got asthma, you gotta carry one!"

"Back…pack…where's…back…"

"Christ! It's on the damn chopper!"

"Gotta…have…" Parker fell back on the sofa, hands clutching his throat. Now his nails were blue. And Sam Carver, not that that was his real name, was in deep shit. When this employer said keep a mark healthy, he damn well meant it.

"Hang on, man! I'm going, I'm going!" He tore out the door, leaving it wide open, and raced back to the helipad.

Parker's hand moved to his jeans pocket. Damn, but this was cutting it close. His fingers were almost too numb to feel the fabric. He fumbled, tried to grasp. His fingers slid off the slick sides of the bottle. He knew he only had time for one more try before he passed out.

There! He brought the magic bottle to his mouth and pressed down. *Hsssssss.* One more hit. *Hsssssss.* The magic vapor rushed through his lungs, banishing the elephant crushing his chest back into invisibility. Ordinarily, after an attack this severe, he'd lie back a few minutes and recoup. He didn't recall an attack this severe, not since he was a kid and asthma first raised its ugly head, and the severity was completely his fault since he'd let it go on so long. No choice there, though, and his lucky day he'd even *had* an attack, he had them so seldom. Hell, even Katherine had never seen him have an attack. Coulda probably faked it, but it just wouldn't have had the same effect. Nobody fakes blue lips.

Okay, all the recovery he had time for. Up and at 'em. His eyes raced around the rig's old office. He needed something heavy enough to knock that fake pilot out as he came back through the door. But the office held only the mildewed sofa and rusting desk, not even a desk chair. Under ordinary circumstances, he might have tackled him as he came back in, but these circumstances weren't ordinary, and Parker wasn't quite back to prime peak performance. Next plan. Just get out the damn door, find a weapon, 'cause surely on this mostly metal rig, there'd be a nice heavy piece of loose metal, and wait his chance.

Parker peered out the open door and looked around. Sam Carver or whatever his name was still had his back turned, leaning over the passenger seat of the chopper, arms moving wildly as he searched. Parker grinned, glad he'd tossed the bag over the seat and not just dropped it in the floorboard. Sure would've been nice if the helipad was a bit farther away but it was where it was. And it was time to go. He slipped out the door just as Carver turned.

"What the—stop! Stop, dammit! Don't make me shoot you, man!"

Ping! Ping! Two bullets ricocheted off metal. Parker didn't slow in the slightest, heading for the turn that would take him out of sight.

Ping! Ping! Ping!

Parker tried to think. How many shots in a Glock magazine? Hell, he didn't know, and assumed it would depend on the model. Which he also didn't know. He'd recognized it as a Glock, but he hadn't really looked at it that close, all things considered. Like trying to breathe. Hell of a lot more than five, though, and he seriously doubted his abductor had only one clip. So counting bullets was out. Just keep going. The best of all possible plans.

Except for one slight problem. This walkway dead-ended into nothing but an open platform. Maybe it had descending ladders, though.

Ping! Ping! Ping! "Don't make me shoot you, man!"

Parker doubted seriously if killing him—at least this early in the game—was the prime objective but didn't doubt for a minute shooting him would be considered a viable option. But this wasn't an old western movie and nobody taking a bullet from a Glock was going to utter a mild 'damn', calmly wrap the bullet hole with a bandana, and keep on running. More likely they'd be writhing in a prone position with a shattered bone while they bled to death.

Ping! That one was aimed closer, almost at his feet. Much more of this and a ricochet was going to get him if the actual bullet didn't. Enough already. Parker swerved to his left and dived off the walkway into the Gulf waters below. His abductor's shout followed him down.

"Are you fucking *crazy*, man?!"

Parker's eyes widened. That damn fake pilot might have something. Only a crazy man would've dived off a metal rig's walkway without checking to see what metal might be lurking beneath. Well, only a crazy man or one being shot at. He tried to pull his legs, turn his body, but no way was he going to miss it completely. The big support girder below him rushed forward, and his legs exploded into agony below the knees. He fought to retain consciousness as the water closed around him and struggled back to the surface, using his shoulder and arm strength. His legs weren't cooperating, they were numb. Broken? And if they were, was it a compound fracture, blood from torn flesh pooling in the waves around him, turning him into shark bait? He couldn't worry about that right now. He had to get back to the support beams to find something to hang onto before he'd have the luxury of assessing the damage. Damn good thing he worked out with weights regularly. No time to lose, either; he could hear the pounding of running feet on metal, his kidnapper racing to the edge to check his whereabouts. Parker maneuvered toward the closest underpinning and disappeared beneath the walkway just as Sam Carver raced to the edge and peered down.

Sam shook his head. *Damn, damn, damn.* Talk about things going to hell in a hand basket. Where the hell was Drayton? Had he even come up? Shit, there was a steel support girder right in the way. If he'd conked his head on that on the way down, he was unconscious at best, dead at worst. And if unconscious, he was a drowned rat by now for sure. The boss was *not* going to be happy. Maybe he didn't even need to tell him?

Carver trotted back to the helicopter and picked up the radio mike. Play by ear time. Keep the boss happy—and for now, ignorant— and then he'd have time to start looking around, see if he could spot Drayton anywhere. Though how he was going to retrieve him if he did spot him, he didn't have a clue, seeing as how Drayton wasn't going to be particularly cooperative about it.

"Okay, we're on the rig. Waiting orders."

"Drayton conscious yet?"

"No."

"How much you give him, for crissakes? He shoulda been awake by now. I got to let baby boy talk to Daddy before too much longer, Daddy ain't no fool. He wants proof his boy's alive."

"Maybe he's got a lower tolerance than most guys. It happens."

"Check in when he wakes up."

Carver grimaced. *Well, just shit.* "Will do. How long am I sitting here?"

"You're the pilot, look at the damn flight plan. This is an initial inspection, two-three hours each at the first three rigs in the line. You been there how long? Twenty minutes? You need a calculator?"

Damn, only twenty minutes? "Just seems like it's been longer, is all."

"When he wakes up, you'll have somebody to talk to. Not that he's gonna be particularly friendly, I wouldn't imagine."

"Nope, that's for damn sure."

"So just sit there. Check in with me as soon as he's awake enough to be coherent. Which oughta be damn soon. And stick close to the radio 'cause I'll be checking in with you."

Sam winced as the radio signed off. The boss didn't know the half of it. He grabbed the binoculars from the chopper and walked back to the site of Parker's disappearance. The only thing he could think of was a cruise up and down all the platforms. What he'd do if he sighted a floating body, he didn't know, since he had no means to retrieve it. No matter whether it was alive or dead.

Underneath the rig, Parker clung to the support girder and studied the understructure. Not exactly the type of inspection he'd had in mind on this trip. On the up-side, this was a damn sturdy rig, holding up nicely against the relentless ocean. He'd heard the pounding of running feet over the walkway but hadn't heard any sounds of movement in the last several minutes. And probably wouldn't unless the pilot decided to start running again, and why would he? No, he was cruising the walkways slowly, hoping for a sighting. A sighting he wouldn't get because no way was Parker moving into view.

His legs ached like a bitch, the left worse than the right, but there weren't any streams of blood swirling around him in the water. His left foot felt numb, too. He needed to get out of the water, assess the damage. And think. Horizontal girders stretched above him. If he could just reach high enough…nope. Wasn't going to happen. He squinted and focused on the platform he'd been heading for when circumstances forced the nose dive into the Gulf. Just as he'd thought. Descending ladders. Not that they did him much good. His legs weren't going to be of any use in climbing it, not right now, anyway. He had hopes his right leg was just bruised but didn't hold much hope the left leg wasn't at least cracked. He felt the flesh swelling out, tightening his jeans. It'd take a while to climb it using just his arms. Too long. It wouldn't take the pilot long to climb down it, though, not if he decided to. But that pilot wasn't too damn bright. Still, best to keep an eye out for him, just in case.

So. Somebody'd gone to a hell of a lot of trouble and pre-planning to kidnap him. There wasn't much reason to kidnap him unless somebody wanted something. Money maybe. Maybe something else. What they wanted was irrelevant. To get it, they'd have to contact his father. If they'd already made contact, his father wouldn't be taking this lying down. He'd have already brought in the proper authorities. And if he knew his dad, those authorities wouldn't be the ones most folks would think of, and he wouldn't be contacting the main switchboard number, either. He'd be using some private unlisted ones. The pilot wasn't bright enough to have done this all by his lonesome, so the question now was—had they already contacted Justin? If they had, all he had to do was stay alive till they got here. One thing about GPS trackers, they'd know for sure the chopper had been at the first rig. But if they hadn't, they could just abort the whole thing, ditch the chopper, make it look as though there'd been a crash, and who'd be the wiser? Parker sighed. It was gonna be a *long* day.

Chapter Thirteen

Special Agent Man

Katherine gave them a few minutes before tapping their shoulders.

"You two might want to come up for air, you think?"

Carrie pulled out of Austin's embrace.

"That was unfair advantage."

"Was not."

"Was too. And you got a hell of a lot of explainin' to do. Like why you're here askin' Kat about that slimeball Quentin Ashland."

"And I've got to say I'd be very interested in that answer myself," Katherine said.

Austin Williams, the man, engaged in consultation with Austin Williams, Special Agent. The struggle was visible. His lips tightened.

"That's classified."

"Well, son, you'd best be declassifying it pretty damn fast. 'Cause Aunt Lillian's got you dead to rights. You aren't here to ask for Kat's cooperation. You're here to get her in an interrogation room. Aren't you?"

"That's not exactly—"

"Then what—*exactly*—is it?"

Austin looked at the three faces staring him down. Special Agent Williams was outnumbered. Time to retrench and shift strategy. Especially if he wanted to make it out of the room alive.

"Okay. Can we all sit down? I'll tell you what I can."

"That'll do for a start." Carrie sat down and motioned Katherine and Aunt Lillian to sit on either side of her. "Then we'll go from there."

Austin sighed. "Ashland's been on our radar for a long time. See, the thing is—he doesn't just defend his clients. He uses them. Very, very profitably."

"Of course," said Katherine. "And that's what I never actually let myself realize. In fact, I guess that's one of the reasons I left when I did, before it got to the point where I'd actually have to figure that out."

"So, can you tell me exactly why you did leave when you did?"

"I told you. A dream. A dream that made me realize he wasn't a good man."

"And that's it?"

"That's not enough? Realizing the man you're planning to spend your life with isn't a good man? Because Agent—if a man's not *good*—it's rather a given that he's *bad*. Don't you think?"

"Well, here's the thing, Ms. Shipton. Anyone associated with Ashland automatically puts themselves on the radar, too. And stays on the radar until such time as they've proven they don't need to be on the radar. If you'd left Ashland and three months, or six months, or a year later, gotten engaged to Joe Shmo from Arkansas—that'd be one thing. But within three months of leaving Ashland, you're wearing Parker Drayton's engagement ring. The Draytons being one of the United States' wealthiest and most influential families. Movers and shakers. You, ah, begin to see where I'm goin' with this?"

"Not really, no."

Carrie snorted. "Well, I do! Oh, for God's sake, Austin! Kat's an artist! She lives in her own little world. That would never have occurred to her!"

"*What* wouldn't have occurred to me?"

"No, I don't think it would. Not now, after talking to her. But you got to understand, honey. The Agency doesn't know Katherine. They only know nine times out of ten, if there's smoke, there's fire. We follow the odds. It's how we break cases."

"Will you two stop talking over my head and tell me what the hell you're talking about?"

Aunt Lillian took over. "They think you finagled that meeting with Parker. That he was a target. That you set him up for Quentin!"

"*What?* And why? What could I possibly be setting him up for?"

"Kat. C'mon, you're not that naïve. For insider knowledge. For influence. To use him. And the Drayton business empire." Carrie looked over at Austin. "Am I right?"

"More or less."

"What's the more part and what's the less part? 'Cause something had to have happened to make you show up on the doorstep."

"That's—"

"Don't you dare. 'Cause if you tell me that's classified, I'll slap you silly, I swear I will."

"The thinking was more on the order of leverage, actually. That getting close to Parker Drayton would give Quentin leverage to use for whichever of his on-going deals might need it at the time."

"Double-talking time is done. What happened to put you on this doorstep right now?"

Austin looked from one woman's face to another. Trapped. The Agency was wrong on this one; he knew it in his gut. Still, there was that pesky detail gleaned from the quick check of her phone records he'd done before landing on her doorstep.

"Ms. Shipton, when's the last time you talked to Quentin Ashland?"

"Yesterday. Yesterday morning. I always knew I'd hear from him again, of course. It's not in his nature to just leave things alone."

"So it was just a social call?"

"It was—ugly. Venomous. Disguised under pleasantries, of course. Like everything Quentin does. Congratulating me on being smart enough to trade him in for a better opportunity, I guess is what it boiled down to. He accused me of being involved with Parker while we were still engaged and swapping him in for more money."

"But you already knew Quentin called her yesterday, didn't you, Agent Williams?" Aunt Lillian asked. "Because you checked her phone records and wanted to see if she'd lie about it."

"Yes, ma'am."

"And she didn't. And those phone records also show that's the only contact she's had with him since she left him, don't they?"

"Yes, ma'am."

"So are you satisfied now?"

"Well—there's still that little thing about pre-paid disposable cell phones. And records we can't check."

Carrie snorted. "So after months of staying in contact with pre-paid disposable cell phones, he calls her real phone? You think? Really?"

"No, not really."

"So give it up already. What's happened to put you here?"

"Parker Drayton's been kidnapped. Ransom is use of the Drayton transport fleet to move some shipments. That means one thing. Drugs. Lots of them."

* * *

Tony DiNitzi lay back on his pillows, paradise coming into view.

"You got it, baby, don't stop, don't stop!" Yeah, nothing got a man in the mood like a plan coming together.

Above him, his live-in increased her rhythm. Paradise didn't seem too far off for her either. "Not…a…chance."

The door crashed open.

"Hands over your heads! Hands over your heads *now!*"

"What the *fuck?!*"

Live-in screamed and flung herself off Tony, grabbing for cover.

Five men in Kevlar vests surrounded the bed, guns trained on its occupants. The lettering across the front read "DEA", so Tony didn't have much doubt about their affiliation. Well, just shit, damn, hell and what the fuck.

"We knocked, Tony. You musta been too preoccupied."

Live-in clutched the sheet to her impressive chest. "Tony, what the hell's going on?"

"Can't you read, bitch?"

"Don't you talk to me that way, you asshole!"

One of the agents picked up live-in's robe and tossed it to her.

"Get out of the bed, ma'am. Nice and slow."

"What? You guys can't get any on your own? Gotta barge in and share my view?"

"Very funny, DiNitzi, outta the bed." Special Agent Thompson tossed him his discarded pants and shirt. "And get dressed. We're taking a little trip."

"How 'bout my underwear?"

"Since there's none on the floor, you must like commando. Now move it."

"You ain't shown me a search warrant."

"Nothing like a jailhouse lawyer." Special Agent Thompson whipped out the piece of paper he'd stashed in his belt. "Satisfied?"

"Whatever you're looking for, it ain't here."

"Wouldn't bet on that if I were you. Move."

Tony heard the sounds of a search in progress as they came down the steps, then the sound of a ringing phone.

Special Agent Anderson, the agent nearest the desk, whipped open the top drawer and smiled. Then he pocketed his own phone, the one he'd been holding in his hand. The one he'd dialed Parker Drayton's number with. His gloved hand picked up the cell phone in the drawer and dropped it into an evidence bag.

Special Agent Thompson laughed. "Careless, careless, Tony. I'd have expected better from you. I mean, you could have at least turned the damn phone off when you weren't using it."

"It's not what you think."

"Sure it is. You aren't screaming for your lawyer yet? That douche-bag Ashland?"

"I got information. You guys are the ones gonna be screaming for Ashland. Let's get this show on the road so you can hook me up with the big guy. The one with the bargaining power."

"You don't say? Then let's get this outta the way while I've got lots of witnesses handy. Tony DiNitzi, you're under arrest. You have the right to an attorney…"

* * *

Tony DiNitzi sat alone in the standard interrogation room. What a fucking rookie mistake for him to make. And for damn sure, he'd underestimated his mark. He'd never have thought Justin Drayton would have called in the feds, certainly not that early in the game. He'd obviously underestimated the man's contact base, too. He had to have started damn high up the food chain to get a DEA SWAT team on Tony's doorstep within an hour of that first call. Damn Ashland. Though in all honesty, he couldn't blame Ashland for his own mistakes. He could have made that call from another location and then smashed the cell and thrown the pieces in a dumpster. He could have gotten another one to make the second call. The call he'd never be making now. He'd just wanted that side-trip upstairs before he left the house. And then to just leave the damn thing on. Oh, well. The best laid plans of mice and men and all that happy shit. Tony was a businessman in an unforgiving business. The thing now was to salvage as much as he could.

The door opened. Finally. Just great. A female prosecutor. In Tony's experience, they were a hell of a lot tougher to deal with than male prosecutors. Seemed like they had an ax to grind, or something to prove. On the other hand, they were easy to fluster when things didn't go exactly their way. This one looked tough. For one thing, she was a gorgeous woman and she didn't downplay it. Great hairstyle, great make-up, great suit that fit like a glove. Lots of self-confidence that didn't seem fake.

She sat down in the chair across from him. She didn't introduce herself. She didn't speak. Oh, yeah. She wanted to play tough. He could do that. Nothing he liked better than getting under a tough broad's skin.

He smiled at her. More of a smirk than a smile. "Nice weather we're having for this time of year, huh?"

"Very."

"I'm Tony DiNitzi. What's your name? Wouldn't mind having your phone number, either. Your personal one, I mean."

"Brittany Spears."

"Funny lady."

"I can be, but not in this case. You think there're copyrights on names? I'm older than she is, if the name was copyrighted, I'd sue her and win."

"Okay, funny lady. I suppose your phone number's unlisted too, huh?"

"Not at all. It's 555-Ballbuster. For someone who said they have information, you seem to be asking a lot of questions."

"You Fed or state?"

"Fed."

"Kidnapping doesn't fall into Federal jurisdiction for twenty-four hours."

"You know, nobody's even mentioned that word, kidnapping. Not till you just did. I must say, you do know your Lindbergh law, don't you? And I do adore jailhouse lawyers, I never cease to be amazed at what total bullshit they can pull out of a half-assed, uninformed and uneducated interpretation of the law. However, the exact provision specifies that when the whereabouts of a kidnapping victim is unknown, it falls under federal jurisdiction after twenty-four hours because after said twenty-four hours, there's a rebuttal presumption the victim might have been transported over state or international lines. 18 U.S.C. Section 1201. Notwithstanding that, in this case, we know Parker Drayton was on a helicopter. One with a GPS. Which shows it's currently in the Gulf of Mexico. Twenty-four-hour time limit is therefore irrelevant."

"Is that chopper more than twelve nautical miles into the Gulf, sweetheart?"

"Of course not. And you know it. Because you know it was headed to a line of disused oilrigs that are roughly two miles offshore. That being conceded, *sweetheart*, those oil rigs are off the coast of Louisiana, not Texas, from whence he was abducted. Therefore, state lines have *been* crossed. Checkmate. Like I said, it's amazing what half-assed interpretations of the law a jailhouse lawyer can come up with. Not to mention you're in Florida. What else you got for me, wonder boy?"

Tony glared. *Smart-ass bitch.*

"What? Cat got your tongue. You said you had information for us. I'll forewarn you, Mr. DiNitzi. We know a lot about you already. None of which has been sufficiently earth-shattering in the general scheme of things for us to bother with. You see, you're *predictable.* And quite useful to us in tracking the ebb and flow of the various business dealings you're engaged in. You're *bait* for us, Mr. DiNitzi. You help us catch bigger fish. Your continued freedom and ease of movement really doesn't endanger the public, not even your—shall we say— termination services. That gun for hire thing. Because so far, it's only been used to level the playing fields in the trade, so to speak. You've saved the taxpayers a good bit of time and money that would otherwise have been expended in long, drawn-out trials and delivered a few final sentences a hell of a lot more permanent than any the courts could deliver. But now you've crossed that line. Big-time. You picked the wrong family to shake down. I can only assume some deal's going down somewhere that's big enough to justify that risk. So if you have information, please start talking and stop wasting my time. Because frankly, I've got better things to do than sit here and watch you glare at me. I haven't eaten lunch yet, and I was planning on getting a manicure, too." Brittany Spears lifted her hand casually, curled her fingers and inspected her nails.

"What'll you give me?"

"Give you?"

Tony leaned forward. "I want a deal. No prosecution on any of this kidnapping thing."

ADA Spears leaned forward to meet him. "I don't make deals. I make promises. And I promise you if anything happens to Parker Drayton, you'll never see the light of day outside of a prison yard again."

"Not even if I can give you Quentin Ashland?"

"Wonder boy, I don't want Quentin Ashland. Because the exact same thing applies to him as applies to you. There's nothing on earth as useful as an arrogant asshole who thinks he's too smart to be caught. We track a lot of activity through Quentin Ashland. We already know it's a safe bet he's involved in whatever shipment's coming in, and he probably masterminded it to boot. Because honestly, *wonder boy*, you're just not that smart."

"Yeah, well, old man Drayton'd be pretty damn grateful to me right now, lady."

"And why is that?"

"Because if I'd done what Ashland wanted, his little boy would already be dead."

"Really? Ashland wanted to get rid of his insurance before the shipment came in. That's odd. Because Ashland really isn't that stupid."

Tony slammed his hand down on the table. "Look, lady! This shipment's all mine! *Mine!* Ashland's not involved with that end at all! He wanted Parker Drayton dead! Don't you get it?! He ordered a *hit*, not a kidnapping! So I oughta get a damn *reward!* If Ashland had picked some other guys I know for this, Drayton'd be dead already!"

"Whereas you, because you could see the wasted potential of just offing the guy, saw immediately that you had to keep him alive. At least until your incoming shipment cleared the US."

"Damn straight I did!"

ADA Spears stood up. She made a gun with her thumb and index finger and pointed it at Tony. She smiled as she blew imaginary smoke off her fingertip. "Gotcha. Gotcha both."

"Hey! Wait a minute! What about my deal?"

The door slammed behind her. Tony slumped in his chair. That hadn't gone exactly as planned. Maybe it was time to switch-up tactics.

* * *

"But he's such a good boy. He just got in with the wrong people!" The woman sitting in

Quentin Ashland's client chair wiped her eyes and blew her nose loudly.

Quentin winced imperceptibly. Why the hell did he have to get all the honkers? The woman should patent that honk, it'd make a hell of a duck call. "Well, Ms. Arnold, I don't really think you've got to worry too much. This is Todd's first arrest and you realized right off y'all needed a lawyer. You'd be amazed how many folks don't realize that and try to handle it themselves. Now all I need to get started is my retainer."

"Oh! Of course!" Ms. Arnold fumbled in her purse and retrieved her checkbook. "How much do I—"

"The standard is $50,000.00 when you engage my services but as this is a first offender case, I'll accept $30,000.00 for now."

Damn, he enjoyed watching folks' eyes widen when money entered the picture.

"I had no idea—"

"Ms. Arnold, this is a RICO charge. The government doesn't take RICO charges lightly. And—"

The office door flew open and banged against the back wall.

"What the—who the hell are you?"

"I'm sorry, Mr. Ashland! I *told* them you had a client!" Quentin's secretary fluttered her hands behind the two men who stood, smiling, behind the client chairs. Same build, same haircut, same air of detached professionalism. One wore a gray suit, the other a black. They flipped open the badge cases held ready in their hands. Twin movements. Shit. Law enforcement. Federal. Staties didn't move with that precision.

"DEA. Now, Quentin. How professional is that? Such language from an attorney-at-law, an officer of the court. What will this nice lady with her open checkbook think? Ma'am, I'd suggest you go find yourself another lawyer. 'Cause this one's under arrest."

Ms. Arnold slammed her checkbook shut and ran from the room.

"Smart lady. You have the right to an attorney..."

"I *am* an attorney!"

"Yep, that's why we're not about to give you a technicality. If you can't afford an attorney, one will be appointed for you..."

Quentin blew an exaggerated breath and waited for the whole spiel from gray suit while black suit cuffed him. "Are you *quite* done now?"

"Not my idea, just something you lawyers came up with."

"What is this, some moron's idea of intimidation? If you're trying to shake me down to get attorney-client privileged information, you're wasting your time. I take my Attorney's Oath very seriously. My clients are entitled to a defense just like every other American citizen! This isn't the Middle East, or didn't you get the bulletin?"

"How does conspiracy to kidnap and conspiracy to commit murder grab you, buddy? Kinda like the sound of it, myself."

"You're insane!'

Black suit shrugged. "The source isn't one I'd usually consider stellar, I'll give you that."

"Source? You've been talking to one of my clients without me? I'll have your badges for this, I'll—"

"You'll nothing. This client doesn't want you, Ashland. He's too busy singing like a canary. Name Tony DiNitzi ring a bell?"

Chapter Fourteen

White Magic

Sam Carver paced the rig's walkways, turning side to side, adjusting the binoculars. Nothing. Drayton was gone. Drowned, almost certainly. Unless, of course, he was grabbing onto the under-pilings for dear life. A few of the walkways ended in ladders but what the hell good would climbing down do? If Drayton was dead, he was dead. If he was alive, he sure wouldn't be cooperating with getting hauled back up. So where did that leave him? Holding the bag, for damn sure. Justin Drayton already knew his son was in trouble. And it wouldn't be long till the Boss knew his bargaining chip was AWOL. The Air Service company knew exactly where the chopper was, roughly two nautical miles off shore. Ergo and therefore, they knew where he was, so it didn't take a genius to figure out he didn't need to be there much longer. He scanned out over the water again with the binoculars.

Swimming was out. He could try and disable all the locators on the chopper, but with all the backups and advances in technology, he wasn't sure he could. Probably it'd just trigger an alarm and bring a search down on him that much quicker.

Nobody'd left a boat lying around the rig. The chopper would have both life vests and a life raft, but he sure as hell didn't like the idea of floating around on open ocean. No help for it. He'd fly straight in to shore, look for the best landing spot he could find, considering it'd have to be away from populated areas, land, and run like hell.

Underneath the rig, Parker waited and listened. His right leg slowly recovered a good bit of feeling. On the upside, that meant it gained a greater degree of mobility with every passing minute. On the downside, it hurt like hell. Not as much as the left though; that leg was gone for sure. At least cracked, if not actually broken.

His ears, tuned to frequencies he didn't know humans had, caught the first faint whirl of chopper blades. The pilot must be abandoning ship. The engine roared; the whirring blades increased cadence. He waited till the noise faded away, until the only sounds were the waves slapping against the under-structure, and the occasional squawks of the gulls who'd stumbled on this offshore resting place. He turned loose of his girder and struck out to the next one. From there he'd go for the next one. And the next. Until he reached that ladder to salvation. It'd be hell to climb with these legs, but he'd make it. Somehow, he'd make it. For his Dad. For Katherine.

* * *

ADA Brittany Spears stood outside the two-way mirror of DiNitzi's interrogation room with the DEA agents who'd just booked Quentin Ashland.

"Think he's stewed long enough?"

ADA Spears shrugged. "One way to find out. Later, dudes."

She opened the door and went in.

"Well, hey, Tony. You miss me?"

"Yeah, I got a thing for black widow spiders. They turn me on."

"Delighted to be of service. I think it's time for us to have a chat."

"That didn't work real well last time. You must've not been paying attention. Or you weren't ready to negotiate yet. So what kind of deal are we talking about?"

"Thought we'd covered this. I don't make deals. I make promises. And I promise if Parker Drayton doesn't come home safely, you'll like how that filters down to you a hell of a lot less than if he does. That's the best you're going to get. Now, if you'd like to talk to your lawyer about that, we've got him real handy. Like in the next room. He's not as popular as you are, though. He's still in cuffs. That's 'cause you don't give in to temptation and smart-mouth like he does. At least, not as much. So you tell *me* the deal, Tony. You were hired to make a hit. You put a change of plans in effect. We know the chopper's on the first rig. Obviously, you're the man in charge, even if Ashland thought he was. When are you supposed to contact your fake pilot again?"

"What's it to you?"

"Well, let's see. If the pilot's expecting to hear from you and doesn't, he might panic. And if he panics, he might kill his hostage and ditch the evidence. That would be a murder charge, not a kidnapping charge. And guess what? Any deaths that occur during a kidnapping are deemed murder one. As to *all* conspirators in that kidnapping, not just the guy doing the deed. So you see, I'm not just talking to hear myself talk when I tell you anything you tell us, anything you do that gets Parker Drayton home alive is very, very much to your advantage."

"I done told you, it's not any murder thing! Never was, not to me. That's Ashland's thing!"

"That's not going to cut any mustard with a judge charging a jury. You do know what that is, don't you, Tony? When he lays out for the jury exactly what charges they're considering and exactly what verdicts they can render for it? If Drayton doesn't come back alive it's murder one, babes. Florida has the death penalty. And isn't as shy about using it as some states I could name. So if you're even a tenth as smart as you think you are, you'll tell me when you're supposed to contact that pilot. And you'll contact him. And sell him out like Judas. 'Cause you're going to tell him *exactly* what I tell you to tell him. *After* you tell me exactly what the actual plan is. If anything you engineered can be dignified with the word 'plan'. *Capiche?*"

Tony glared. "*Capiche.* He's supposed to stay put for an hour, hour and a half. And then move Drayton to the second rig. You know, follow the flight plan exactly."

"Brilliant. Be right where he's supposed to be. Because for sure a man as rich and powerful as Justin Drayton's just going to fall all over himself doing exactly what he's told. I mean, he couldn't possibly have contacts so high up it'd give you altitude sickness."

"So whatda'ya want me to do? I can't exactly contact him from here. Can't do it by cell phone. Don't guess you thought of that."

"As a matter of fact, I did. And you're in the right place. Law enforcement's one profession where cellular hasn't completely replaced good ol' radios. Never will be. You know why Ashland ordered this hit? I have no trouble believing it, you understand, but he's a businessman. Whatever increases his bottom-line. Even you understood the potential uses. So why does he want Drayton dead?"

"Oh, I get it. That motive thing. You need a motive."

"No, I don't really need a motive. I got you. Just personal curiosity."

Tony laughed. "Now that is funny. Had trouble believing it myself."

"So—why?"

"A dame. Can you believe Ashland had the hots for a dame that bad? His fiancée ditched him for Drayton. Traded him in for a richer model. Way he tells it, anyway. Don't know about that personally. He's sure as hell mad at her though. Turns all red if you mention it."

"Interesting. Don't know how useful. But interesting."

Ten minutes later Tony sat in front of a radio, fine-tuning frequency, and achieving the same results over and over. Nothing.

"He ain't gonna answer."

"Then Tony, I suggest you get ready."

"For what?"

"To lean over and kiss your ass good-bye."

Brittany looked up as the door opened. Black suit DEA guy motioned her outside. What had he said his name was? Oh, yeah.

"Agent Thompson. You got something for me?"

"The chopper's not on the first rig anymore. It's headed straight in to the Louisiana coast. Straight as the crow flies."

"Not good. That wasn't the plan. And DeNitzi can't raise the pilot on the radio."

"Pilot must not want to talk."

"Safe bet."

"And he wouldn't want to talk if—"

"I don't require a diagram, Agent Thompson. Best case scenario is Parker

Drayton's on that chopper and the pilot's gone rogue. Worst case scenario is he's dead and his body's back on that rig. Or badly hurt, which is probably worse than dead, if we don't get there damn quick. And the pilot's cut his losses and run."

"Or—"

"Or, it's a big rig. If he managed to get away, there'd be lots of hiding places. Lots of places to ambush, too. Even for an unarmed man. I do my research. On all parties involved in one of my cases. Parker Drayton doesn't have a reputation as a wuss."

"No, just the opposite. He's a physical fitness nut, likes to ride the edge."

"We've got to be ready. Everywhere. When is the chopper going to clear the Gulf and hit land? We need a swat team ready the minute that chopper lands—"

"Ms. Spears, they were only two nautical miles off the coast. The chopper was on land almost as soon as they picked up movement. There was no way in hell to get anybody there in time to intercept."

"Where is it?"

"Cameron Parrish. And I'll save you your research time on that. It's got the most land and the least population of any Parrish in Louisiana. Almost half of it's swamp, marsh and water. But it's got lots of elevated ridges. *Cheniers*, I think they call 'em. Good landing spots. Chopper's sitting on one. Right in the middle of nowhere. A team's on the way but no way in hell are they going to get there until that pilot—and Drayton if he still has him—are long gone. And it'll be looking for needle in a haystack."

"Get a K-9 unit in there."

"I don't need a diagram either, Ms. Spears. But marsh, swamp and tracking dogs don't get along that well. Not impossible but not guaranteed."

"Shit!"

"Yes, ma'am."

"But he could still be on that rig."

"He could. Can't ignore the possibility. Coast Guard's on the way. And they can check that rig a hell of a lot faster than we're going to search a damn swamp."

"So now, we wait."

"We wait."

"And by the way, you can call your dogs off Katherine Shipton, too."

"Why would we do that?'

"Because she's got nothing to do with it. Not the way we thought anyway. She ditched Ashland. And he wants revenge. Simple as that."

"How do you know?"

"DiNitzi said so, weren't you listening? Ashland ordered a straight-up hit. This little side venture was all DiNitzi."

"Not exactly the most reliable source."

"No. Just too greedy to have ever come up with that story unless it was true. Call your dogs off."

* * *

Justin Drayton waited, too. Not patiently. Patience had its place in a successful businessman's repertoire, and he'd learned to practice it when necessary. It was an acquired trait for him, though. He paced restlessly, his eyes focused on the phone in a glare that had toppled conglomerates.

He pounced in the first seconds of the shrilling ring.

"'Bout damn time! Talk to me, Bob! What the hell's going on? Is Parker all right and where the hell is he?"

"Well, that's kind of complicated."

"Uncomplicate it. And don't sugarcoat it."

"We don't know if Parker's all right or not. We hope so. As to where he is—he's in one of two places. And we don't know which."

Justin's grip tightened on the phone through Senator Withers' explanations, knuckles whitening.

"I told you not to sugarcoat it, Bob. If the pilot headed back to shore without waiting to contact his boss, there's a third place he's likely to be. Floating in the Gulf. Dead."

"It's possible. Also possible he got away and he's hiding someplace on the rig. That'd put the pilot in a panic, too."

"In which case, he's probably hurt. 'Cause they wouldn't have made it easy for him, and he sure as hell wasn't gonna go down without a fight."

"The Coast Guard's almost at the rig, Justin. A search team's already on the ground at the chopper."

"Been putting off calling Katie, but I can't put it off any longer. The press is gonna get this pretty quick, with the rescue teams out. Surprised they haven't already. Can't let her hear it that way."

"Justin don't do that! The dirty attorney I told you about, the one behind the whole thing—Justin, he's Katie's ex-fiancé! Didn't want to throw anything else at you if I could avoid it, but it's possible Katie's been involved in it from the start, setting this up! They sent an agent to the house right away."

"They sent some damn *interrogator* after my daughter-in-law?"

"She's not—"

"Close enough. And I knew who Ashland was soon as you said his name! Katie never tried to hide anything, not from Parker, not from the family. Damn few folks come wrapped in cellophane these days, not Katie, not Parker."

"Justin don't do anything stupid. You let the experts handle—*shit!*" Senator Whithers hung up the phone. No point talking to dead air.

* * *

Katherine jumped when her phone went off.

"Oh, God! That's Justin's ringtone! What do I say, does he know, what do I say?"

"Yes, he knows." Austin's phone, silenced, vibrated in his pocket. "Just talk to him. I've got a call I need to take. I'll step out, so we won't be talking over each other."

"Justin—"

"Katie, you put whoever they sent out to the house on this phone right now!"

"I can't, he just got a call himself. How did you know—"

"No point in having connections if you can't use 'em, Katie. I went straight to the top the minute I got the first call. But I never thought the fuckin' idiots—sorry, that just slipped out—would ever think you had anything to do with it."

"That doesn't matter. All that matters is Parker. Do you know anything?"

"A little. And what I know might be why your watchdog just got a call. Is he off yet?"

"No, not yet—wait a minute, he just came in."

"Put us on speaker."

"Okay. Austin, he wants to talk to both of us." Katie held the phone out and punched the button. "Done. Go ahead, Justin."

"Son, you just get an update call?"

"Yes, sir."

"First off, you back off my daughter-in-law. She's got nothing to do with this."

"I already know that, sir."

"Officially?"

"I knew anyway. And not completely officially, no, but I'm advised they're seriously re-thinking their position on that."

"Then let's make sure the right hand knows what the left hand's doing." Justin ran through the current scenario. "That jibe with your understanding?"

"Yes, sir. So we're just in a holding pattern right now till we hear from—*Katherine!*"

Carrie and Lillian raced to catch her as she fell and managed to veer her in the direction of the couch.

"*Kat!* Don't you faint on us now!"

Katherine shook her head and tried to sit up.

"I'm not going to faint. He's at the rig. Not on it. Not exactly. And the Coast Guard needs to hurry!"

"They're going as fast as they can, Ms. Shipton, I promise you."

"Unless we do something, they're not going to be fast enough!"

"Ms. Shipton, from here there's nothing we can do, you have to know that."

"Yes, there is." Carrie sat down beside Katherine and took her hand. "Concentrate, girl. We're going to send him everything we've got."

"Have you two lost—"

"No, Agent Williams. They haven't lost their minds." Aunt Lillian shoved him out of her way, took each girl's free hand and made a circle. "They've finally found something. Stay with me here, girls. And *concentrate*. Concentrate the power."

* * *

Finally. The end was in sight. Home plate, goal post, final basket. A mixed bag of metaphors, for sure, but Parker didn't care. He'd worked his way down the line, girder to girder. Next stop, ladder. And then the fun would start, because it'd be a hell of a workout getting back up it with this left leg, but he'd manage.

And he'd better manage damn quick, too, because he didn't much like the way the waves were moving. Well, that wasn't exactly right. He didn't like the way something in the water was making the waves move. Because they weren't moving naturally. Something was cutting through them. Something big. The Gulf was full of whale sharks, the biggest of all sharks and the most common in the Gulf. That's probably what it was. He hoped to hell that's what it was. Parker'd been born and raised in Houston, an hour's drive from East Beach and Stewart Beach. He'd grown up in the Gulf. He lived in Tampa Bay now. He knew his sharks. Whale sharks were great. Filter-feeders. Didn't even use their teeth to feed, just sucked stuff through them. He'd caught rides with young whale sharks before.

Almost there.

Just keep going, just keep going...

His head jerked around. Katherine? He reached up for the highest ladder rung he could grab. Got it! He pulled his legs through the water, seeking the highest underwater rung he could use to pull up.

Stabbing pain shot through his left leg. What the hell? He'd thought it was pretty much numb. He'd thought wrong. Something was holding his leg. Something was *in* his leg. He looked down and saw red seeping into the water. He'd impaled himself on an underwater metal projection of some sort and it was still in his lower leg. He turned loose of the ladder rungs, pushed himself off and fell back into the water. He felt metal sliding out of flesh, then the burn of salt water, so agonizing he almost fainted. He broke the surface and lunged for his handhold on the ladder again, not as high up this time. He had to be able to angle his legs in toward the ladder a lot slower. No sudden forward jerks this time. Especially since a quick glance confirmed—there was a lot more red in the water. And whatever was moving through the waves knew it. Something was coming straight for him. Hand over hand, he powered his way up the rungs by brute force shoulder strength, making his aching right leg take his weight as he dragged his almost immobile left leg up behind it.

Don't look down, Parker, don't look down!

Katherine? No way. But he couldn't have heard her any more clearly if she'd been beside him. His right leg cleared the second rung above the water. But that left leg—it just didn't want to go.

No excuses, Parker! Reach for it! No pain, no gain!

He shook his head. He was losing it. Completely. He dragged his left leg up. More precisely, *something* dragged it up. He'd have sworn he felt hands pulling the leg up. Now it dangled, out of the water. He felt the blood running down from the stab wound caused by that underwater metal shard. That explained it. Hallucinations caused by stress, pain and blood loss. He turned his head and looked down.

Bull sharks. Considered by some experts to be the most dangerous and aggressive in the ocean. Not that big and only two of them for now, but they'd have company pretty quick. Bigger company. He wasn't far enough up. And for damn sure he couldn't get careless and lose his grip. But he just couldn't—

Parker! Move your ass! Do you hear me?

He managed a few more rungs, certain he felt invisible hands cradling his leg, pushing him from his rump. He had to rest. He was getting woozy, too. That damn blood loss, probably. He hadn't hit an artery, obviously, or it'd be pumping blood and he'd already have bled out, but he was losing enough to worry about, especially stuck in this straight up position. Beginning to hear things, too, other than Katherine's voice, scolding like a personal trainer turned drill sergeant. This noise sounded like a big engine. Maybe even whirling chopper blades.

He looked out over the water. Oh, yeah. He was hallucinating. A Coast Guard cutter headed straight toward the rig. He looked up. A Coast Guard chopper hovered above. He was either saved or totally round the bend.

A megaphone sounded from the bow of the cutter.

"Parker Drayton! Stay still! Repeat! Stay still! We've got you!"

Chapter Fifteen

The Wedding

Six weeks later, Parker and Katherine Drayton stood close on the deck of the Tampa Bay Watch Lighthouse and watched their family and wedding guests mix and mingle and laugh against the perfect backdrop of an ocean sunset.

Parker, arms around his bride, rested his chin on Katherine's head and laughed. "Is it just my imagination or is Dad really hitting it off with your Great-Aunt Hattie?"

Katherine turned and threw her arms around Parker's neck. "I think he really is! Isn't it wonderful? Aunt Hattie hasn't *looked* at another man since Uncle Henry died five years ago."

"Honey, Dad hasn't looked at another woman since Mom died *fifteen* years ago. So let's keep our fingers crossed and don't jinx it by talking about it."

"Agreed. But isn't it just amazing how well our families are getting along?"

The intricate and far-flung Shipton clan had arrived *en masse* from Calgary and other points north—and in the case of a few cousins currently residing in Australia, points south—two days prior to the wedding. They'd hit the airport at pretty much exactly the same time the Drayton clan had arrived *en masse* from Texas and other points south due to the Drayton oil empire's interest in Latin America—and in the case of a few cousins tending to Drayton oil interests in Canada, points north. No Shipton had ever, in family memory, met a stranger. The Draytons were Texans in their hearts, no matter where their immediate family branch lived, and certainly no Texan had ever met a stranger. Accordingly, when the two clans met at the designated spot to wait for the vans Justin and Parker had arranged for transport from the airport to the Azure Bay Beach Club Resort where they'd booked an entire floor for each of the big families, the result was inevitable. Within five minutes, the Shiptons and the Draytons were hugging, handshaking, and intermingling so fast and furiously only their accents gave any clue as to who belonged to which family.

"It's great how much the families like each other, but I don't think it's *amazing*. I mean, if we're being honest, two words apply to pretty much everybody in both families. Independent and stubborn with a touch of eccentric."

"That's three words."

"If you want to get technical."

216

"I'm eccentric?"

"You're an artist. So isn't being eccentric required?"

Katherine laughed. "Maybe. A little bit, anyway. But so are you or I'd drive you nuts. I thought the band's manager was going to gag when I gave him the play list we put together."

"Proof that while money can't buy everything, it can make sure your wedding has everything from swing jazz to country."

"With 60's rock and disco thrown in for good measure. Oh! Look at Mimi and Poppy!" Katherine pointed to Bill and Mina Shipton, swaying in perfect unison to the tune of *That Old Black Magic.* "Would you believe me if I told you I threw that in just for them?"

"Of course I'd believe you. After all, that's the strongest genetic trait in your family, isn't it? Magic?"

"Excuse me?" Katherine's conscience twitched. She really did need to tell him the truth. Just not today.

"Magic. It's more than just a word for your family, isn't it? Are you ever going to tell me about it?"

"Tell you—what?" *He knew. He didn't know exactly what he knew, of course, but he knew something.*

"About how you were out there, how you were with me in the Gulf. And who was out there with you. 'Cause darling, you weren't alone."

"I don't know what—"

"I'm talking about. Of course you do. You always do. You even know what I'm *thinking* about."

"Because I love you. People in love can do that."

"Absolutely. And sometimes I know what you're thinking, too." He kissed the top of her head. "But no way could I have told you to move your ass when I was three, four hundred miles away from you. Or helped you move it."

"You *heard* me?" *Oops. And just shit!* Katherine clapped her hand over her mouth.

Parker laughed. "And that's called letting the cat out of the bag for sure! Heard you? Honey, I *felt* you. Hands on my legs, pushing me up. Not just yours. Couldn't figure that out, till I found out your Aunt Lillian and Carrie were here. No, that was a combined effort. Though I'm hoping your hands were the ones on my actual ass and not Aunt Lillian's. Tried to tell myself it was just my imagination, but it wasn't. Was it?"

"It—it runs in the family. That portrait I finally finished?"

"Of that wonderful old woman. Yes. The wisdom of the ages is in that face, in those eyes. That might be the best work you've ever done. Though that's fitting since it's for Mimi."

"That old woman—she's the family matriarch. Ursula Sontheil Shipton. To history, she's known as Mother Shipton. You can look her up, she caused quite a stir in her day. Her prophecies almost got her burned at the stake. And she's a real character."

"Sounds like you've got a personal acquaintance with the lady."

"Mayhap I do."

"Right down to her speech patterns, huh?"

"All the women in the family do. It passes from her to us. The gift of prophecy. The gift of magic. And to some of the men, too, it's not really gender specific. Poppy's got it, I'm pretty sure, but he's never, ever admitted it. I think men have a harder time accepting it. And I don't have room to talk, it took me quite a while to accept it and once I did, I realized it was something I'd actually known subconsciously all my life."

"Well, that's something to look forward to. Will our little girls levitate in their cribs?"

"God, I hope not."

Carrie and Austin danced near. Carrie waved as they passed.

"Hey, Mrs. Drayton! Great wedding!"

"Hey back, Mrs. Williams! Yours was, too!"

"That still floors me." Parker shook his head. "Super-model Carrie Bennington's a country girl from the wrong side of the tracks. The tracks of Plumnelly, Georgia, no less. Who married the boy next door turned DEA agent. Aunt Lillian I get, her being blood and all. That she was out there in the Gulf with you. But Carrie?"

"The gift isn't exclusive to the Shipton line. Many people have it and probably most of them don't have a clue they do. But those of us who have it and know it—and most of us who admit it are women—blood or not, we're sisters. Sisters of Prophecy."

"And what's that gift told you lately?"

"That some things are just meant to be."

"Like us."

"Like us."

* * *

Lillian stood at the bar getting her Long Island Iced Tea refreshed. She was reminding herself firmly she was *not* to get another because she wanted to be capable of snapping candid pictures of the rest of the reception and the departure of the bride and groom when Irene walked past, cell phone at her ear. Even without the family gift, as Parker had so aptly pegged it, Lillian's big sister instincts by themselves shouted that something wasn't quite right. Combined with the family gift, that big sister instinct revved up into a high-pitched scream. She followed Irene farther down the beach and caught the tail-end of her conversation.

"…know you know what you're doing and of course I know you've been doing it almost since you could walk. I just worry sometimes, is that so strange? And it would have been nice if you'd taken off a couple of days from practice and come to the wedding with me but of course

I understand why you couldn't. Kat's only my baby sister *and* my baby niece *and* my constant companion and best friend growing up after all, that certainly doesn't compare with getting ready for the Calgary Stampede!"

Lillian hung back. *My, my, my. Trouble in paradise? Haven't heard Irene being that bitchy in a while.* Irene was talking to her fiancé, Matt. One thing this family didn't lack was variety. Katherine had just married the heir to an oil empire, Irene was about to marry a rodeo cowboy, a bronc riding champion, to be precise, named, of all things, Matt Dillon, courtesy of his father's love for classic American western television shows. A cowboy who'd be risking life and limb very shortly in the upcoming Calgary Stampede. Irene knew she was marrying a cowboy, and she wasn't upset that Matt hadn't come to the wedding with her. Lillian knew her little sister better than that. Something else was up.

"...don't need you to meet me at the airport, I'm not the only one coming back tomorrow, I'll get a ride...of course I'm not coming back early because I'm mad at you! Do you seriously think Kat and Parker want company on their honeymoon? Yes, I'll call you as soon as I land."

Irene stabbed her phone viciously when she ended the call and pulled her arm back as though she was about to toss it into the ocean. Then sanity apparently returned and she dropped her arm. Lillian smiled to herself and started walking toward her sister.

"Well, I'm glad you managed to restrain yourself. That'd have been quite an expensive throw if you'd tossed that phone in those waves. What's the matter, honey? And don't try to tell me you're upset because Matt didn't come with you, I know better. What's up?"

Irene leaned her head onto her older sister's shoulder. In some ways, Lillian knew her better than their mother did. Being fifteen years older placed Lillian in the unique position of being surrogate mother and, as Irene grew up, close friend as well as sister. Irene flashed back to last night's dream, the vision of Matt's broken, bloody body on the dirt of the rodeo ring, the pounding hooves of the enraged bucking horse, the waving arms of the rodeo clowns trying to pull the maddened horse away from Matt, the sound of her own screams from the stands as she tried to fight her way down to him.

"Well, I really am just a little bit pissed he didn't come. The Stampede's not for a couple of weeks, after all."

"I know. But Matt's a cowboy. You know? The idea of a society wedding, even Kat's—you know as well as I do, he'd have felt like a fish out of water. We Shiptons might prefer the simple things of life—and after meeting Parker and all his family, I'm pretty sure they do, too— but we can adapt to any scenario life might put us in. Which for the Draytons mean big parties for social events. But Matt would have been miserable. And that's still not what's really upsetting you."

"I'm just tired, Lilly. Work's been rough, and all the wedding planning, and Kat's wedding—which I wouldn't have missed for the world, don't get me wrong, even if she'd made me wear a really hideous bridesmaid dress instead of this pretty thing." Irene stroked the silk of the simple cream sheath. The neutral color and classic design had set off the natural beauty and coloring of all Kat's attendants.

"It's been really hectic lately, I know." *And you aren't fooling me one-bit, young lady. But I'll let it go for now.* Lillian squeezed off a hug. "And I want you to promise me you'll get some rest when you get home. I'll be home to help soon, I'm only staying behind to make sure all the after-wedding chores here get handled and to house-sit till Kat and Parker get back from Maui."

"You don't have to hurry on my account and you don't have to worry about me, either. I'm fine. Really."

"I know you are, honey." *And I've got some beach property in Arizona to sell you too, little sister.*

Chapter Sixteen

Irene

Lillian hummed to herself as she pulled open drawers in the guest room bureau and transferred her clothes from the bureau back to her suitcase. Katherine and Parker were due back tomorrow and though they'd asked her to stay over with them for another week, they were still newlyweds, even if they were back from their official honeymoon. Three was still a crowd and it was time for her to go.

Her cell phone started twanging Garth Brooks' *Rodeo*.

Irene. She grabbed the phone before the end of the first ring. "Hello?"

"Lillian, when are you leaving Tampa? "

Uh huh. Trouble in paradise for sure. Haven't been able to get her off my mind all week. "I'm packing right now, my flight's leaving tomorrow at 11:30."

"And you're coming straight here, right? You're not stopping over anywhere?"

"I promised I would, honey. Are you having problems with any of the wedding plans?"

"I'm beginning to think there isn't going to be a wedding."

"Excuse me?"

"I don't know if we'll even be getting married. And I—" Irene broke off with a loud sniff. "I need you."

* * *

Irene pulled herself together. After all, they were still a couple—at least for the time being—and Matt should have already been here. She sure couldn't fuss at him for being late, time had slipped up on her, too.

"Sorry I'm late." Matt strolled into the kitchen of Irene's downtown apartment and slipped his arms around her waist, drawing her back and nuzzling her neck.

"Actually you're just in time." Irene turned into his arms, lifted onto her toes, and planted a kiss on his lips. "I got caught up fixing the guest room for Lillian and nearly forgot to put the roast in the oven."

"Smells great."

"Good. I'll just turn off the heat and let it rest. Want a beer?"

"Yes, ma'am. I sure do. It's been one hell of a day."

Irene grabbed a couple of bottles out of the fridge, handed one to Matt and kept one for herself. "Let's take these outside. I'm ready for a break too."

The apartment balcony looked out over the garden and swimming pool and provided a cool respite from the uncharacteristically warm Calgary heat. "I love it that we're having such great weather for Stampede." Irene snuggled up beside Matt on the swing." I just wish it wouldn't get quite so hot inside the apartment."

"It is hot in here. Oh, well, once you're moved out to the ranch all you need do is open both sets of doors and let the wind blow through. It never gets too hot in the ranch house."

"I can hardly wait. Meantime though, I need to pick up another fan so Lillian doesn't suffocate in that bedroom."

"Speaking of Lillian, don't forget I've got tickets for both of you in the family section tomorrow afternoon."

"Oh. Thanks, that was thoughtful. But I wonder if she'll feel up to it?"

Matt frowned. "Why wouldn't she?" He ran his hand along one of the waves of Irene's long red hair, smoothing it back from her face and looking down into her eyes. "You've been making excuses every time I mention the Stampede. Is something wrong?"

"Nothing's wrong." Irene's voice sharpened and she ducked her head to avoid Matt's eyes. "It's just that Lillian's flying all morning to get here from Tampa Bay and I'm not all that sure she'll feel up to dumping her stuff and heading straight out to the rodeo."

"What time is she getting here? I thought she had an early morning flight."

"She does, but it's still nearly a four-hour flight. She's getting older, you know?"

"Irene, she's only fifteen years older than you are! And you'd better be glad she didn't hear you say that. Besides, she'll never get old. You're more of an old hen than she'll ever be."

"What did you just call me?" Irene punched him in the arm.

Matt laughed and grabbed her hand. "Just kidding. Hey, let's be serious. I don't believe this has anything at all to do with Lillian. You've been changing the subject every time I've mentioned the rodeo. Like you don't even want to think about it, let alone talk about it. Something's going on, and I'm not letting go of you until you tell me what's wrong." He pressed her against the back of the swing and gave her a long and very hungry kiss.

"Are you sure you want to talk about the rodeo right now?" Irene mumbled against his lips, and then deliberately slid her hands underneath his shirt, up his bare back and around the front until her fingers brushed against his nipples.

"Hey, that tickles."

"It'll do more than that soon." She rubbed her palms back and forth until she had him squirming in his seat.

"Let's take this inside."

"I thought you'd never ask."

Later, after a very satisfying hour in the bedroom, Matt sat up. He climbed over Irene and straddled her legs, planting his hands on either side of her head. "Now that I've got you where I want you, let's have an answer to why you've been avoiding any mention of the rodeo.

"I haven't been avoiding," Irene started to protest when Matt's cell phone belted out *Beer for My Horses.*

Matt grabbed the phone from the bedside table and flipped over onto his back. Irene grinned and jumped out of bed.

"I'll be in the shower."

When she came back five minutes later wrapped in a towel, Matt was already fully dressed.

"That was Brett. They've called a meeting and they want everyone there who's riding tomorrow. Something to do with safety and how to deal with possible interference from demonstrators. Damn, I hate that shit. I mean, most of us take care of our horses like they were our kids, sure would make life a hell of a lot easier if people believed that."

"Sorry. I know it's troublesome. Will you be back, or do you have to go out to the ranch?"

"I'd better go to the ranch. I still have some stuff to pick up and this is probably going to end up being a late night. No use disturbing you when you've got Lillian coming tomorrow. I'll have your tickets waiting for you at will call. You'll be there right?"

"I'll try." Irene ducked her head to keep from making eye contact.

"That's crap, Irene. I'm going to expect to see you there and if you don't show up then it appears to me, we've got some problems need to be worked out before we do any more wedding planning."

With that Matt stormed out the door leaving Irene to throw herself down on the bed and burst into tears.

Chapter Seventeen

Sisters

Well, I don't know quite what I was expecting, but it wasn't that. Lillian buckled her seatbelt and settled back to ponder the sudden turn of events between Irene and her fiancé Matt Dillon.

Even under the present circumstances, she couldn't stop the grin that always occurred when she said Matt's full name, even to herself. When her sister Irene first introduced Matt to the family everyone thought he'd made it up as a stage name, him being a rodeo star and all. But nope, just nutty parents who were western fans. It said a lot about Matt he hadn't been traumatized for life growing up with that name.

Lillian had no idea what could have gone wrong between the two, but she knew for sure it hadn't been because Matt hadn't come to Kat's wedding. Irene and her cowboy had been thick as thieves for nearly two years, and their engagement last Christmas had been expected and applauded by everyone who knew and loved them both.

"And what be abrew to put such a look on your face, my girl?" Mother Shipton materialized in the seat next to Lillian.

Lillian started and caught herself before she spoke out loud, switching to a whisper in the nick of time. "Heavens, Mother, you scared the living daylights out of me. I'm assuming I'm the only one knows you're here, right?"

Mother Shipton's grin showed a mouthful of surprisingly white teeth. "For now. Though I've a mind to flash this smile and see if I can still garner an appreciative glance from a handsome lad. How do ye like it? I tried a wee bit o' that white potion I found in Katherine's bathroom in the strange jar. Very tasty, it was. Didn't expect my teeth to change color, though. Wondrous things this century has, just wondrous."

"That's tooth whitener. You're not supposed to eat it. And it's not polite to take other people's stuff. Besides, what would your Toby say about you flashing your smile around at strange men? I'm surprised at you, Mother, for shame."

Mother waved a hand in dismissal. "Chill out, child."

"Chill out? Did you seriously just tell me to chill out? Wherever did you hear that?"

"It's old I am, child, not stupid. I still have my ears and wits about me. And it's many years I've been without my Toby and no man I've ever met or ever will meet can hit his measure, for certain sure. It's just a bit of sport I'm having. And my Toby wouldn't be saying a word, it's laughing his arse off at me is what he'd be doing."

The man across the aisle gave Lillian a questioning look. "Notes for a scene that just occurred to me!" She held up a small recorder and nodded at her fellow passenger. "I'm a writer." He smiled and nodded back.

"What are you doing here?" Lillian turned back to Mother.

"Why, it's going with you I am! I'd think that'd be as clear as the nose on your face."

"What?"

"I like it here. Or more proper to say, I 'spose, is I like your now. Your time, this century. Contraptions such as this plane. 'Course, I could just pop over to Calgary all on my own, but I wouldn't be enjoying your company then, would I? My time's lonely. And dismal. And boring. Has been ever since I lost my Toby. And without—" Mother paused and played with the buttons of the arm rest.

"Without what?"

"Family, girl. Without family, a body's life t'aint worth living. And now here I be. With my family. You'd not deny an old woman her family, now would ye?"

Lillian sighed. "Okay. But you stay out of sight. Irene's the skittish type. One glimpse of you and she'll freak out."

"You always did baby that one." Mother crossed her fingers and held them in front of

Lillian. "Don't banish me. Mayhap you'll find me helpful."

"Did you just make the sign of the evil eye at me?"

"Heavens no, child! I made a sign to keep your evil eye off me!"

"Wait a minute. How do you know I baby Irene? Which I don't. And don't be popping off and scaring the daylights out of Mom, either!"

"*Pssshaw.* As if she doesn't know good and well who I am and where all of you come from."

"Excuse me? Really? She knows about you. How? And you didn't answer my question. How do you know I baby Irene?"

"An' who do ye think helped keep your Mum out of the loony bin when Edward and Alice were killed in that auto accident? You were just a teenager yourself, although there's no doubting you're the one who held the family together. Bill and Mina both in pieces, just shattered they were, no parent should have to feel that pain. And your mum, with six young'uns still at home and now a grandchild still a holding babe to take care of to boot—I tell ye, it was touch and go for a while. She needed me."

"Wait a minute! You *talked* to her? She *saw* you? But how? She's not actually Shipton blood."

"And that beautiful giantess Carrie, she who guarded Kitty-Kat on her junket through time—it's Shipton blood that runs in her veins?

No, she be a sister of the heart. And sometimes, that be stronger than any blood ties. Mina, she has her own power, strong and pure."

"Why didn't she tell me?"

"'Tis not the kind of thing to be telling a young girl already shouldering too heavy of a burden. No, I had the devil's own time convincing Mina she hadn't lost her own sanity. For certain sure, she wouldn't relish having her own daughter thinking she'd gone round the bend."

Lillian scowled. "So—you're telling me you've always been able to watch the family? That you've been watching us for years? I thought Katherine was the first. The pivotal key. The only one who could change the family destiny to ensure the family even existed."

"And for certain sure, she was, child! The only one in all those years who could travel back with me her own self. 'Twas that what was needed to save the family, nothing less. A rare talent indeed, and only given to those born under exactly the right alignment of the stars. A blessing and a true miracle her friend Carrie had it, too, to help keep our Katherine safe on that adventure. Ah, what a beautiful giantess that girl is! Sisters of the heart indeed, those two! But since 'tis a talent I have myself—well, once I knew I had it, I couldn't be so wasteful as to not put it to good use, now could I? And it just depended on the situation, it did, whether anybody ever knew I was there or not. Now don't fret. I'll stay out of sight unless I'm needed."

"I don't believe this! You've been spying on us for years? And you're just now *telling* me this, after acting like everything you were seeing was all new and shiny and oh-so-strange? Including that bit about teeth whiteners when you finally decided to let me know you were hitch-hiking? Air-hiking? Whichever."

"Not spying, m'dear. Guarding. Quite another kettle of fish altogether, don't ye know? Don't be so quick to judge. 'Tis handy I am to have around when there's hanky panky afoot."

"There is no hanky panky. Matt is a perfect gentleman, and whatever is going on with those two is bound to be nothing more than a misunderstanding."

"All righty then, 't'won't take long to find out the right of things, and then I can have a catch up with Mina. And then we'll see what we be needing to set this branch of the family aright."

"That's what I'm afraid of. What we'll see."

* * *

Lillian smiled at the sandy haired young man who'd just inspected her passport and given her the go-ahead to retrieve her luggage and proceed through Customs at Calgary International airport.

"And where are we off to from here?"

Lillian glared up at Mother, perched atop the luggage cart she'd just snagged from the cart carrier. "Where—how on earth did you get up there? We're going out those doors and down the ramp to meet Irene, and what are you doing on top of the cart? Don't you think I have enough to push as it is?"

"*Pshaw*. You know full well this isn't a corporeal body with any weight. And even if it did have weight, how much could this frail old thing weigh?"

"Well, it feels like you weigh plenty. Must be all those knickknacks you kept putting in my basket at the gift shop. And where'd you learn about stuff like corporeal bodies anyhow?"

"And ye think I'd let all our girls go off to those colleges by themselves without anyone to keep an eye on them? Regular dens of iniquity those things are, oh, the things I could tell ye! Oh, wait, I don't have to! All the times you ended up studying in the library when that roommate of yours played the tramp in your room with that Joe Whit—"

Lillian stopped the cart. "That's enough, thank you! And really? You've been going to university with me? All the kids?"

"Oh, for certain sure! Couldn't pass up such entertainment! Not to mention all the things I've learned over the years. No one's ever too old to learn, you know. And I told you already, just because Katherine's the only one capable of negotiating the time-space continuum doesn't mean—"

"Negotiating the time-space continuum? You're a fraud, Mother, that's what you are! Oh, yes, you've just missed Toby so much, and here you've been hi-jacking college life! You can speak perfectly modern English when you want to, you slipped up big time with that little speech! You've even been sitting in on science classes!"

"Idle hands are the devil's own workshop. Idle minds, too. Science comes easy to me. Has a lot of magic in it, though most folks don't have a clue it does."

Lillian came to a full stop. "Wait just a minute! I specifically remember the girls telling me they came back from one of their Fifteenth Century jaunts and found you in hysterics over MTV! That you called it a 'devil box' and it'd scared you to death! The hell it did, not if you've been hanging out in college dorms!"

"*Pfft!*" Mother waved her hand in dismissal. "I could tell they were on their way back and I wanted to give them a bit of distraction, get their minds off the journey. 'Twas still very new to them and it doesn't do to let yourself be overwhelmed. And 'tis very fond I was of the Drama Departments at those colleges, too. Besides, modern music's suffering, my girl. That whole scene needs a trip back to Gershwin. Now that was music! Though I did acquire a taste for the Rolling Stones."

"The Rolling Stones?! And did you disco, too?"

"For certain sure! John Travolta in his young days, ah, that was a treat! Quite the dancer! Though of course he pales when compared with Patrick Swayze, Lord bless and keep his soul."

"Mother! Have you no shame? What would your Toby say?"

"It's old I am, child, not dead. Well, scratch that. Yes, I am. But Toby never expected me to sit like a coal lump and twiddle my thumbs. Knew full well I wasn't about to, either! I've had lots of time to fill. Kept a close eye on all my girls."

"You are the most infuriating…Oh, sorry!" Lillian spoke to the elderly man in a big white cowboy hat who stepped forward to offer a hand with her cart. "I was talking to my nephew." She pointed to the Bluetooth device attached to her ear. "He's gotten up to a bit of mischief while I've been gone."

The white hat – a member of the traditional greeting group that volunteered to meet visitors to Calgary with a warm smile and a helping hand – smiled at Lillian and nodded. "Oh, they'll do that all right, those young ones will. Will you be wanting a taxi or a shuttle perhaps?"

"No, I'll be fine, thanks. My sister is meeting me. There she is over there." Lillian pointed toward the speeding bullet who'd suddenly taken the form of a drop-dead gorgeous redhead blasting down the aisle towards them.

"Well, I certainly see the resemblance." White hat stepped back to avoid a collision as the redhead launched herself into the older woman's arms, nearly toppling themselves off their feet. He smiled, nodded to both of them and headed towards the next arrivals.

"I thought you'd never get here." Irene wrapped her arms around her sister and hung on like a limpet.

"Irene. What in the world is the matter? You'd think it'd been two years since you've seen me, not two weeks."

"It's awful. I don't know what to do. Everything was so perfect, we had the wedding all planned and we were so happy, and now we're doing nothing but fighting and everything is ruined. I don't know what to do."

"Major trauma going on here." Mother said into Lillian's ear.

"Shush!"

"What? Why did you say that?" Irene sobbed even harder.

"It's okay. Don't cry. That wasn't meant for you. I was talking to Mother."

"Mother? But Mimi's not here and you call her Mom, what's up with Mother? Are you okay, Lillian?"

"No. Not our mother. I know she's not here. Listen, Reenie, you need to stop crying and we need to get out of the airport. Come on, dry your tears and let's go get the car. There are things I need to tell you and this is not the place."

"But Matt!"

"I know. You're scared to death he's backing out on the wedding, but try to get yourself in hand, and we'll figure it all out. I'm sure whatever it is, it's not the end of the world. You know I'd know if anything was really wrong because he's the man you love."

Irene nodded. "I've been hoping you'd say that. I know you always know with us, but I wasn't sure if it would work with Matt, too."

"Of course it does. It works with everyone we love. Is this yours?"

Irene had stopped in front of a Ford Supercab that looked to Lillian to be a long ways up from the ground.

"It's okay. See? There's a running board. I've been spending a lot of time at the ranch out in Strathmore. The truck is so much handier with the horses and all."

"Very interesting." Lillian said, and covered her mouth to choke back the laugh that threatened to escape at the sight of Mother perched on top of the hood like an out of this world ornament in her black dress and flowing cape.

"What's so funny?"

"I'll tell you later. You wouldn't believe me right now." Lillian patted Irene's hand, motioned to Mother to join them in the cab and settled down to enjoy the ride.

* * *

Irene poured her heart out on the way to the apartment.

"We were supposed to go to the bakery this weekend to pick the wedding cake, but one thing after another kept popping up—or so he said—and he couldn't make it. And then last night, he was all 'you have to bring Lillian to the rodeo'—even though I told him after a four-hour flight you'd be too tired—"

"Excuse me?" Lillian's eyebrows assumed exclamation point position. "What am I now? The resident old lady invalid?"

"I didn't mean that and you know it! But it's just rodeo this and rodeo that and I ask you, what woman can compete with the Stampede, for heaven's sakes?! And he stormed out and didn't even tell me he loved me!"

"Irene." Lillian turned the full force of her hazel eyes on her younger sister's face. "Irene, if you're going to try and lie to me, you could at least try and make it believable. You'd be just as happy if Mom baked your wedding cake. From a Pillsbury cake mix. So stop this babbling about wedding cakes and me being tired from a measly little four-hour flight and tell me what's really going on between you and Matt."

Irene gripped the steering wheel with both hands and fought to keep the tears from flowing. "I knew you'd see right through all of that. I don't know why I even tried."

"I don't either, I'd certainly have thought you'd have known better. Now what exactly is going on with you?

"Wait, this is my building." Irene turned onto Sixth Avenue in downtown Calgary and into the parkade between two thirty-five story cement towers. "Let's wait until we get upstairs to my apartment. Then I promise I'll tell you everything."

"Good idea. I'd much rather you kept your mind on your driving." Lillian looked out the window of the truck and shuddered. "There isn't much space between the rows of parked vehicles from what I can see. You sure you're going to be able to park this big truck in one of those little spots?"

Irene laughed. "Very funny. I'll have you know I've been parking this truck in here for months now and you won't see a single scratch anywhere."

"Admirable."

"I have to admit it's not ideal, but it wasn't supposed to be for very long. We'd already planned for me to give up the apartment since I'd be moving out to Matt's place in Strathmore after the wedding."

Irene's lip started to quiver and Lillian reached over and touched her shoulder. "Let's not think about that right now. We'll talk everything through once we get inside. You just concentrate on getting this monster settled, and then maybe I can get you to fix me a decent cup of tea. It'll be the first decent cup I've had in almost three months. They don't do hot tea down South and you've no idea what that sweet syrup they call iced tea tastes like!

* * *

"What a nice comfy apartment you have." Lillian followed her sister down the hallway to the rose-colored bedroom, the one Irene had dubbed *Lillian's Room* the day she moved in because of the delicate, rose-colored walls set off with gleaming white molding. True to the apartment's theme, Irene had selected a goose down duvet covered with twining roses. And, of course, a dozen multi-colored roses adorned the white and gold dresser.

"I know you have to put your things away before you'll enjoy your tea." Irene, well acquainted with Lillian's habits, placed her sister's suitcase on the bench at the foot of the bed and stepped back. "I'll be in the kitchen getting things ready. Come on in when you're finished."

"Didn't I tell you what a lovely girl she was? And will you quit jumping on my bed!" Lillian shook her finger at Mother, who was bouncing up and down in the center of the bed in a very unladylike—and very non-elderly—manner.

"What's that?" Irene called from the hallway.

"Nothing, dear. Just talking to myself."

Irene's laughter echoed down the hallway.

"This has got to stop. I'll have to tell her about you at tea, otherwise, it won't be long till she's convinced I've gone completely round the bend."

Mother stopped mid-bounce and cackled. "I 'spose I could, but 'tis possible she won't be able to see me even if I do try to show myself."

"What do you mean? Can't you just materialize? Whenever you want to?"

"'Tis not that easy. First, I've got to put myself into the person's head. I did that with you. You were easy."

"You know, that sounds rather insulting."

"Oh, no, m'dear, not at all. The more in-tune a body is with their power, the easier 'tis to make them see me! Then once I'm in, I just plant a little seed of an idea there's something they need to be looking at. And 'tis a lot harder with some folks than others. I had the devil's own time with Katherine, she didn't have an inkling of her own power, much as she has, and I never did manage to get inside her Parker's head, 'tis just plain stubborn those Drayton men be."

"Well, this is entirely different. Irene is family. Besides, she has the gift. And I'm almost certain she knows it, but she's scared of it. That's why I know there's a heck of a lot more to the trouble between her and Matt than any stupid rodeo tickets. She's always had a streak of mule in her, that girl has, and we need her to open up about the real reason she's putting up all these roadblocks about even setting foot on Stampede grounds. For heaven's sake, she's been on the back of a horse since before she could walk. She loves the rodeo, and she loves Matt Dillon. Something's going on here, and we're going to go into that kitchen, sit down with a decent cup of tea, and you're going to make yourself visible and scare the life out of her."

"Yes ma'am." Mother floated off the bed and dipped into a curtsy in front of Lillian. "'Tis me best I'll be doing then. See?" Mother stretched her mouth with two fingers and stuck out her tongue. "I've got my scare face on."

* * *

Lillian paused in the kitchen door and took a deep breath. *Here goes nothing.*

"Reenie bring the tea over and sit down with me. There's something we have to talk about right up front."

"Two seconds. There! Done!" Irene turned toward the table, a plate of finger sandwiches in one hand and a large ceramic cup of tea in the other. Her eyes widened and her face went white. Plate and cup hit the tile floor.

Lillian rushed toward her younger sister, afraid she was about to follow the plate and cup down to the floor.

"Why did you do that?" she hissed from the corner of her mouth. "I told you to wait till I'd explained before you tried to make her see you! Reenie, don't you faint on me!"

"'Tis not a thing I did, and that's God's honest truth!"

Irene shook off Lillian's supporting hand. "I'm not going to faint, Lillian, let go." She walked slowly toward Mother. "I know you," she whispered. "You used to come see Mimi. When I was a little girl."

"Aye, that I did, m'dear. And you were a very little girl, no more than three. You saw me? And you remember me?"

"Yes, but—you look the same. The very same! And that's just impossible, it's—it's—

"'Tis magic, child. Pure and simple."

"Let's all go sit down at the table, shall we?" Lillian steered Irene toward a chair. "We'll chat while I clean this up and get us all some tea."

* * *

"…so that's the story, Reenie, unbelievable as it sounds. We've got sort of a family guardian. A time-hopping family guardian."

"And that's where it comes from?" Irene stared at Mother in awe and then back at Lillian. "That—thing—you do? Always knowing when one of us is in trouble, always being there?"

"Well, now, 'tis not just your sister has that, dearie. There's not a female born in this family that doesn't have at least a touch of the gift. Some a great deal more than others, mind you. But all of us have it to some degree or another. Starting with my own beautiful Isabelle. I see

246

her now and again in all of you, always lifts my heart."

"You can't go—well, see her? Visit her?"

A shadow crossed Mother's face. "To be sure, I could see her. And I 'spose I could even visit, did I take a mind to, but she and I—we're too—close, that might be the best word. 'Tis the natural course of things that children bury their parents, lead their own lives. So I felt it best to leave her alone and let her live it. 'Twas a dark time and my Isabelle didn't have the gift of travel. Told you, in all this time, none of our blood but Kat's ever had it. 'Cepting my own self, that is. Sometimes 'tis best to leave behind things can't be changed and concentrate on the things that can."

"But what happened to her?"

Lillian felt sorrow pour from Mother's soul. "Reenie. That's Mother's business and none of ours. Let's just be grateful our guardian's now made herself visible. She's very handy to have around." Enough sentiment, it was time to balance out the emotion that had streamed into the room from Mother when she spoke of her daughter. "Also frequently annoying as hell, mind you, but handy, I have to admit that."

"And 'tis very fond of you, I am, too, m'dear." Mother Shipton smiled at her across the table and Lillian knew she realized exactly what Lillian was doing. And was grateful for it.

Irene jumped to her feet. "Look at the time! I need some family magic fast. Our company's going to be here in just a few minutes to watch the Stampede Parade with us. And I don't have all the food out."

"Ah! Kitchen magic!" Mother stood up and headed to the counter. "The best kind of family magic. Tell us what we need to do, dear heart."

* * *

The Stampede's opening day parade went straight down Sixth Avenue, which meant that visitors to Irene's 14th floor apartment were able to sit out on her large balcony and watch all the action. Matt should have already been there, helping with Irene's planned family brunch, but so far he was a complete no show. Irene was determined not to show how worried she was about that and had on her British game face, the one telecasting that everything was just perfect, thank you very much. It might have even worked with any other family, but in this one, that game face didn't have much of a chance.

The first guest to arrive was Shipton cousin Tami Cartwright, a fellow Calgarian and very close friend of Irene. Not five minutes after sharing welcoming hugs with Irene and Lillian, Tami marched directly over to the stool Mother had chosen as her seat to view the action.

"You must be Mother Shipton." She held her arms out and leaned forward. "I've been dreaming about you a lot lately."

"*Ahhh*." Mother smiled and raised her own arms to meet Tami's hug. "So you're the one that's been coming along on my walks. I wondered when we'd meet in person."

"I don't get it." Irene followed Tami over to the table and swiveled her head back and forth between the two women. "You can see her?"

"Of course I can see her." Tami laughed. "If you'd listened to me when I told you about my last dream workshop, you'd have remembered me telling you I'd been spending time with family."

"I did too listen." Irene tossed her head. "I thought you meant a *real* family member."

"Oh, so it's not real I am?" Mother tossed her head indignantly.

"I'm sorry, Mother. I didn't mean that."

"You'd best be saying that. Nice save." Tami nodded her approval. "I see Matt's not here."

Irene blushed. "It's stampede week. You know how it is."

Tami put her arm around Irene and hugged, taking the opportunity to whisper in her cousin's ear. "We need to talk."

"Sounds like the rest of your company." Lillian called from the living room and pointed to the TV screen, now flashing on the lobby and a group gathered in the entryway. Tami's husband picked up the phone receiver from the lobby panel and the phone rang in the apartment.

"Okay. When it settles down." Irene tossed the words at Tami, before heading for the phone to enter the buzz-in code.

Within minutes the apartment walls echoed with happy voices sharing *remember when's* and fresh squeezed Mojitos made by Tami's sister Billie, who had flown in from Oregon the night before. Tami'd made sure there was a "properly prepared" pot of Red Rose tea for Mother, and there were enough snacks to feed half the parade crowd.

Mother seemed to be in a different spot every time Lillian saw her, but then anyone capable of time travel was certainly capable of transporting in a flash from one location to the other.

"You're making me dizzy," Lillian whispered when Mother materialized on an empty cushion beside her.

"'Tis a grand thing, family. And it's not too many chances I get to view so many of you together in one spot. Let an old woman have her fun."

"Fine with me. As long as that fun doesn't involve any sudden appearance to a poor unsuspecting soul and giving them a heart attack."

"I would never."

Irene flitted around here and there, inside and outside of the patio filling drinks, and taking care of her guests.

"You're not getting to see much of the parade yourself." Lillian placed her arm around Irene and motioned for her to take a seat at the heavily laden table. "Stop. Let me fix you a plate from all this wonderful food you've set out. Have a Mojito, don't they look tasty?"

"Oh, I'm sorry, Lillian, would you like one? You don't have to just drink tea, you know, we just wanted to be sure you had it if you wanted it since you've been without proper tea for so long."

"No, thanks. They look wonderful, but I'll stick to my tea. You didn't answer me about sitting a spell, watching these spectacular floats, and letting me fix you a plate."

Irene bent down to her sister. "I'm sorry Lil, I can't. I'm worried sick about Matt. He didn't call last night. He didn't even check to see if you made your flight okay. And this morning when I called his cell phone, it went straight to voice mail."

Tami caught the edge of the conversation and joined the group. "Maybe he's just overwhelmed with preparations for the first day?"

"That's just crap. He's never failed to return my calls, no matter how busy he is down at the grounds. No, something is wrong. I know it. I feel it and I've already called down to the barns. They said Matt's been there since early morning but he's not taking any calls. He left a message for me to pick up my tickets at Will Call. He'll wave to me from the infield and see me after his first ride."

Lillian shook her head. "That sounds a bit like an ultimatum."

"That's just exactly what the fuck it is! An ultimatum! And you know I'm not going to cave in and meekly trot myself on down to the rodeo grounds just because Mr. Matt God's Gift Dillon expects me to tuck my tail between my legs and play the good little wifey." Irene's voice rose and with a nod to Lillian, Tami took her cousin's hand.

"Come on, Reenie. Let's go in the bedroom for a bit. Lillian will see to everyone."

"Yes. You two go take a break. I'll handle things." Lillian urged the two down the hall, before turning back to where the parade seemed to be keeping everyone occupied.

* * *

Tami steered Irene toward the edge of the bed and managed to get her to sit.

"Who does he think he is?" Irene snapped. "He's been building toward this, it isn't just a whim."

"Now wait. Let's stop and think about this, Reenie. Maybe Matt needs a bit of reassurance that you're sincere about wanting the same kind of life he lives. Remember cowboys are also ranchers, or at least Matt is. He works long hours and has a lot of responsibility on his shoulders, what with running the family farm. He's also the Canadian National Saddle Bronc champion. That requires a certain amount of commitment. He needs to appear in certain places, represent his sport and his country in quite a few political and charitable functions. You knew that going into the relationship."

"Of course I knew. That's not the problem. I fully support him and the ranch and the life we're going to live, and everything that goes along with it. But the thing is—" Irene jumped up from the bed and started pacing. "The thing is, and you'll probably think I'm nuts, but I've been having the same dream every night since Matt rode at Ponoka. It's the Calgary finals and Matt comes riding out of the chute on a high bucking dream of a horse. Everything's going great when his horse suddenly goes nuts. He puts his head down and goes totally mad, he leaps straight up ten feet into the air and does a full back flip. I see Matt hanging on for dear life but there's no finishing that ride. I don't know why the horse just suddenly turns into a killing machine that's going to get the rider off his back no matter what. And in my dream I scream just as Matt flies over the horse's neck and under the hooves, and the hooves, they don't stop, they just keep stomping, stomping, blood spray's everywhere and Matt's head—it's under the hooves. Everybody's screaming and that's when I finally wake up, soaking wet with sweat."

Irene stopped and wiped her eyes with the tissue Tami held out. "I'm sorry. I know it's stupid. I know it's a dream. But you know how I am. Tami. When I have dreams like this, they tend to come true. I can't go to that rodeo. I know Matt won't stop riding, and I know he won't believe me if I tell about this dream, but one thing I do know. Before this it happened, Matt rode up to where I was sitting and took off his hat. And bowed. To me. And he said, 'This one's for you, lovely lady.' So I was *there*, there when it happened. But if I don't go, it won't happen. Maybe." Irene shredded the tissue in her hand. "At least, that's what I have to believe. That if I'm not there, it won't happen. So I'm not going. End of discussion. Even if it means Matt won't want to marry me."

Chapter Eighteen

Ridin' the Rodeo

The excitement that was always part and parcel of the Calgary Stampede had launched into full scale pandemonium by the time Matt strolled onto the grounds Thursday afternoon for *Sneak a Peek,* the unofficial opening day of the midway and several of the exhibits. Locals and those *in the know* could purchase discount tickets to explore all the stampede had to offer before the official opening. As the reigning world champion saddle bronc rider, the officials expected Matt to join the other cowboys meeting and greeting guests and mingling with the rodeo fans who always looked forward to this opportunity to meet with their favorites.

Matt spent a couple of hours doing his duty and mingling in the Exhibit Hall and then crossed the grounds towards the infield barns. The horses and cattle making up the rough stock for rodeo performances wouldn't arrive until tomorrow morning, in preparation for the afternoon rodeo, but the riders and stock hands made a habit of gathering in the barns on Thursday to meet and greet and catch up on the latest news and gossip.

"Hey, Matt! Been wondering when you'd make an appearance." Steer wrestler Brett Summers, one of Matt's buddies from grade school, strode out of the barn.

"How's it going?" Matt put out his hand. The two men shook and walked together to sit on one of the benches lining the infield. Both of them had grown up in rodeo families who lived, breathed and slept the rodeo circuit. Like Matt's dad, Brett's had named his son after a western character, too – in this case, Brett Maverick.

"Have you seen Chance?" Chance Mayfair was Brett's closest competition in the ring, though out of it, Brett was the favorite. Chance didn't go out of his way to make friends.

"Nope. Been mingling with the fans, I just got here to the real rodeo. Why?"

"He's been running his mouth about how he's going to take you down this year no matter what it takes. I just figured you should have a heads up."

Matt pushed his cowboy hat back on his head and scowled. "I make it a point to ignore his bullshit."

"I know, but I'd keep an eye open if I were you. You know his reputation. The bastard abuses his women and horses both and I'd make damn sure he didn't get anywhere near your rides if I were you."

"I'll keep an eye out. But I seriously doubt he'll get a chance to mess with any of the stock. They keep a close eye on the pens and there's always two or three officials on watch for anything out of the ordinary. Calgary's damn serious about the animals' welfare."

Brett nodded. "I know, and you're right. I just figured better warned than caught off guard."

"Thanks. 'Preciate you, buddy." Matt grinned and gripped his friend's shoulder.

"Enough of a bad subject. How're the wedding plans coming along?"

Matt shuddered. "Don't even ask. Irene's a basket case about everything getting done on time, and on top of that she's got some bee in her bonnet about the Stampede, don't even seem like she wants to show up for any event at all."

"Irene? She loves the rodeo."

"I know. I don't know what the hell's gotten into her lately. Anyway, her big sister Lillian's getting back in town today, I'm sure hoping that'll settle her down."

"Probably just nerves. Women get that way. Laurie drove me nuts the whole month before our wedding. And I'll tell you one thing sure. If I had it to do all over, I'd damn sure elope to Vegas."

"Yeah. I already suggested that." Matt laughed. "You can imagine how that went over with the Shipton sisters."

* * *

Irene stayed true to her decision not to set foot on the Stampede grounds, but as the afternoon stretched past the time of Matt's scheduled first ride, her nerves stretched thinner and thinner in anticipation of what she expected as Matt's reaction, which was absolute silence. Matt wouldn't confront her over the phone or come storming over in a rage. That wasn't in his personality. He'd do worse than that, he'd retreat into himself, hugging his hurt feelings like a child hugged his teddy bear. And there might be nothing she could do to pull him back out of that hurt. After a sleepless night and countless unanswered calls to his cell, Irene joined Mother and Lillian at the breakfast table."

"Irene, would you like some breakfast?"

"No thanks, Sis. I'll take a coffee to go, though. I've decided it's time Matt and I got something straightened out. I'm going to drive out to the ranch. I haven't heard from him since yesterday afternoon and he's not answering his cell."

"Head-on's always the best way to tackle a problem." Lillian smiled at Irene and Mother nodded her head in approval.

Irene's phone rang as Lillian poured coffee into her travel mug.

"Hello." She held the phone with one hand and took her travel mug with the other.

"Hey, Irene, it's Brett here. Do you know where Matt's gone?"

"Exactly what I was about to ask you. I didn't see him last night and he's not answering his cell phone."

"Damn. I warned Matt yesterday morning about Chance. He's been bragging around he intends to take that title one way or another, but you know Matt, he doesn't hear what he doesn't want to listen to. Matt shoulda' had the winning ride, but right after his, Chance came in on a horse that went off like a keg of dynamite. Craziest ride I've ever seen. He got full points, blew right past Matt's score."

"But Matt's been beat before, he's not a sorehead. He still should be at the Stampede this morning. What aren't you telling me, Brett?"

"I know all that, Irene. I don't understand what happened yesterday, what was going on with Brett. Chance pulled a horse that went nuts right out of the chute. Everyone figured he'd just gotten lucky, got a horse that gave one hell of a ride. But then Matt stormed into the barns claiming Chance'd doctored his horse. I mean, Matt even went to the Animal Welfare Vets, but they told him there was nothing wrong with the horse. He didn't like that worth a damn, told them to screw themselves, and then he went looking for Chance. Found him, too. Didn't actually *hurt* him none, but the police are here looking for him this morning, so we're all thinking the ass- hat pressed charges."

"Charges?"

"Yeah, charges. For a busted lip, the damn cry-baby. But since they're here and wanting to

259

talk to Matt, I'm pretty sure it'd be a real good idea for us to figure out where he is before this blows up any bigger."

"Well, I don't know what's going on with Matt, but I do know how he'd handle a situation like you're describing. He'd take it straight from the horse's mouth. If he thought there was something wrong with that horse and nobody was listening, he might just take it upon himself to take some blood and saliva samples from that horse to another vet. Like the ranch vet. You understand what I'm saying, Brett?"

"I never thought of that. You might be right. I'll go on over to the barns and see what I can find out, if anybody's seen him."

"Just make damned sure you don't go saying anything that'll land Matt in trouble or you'll be the one on the wrong side of my temper. And they don't call me Red for nothing."

"Okay, Red. Calm down. I'm just telling you what I know and giving you a heads up. I had to tell the cops Matt'd probably be at your place if he wasn't at home. I'm sorry, but I didn't know what else to tell them."

"Well, I haven't seen him, and I haven't talked to him, but I'm damn sure not going to sit around here waiting for them to come and ask questions I can't answer. My sister's here, and one of my elderly relatives. I'm sure they'll have a great time questioning her."

Irene clicked off her phone and turned to see Lillian trying to keep a straight face.

"Siccin' the bobbies on me are you, lassie?" Mother's eyes twinkled. She reached for Irene's hand and drew her toward the table where Lillian had pulled out a chair.

"Let's have a chat before you go tearing off across the country," Lillian said. Mother nodded agreement.

Chapter Nineteen

Brothers and Wolves

Joe Two-Feather looked up from the chunk of cedar he'd been carving into a stem for his Pipe. The young man walking up the path to his isolated cabin outside Golden, British Columbia, had the black hair and facial features that identified him as "not quite Native" but "not strictly Caucasian" either. Everyone who followed rodeo would recognize the muscular build, handsome face, and steel blue eyes of the reigning world champion saddle bronc rider instantly.

"Matt Dillon, what you doing here?"

"Can't a man call on a friend?"

Joe spat out a wad of tobacco and waved away Matt's question. "You figure I'm getting too thick to remember what day it is? Why in hell ain't you back in town getting ready to ride that bronc of yours?"

Every rodeo fan knew today was Showdown Sunday and no cowboy in the country would pass up an opportunity to compete for the biggest prize in rodeo, and certainly not the current champion, especially since he'd soon have a wife to support.

So as soon as Joe spotted Matt walking up his path at half past ten on Showdown Sunday, he knew something was wrong. The rodeo was a three-hour trip from Golden, and even if Matt had a helicopter stashed somewhere—and Joe'd have heard one of them landing within 50 miles of his isolated Rocky Mountain cabin—there wasn't any way Matt could make it back to ride in the Calgary Stampede finals this year.

Joe wasn't sure what was going on, but the situation didn't smell one bit like a friendly chat between brothers—which they might as well have been, raised together the way they were. Joe had lost his Cree parents in a car wreck when he was only six. Matt's dad, an RCMP officer, had been the first one on the scene, and the one who'd delivered the bad news to Joe and his grandma. From that day onward Joe had spent nearly every weekend with Constable Dillon and his son Matt. So, it had only seemed right that when Joe's grandma left to join her son and daughter-in-law in the spirit world, Joe'd moved in with the Dillons.

"Nice to see you too, Buddy." Matt crouched down beside his brother and watched quick hands run the knife along the cedar shaft.

Joe stopped in mid-peel and focused sharp black eyes on Matt's face.

"What's wrong?"

"Well," Matt propped his back against the wooden stair railing and stretched his legs. "As you might've noticed, today's Showdown Sunday and I'm here and not in the infield."

"Yep. I did in fact notice that." Joe nodded and waited for Matt to continue.

"Somebody's playing dirty, and I'm not sure how I want to handle things. Guess I needed some time to sort it out."

"Dirty how? Who?"

"Chance Mayfair. You oughta know that without asking."

"So, what did he do this time?"

"I don't know, but he did something that made his horse go nuts. I can't prove it of course. But I know he did. I got a good look at that poor bugger when they chased him out of the ring, and I'm telling you, he acted spooked. Chance had to know there was something wrong with that horse but he didn't give a damn, not Chance, the only thing he cared about was pocketing his share of that million."

"So why not turn him in?"

"That's the hell of it. I went and talked to one of the Vets, who took me over to talk to the women from the Animal Advisory Panel. When I told her what I suspected, she asked the Vet if all the horses had been drug tested like usual and he said yes. Since I had no idea what Chance had done to his horse and no proof, I couldn't back up anything. They made it obvious they thought I was just mad because Chance outrode me. They suggested I get a good night's sleep and get ready for today's ride and things would probably work themselves out."

"Oh boy." Joe knew Matt's temperament as well as he knew his own, so he knew how that must've gone.

"I guess I kind of lost it at that point. I told them I wouldn't be riding in any fucking rodeo where they cared more about their image than they did about protecting their stock. I walked out, jumped in my truck and headed out here."

"That's not like you, Matt. If the brother I know thought someone was doing the dirty he'd be like a dog with a bone until he got to the bottom of things."

Matt shrugged. "It seems nobody's interested in what happened out there. Apparently they all think it's just sour grapes on my part."

"Nobody who knows you and knows Chance will have any doubts."

"Yeah. But things are different now. The money makes everything bigger. A lot of riders don't even know each other. It's not the way it used to be. Besides, I did take a stab at getting to the bottom of things, the hard way. Guess I screwed that up, too."

Joe shook his head. "Don't tell me. You always did have a knack for hitting first and asking second. You put him in the hospital?"

"Nope. Busted his lip and wounded his dignity, but that's all. He's telling everyone who'll listen that I jumped him from behind because I'm pissed off about not winning top day money. Says I'm chicken shit and afraid he's going to take my title."

"Want a beer?"

"No. I need to keep my head clear. I think I'll take a walk over to Northern Lights."

Northern Lights was a Wolf Center and a favorite with both men. They'd invested a considerable amount of their time and money helping. Wolves have been hunted to near extinction in the past century, and the species only survived now because of centers like Northern Lights.

"I need to see if any new pups have shown up since my last visit."

"Good idea. I was over the other day. Maybe you'll spot the white male. It seems he's appointed himself leader."

"That I've gotta see." Matt stood, then leaned down and placed his hand on his brother's shoulder. "Thanks, Joe. I appreciate you trusting my word."

"What else?" Joe picked up the piece of cedar and put his knife back in motion.

* * *

Northern Lights Wolf Centre was located a few miles outside of Golden on the border of Yoho National Park. Nestled between the Rocky and Purcell mountains, the scenery was nothing less than spectacular, and being it was midsummer, Matt would have little chance of visiting the center without encountering more than a few tourists. Still, he figured if he took the back trail and worked his way around he might just get a look at the new white wolf, and even if he didn't manage to make it alone, just getting to spend some time among these awesome animals more than made up for any unwanted companions he might encounter along the way.

I know it's stupid. Matt told himself as he headed up the increasingly steep path that led around to the back of the Centre. *I shouldn't have walked out, but what the hell. They suspected I had a reason for claiming Chance did something to his horse but all they care about is keeping their image clean. I hate that political bullshit.*

His self-talk helped take the edge off his anger and by the time Matt reached the far enclosure he'd settled his insides. He'd spend a few hours with the animals and then he'd make his way back into the City. No doubt Irene would tear a strip off him when he got back, but he deserved it and his relationship with Irene was another of the fences he needed to mend.

He leaned against a post and squinted into the sun, watching as the greyish white wolf loped up the hillside and paused long enough to cast an eye over Matt as he stood outside the enclosure.

God, you're gorgeous.

The white wolf watched for a time, until seemingly satisfied with his inspection. Then the magnificent, proud beast turned towards the mountain and loped out of sight.

Wow. Matt let out his breath. *You were most definitely worth the trip.*

Chapter Twenty

Witch Business

"Just what is it you expect us to find down here?" Lillian hissed, running to keep up with the flitting figure of her weightless ancestor.

"I won't know until I find it, now will I, and there's no need for you to be hissing at me, ain't nobody but these horses out here, and even if somebody happened along all they'd see would be a crazy woman nattering away to herself."

"I'm not nattering to myself. Though Lord knows, thanks to you and your disappearing acts, everyone I know probably thinks I've taken leave of my senses what with me always talking when it seems there's nobody else around."

Mother chuckled. "You'd be surprised how convenient it can be having people thinking you're just a wee bit loony. Explains away a lot and keeps them well out of your business if you know what I mean."

"Stuff and nonsense. Okay, out there in those pens is where all the bucking stock is kept and in those trailers in the lot behind the pens is where the riders keep their sleeping trailers. I don't know which one is Chance's, though.

"Don't you worry your head about that. You just go on back home and tell Irene that everything's going to be just fine and she's not to fuss anymore about that dream she had."

"I don't know what you think you can do anyway. With Matt and Irene not speaking any longer and Matt disappearing and missing his chance to ride in the rodeo, there's not a heck of a lot of fixing anyone can do, I don't think. If you're planning on mending things between Irene and her Matt, I don't see any way that's going to happen. Irene believes what she saw in her dream and you know how she is with those dreams. At least you ought to know since you're probably responsible for her seeing them in the first place."

"Nope, that's not me. That's just something most of us have all been born with. One of those blessings or curses, depending on how you look at things, that we've all got to live with. The rodeo's not what's at the heart of this problem. But before we fix the heart, so to speak, we need to take care of the situation that started all this mess to begin with. You see, I fully believe what young Matt had to say about what Chance Mayfair did with his horse, and not only that, I believe I know exactly what kind of tomfoolery caused all this."

"What do you mean, Mother? Caused all what, and what kind of tom foolery are you talking about? I swear you talk around in circles more than anyone I've ever known."

"Just don't you worry your head about how or what, you just leave that to me. I've been pondering all this ever since Tami told us about Irene's dream. Something kept niggling at the back of my mind when she described her dream and then told me about Matt and his horse, and that's when I remembered Andrew Isaacs."

Lillian screwed up her face and looked at Mother like she'd taken leave of her senses.

"Who is Andrew Isaacs and what's he got to do with Irene's dream and Matt's rodeo?"

"It's not what's he got to do with it, Lillian, it's what it reminded me of, what this Chance Mayfair must have done. You see, Andrew Isaacs prided himself on having the finest horses in all of England, and he bet a lot of money on the results of an upcoming race at Doncaster. Word got around however, that a young upstart named Mark Appleyard had a black stallion that could outrun anything on four legs. People claimed they'd seen him out on the moors and there wasn't a horse in all of England that could even come close."

"How does that remind you of whatever it was that Matt thinks Chance Mayfair was doing to his horse?"

"Well, back then there weren't any fancy electronic devices, but Andrew wasn't taking any chances that Appleyard might actually have a horse that could outrun his stallion. You see there's always been certain sounds that spook horses, and one of the worst was the bagpipes. There were a lot of accusations flying around after that race, let me tell you. Mark's horse went flying past Andrew's and he wasn't looking back. Then, just as they got to the farthest turn in the course, from somewhere off in the woods came the worst bagpipe playing anyone had ever heard. Folks all around the racetrack covered their ears, and that there horse of Mark's, he left the track, leaped across the ditches, tossed young Appleyard so far it broke the young lad's neck. There was a lot of bad feelings about that, but nobody could ever prove anything so Andrew got the prize and that was the end of things."

"So, you think maybe Chance Mayfair's gotten hold of some kind of electronic device he's using to drive his own horse crazy, and maybe, given Irene's dream, he'd be thinking of using that same device to do the same kind of damage to Matt that Andrew Isaacs made happen to Mark Appleyard?"

"It crossed my mind, it did. That's why I've got this idea in mind, and with a little cooperation from you, I think we might just put this situation to rest without anybody at all getting hurt."

Mother spoke for several minutes, and by the time she'd finished laying out her plan, Lillian was barely holding in her laughter.

"So, you see, what I want you to do, my girl, is find out where Chance Mayfair bunks for the night and then I want you to go on back to Irene's apartment and leave the rest to me."

* * *

Mother floated over the line of motor homes that filled the area behind the barns, where most of the cowboys bunked out during the ten days of the Calgary Stampede. Lillian had found out from one of the ladies in the Exhibition Hall Café that Chance Mayfair, one of the least popular of the cowboys who came into the small Café every morning for breakfast, was a cheap tipper and all in all, an unpleasant person to be around. Chance kept his truck and trailer behind the barns for sleeping but apparently, he wasn't much into culinary arts, and when he didn't eat in the Café he bummed left-overs off the food vendors in the grounds. A lot of the vendors were generous with whatever was left at the end of the day and Chance made certain to be first in line for any free stuff.

Not a very nice young laddie, but perhaps after I've had a wee chat with him, he'll come up with a whole new change in attitude.

Mother found the trailer, slid on inside the locked doors and pulled a chair up beside the man sprawled across the folded-out double bed, snoring loudly.

"So it's Chance Mayfair I've the pleasure of speaking with today, is it now?" Mother put her mouth next to the young man's ear and raised her voice to a pitch that would easily summon all the cows on Scotton Moor.

"*Hey! What the hell!*" Startled out of a dead sleep, Chance leapt out of bed and towered over the old lady sitting in a chair beside his bed, grinning like a circus clown.

"How'd you get into my trailer?" Chance bore down on the woman. "You better get the hell outta here or I'll be calling security to come and drag you out."

"You mean like this?" Mother swooped out of the chair, flew across the room, and landed on top of the television set up in the far corner of the combination living and bedroom.

"*Hey!*" Chance tossed his hands in the air. "How'd you do that! What are you *doing* in here? I may have had a couple of beers last night but I know damn well I didn't ask no old woman to come on home with me."

"Oh, ye don't like the way I look? Well, if'n that's all that's troublin' you lad, why didn't you say so? How about I just fix myself up a wee bit."

In the blink of an eye the old woman disappeared and a sleek black panther with glowing red eyes and a mouth full of gleaming white teeth crouched in her place.

"*No! Hey! What the hell! Stop it, back!* Get *away* from me!" Chance jumped over the back of the chair where Mother'd previously sat, his face as white as the teeth of the panther.

"Well now. You don't fancy that look either?" Mother turned from the panther back into the old woman and floated down from the TV set to stand on the floor in front of the chair.

"You're a witch, aren't you?"

"In a manner of speaking. So are you ready to listen to a few things I've got to tell you or do you want me to invite a few more of my friends to pay you a visit?"

"No! I'm listening. I'm a *real* good listener. You just go right ahead with whatever it is you want to talk to me about."

"There, there, now that's a sensible laddie. So, first, we're going to have an understanding about the trick you pulled out there in the ring the other day."

"What trick?"

"Did you hear me tell you that I wanted you to listen and not waste my time with any silly denials? As you've already figured, I'm one of the immortal kind, and I don't need you to tell me what you did or didn't do out there the other night. I know what you did. I know everything you did, and from now on I'm always going to know everything you do. Do you understand me now, or do you need me to call in a few more of my friends to help you clear the cobwebs outta that rather thick head you got perched on top of yer shoulders?"

"No ma'am. I mean yes ma'am. I mean I understand and I won't interrupt no more."

"Good, then let me tell you what you're going to do from here on out."

Mother spoke for another twenty minutes, and finally, when she'd finished all she had to say, and just to make darn sure Chance Mayfair would have no illusions about who he was dealing with, she took time out to change into what most humans assumed a werewolf looked like. For good measure, she finished with an incredibly ghoulish eight-foot zombie.

"Oh, it was powerful fun." Mother laughed as she told Lillian all about it back in the apartment. "I suspect he most 'probly had to change his drawers *and* his jeans once I left. I've been wanting to try out that Zombie ever since I watched that silly show on Katherine's television set."

"Oh, Mother! I don't know what I'm going to do with you." Lillian smothered a giggle. "I've got to confess though, I'm truly grateful you've taken care of that dreadful Chance Mayfair. Now all we have to do is figure out how to patch things up between Irene and Matt!"

"Just you leave that to me, my girl. I only wanted to catch you up on me night's work. All you've got to do now is tuck yourself in for a good night's sleep. I'll be gone when you get up in the morning but make me a promise that you'll keep Irene here in the apartment until she gets a call from her Matt. Once she gets that call everything should be set into motion slick as a whistle and before you know it we'll be listening to wedding bells and eating cake."

* * *

Matt Dillon strode along the front porch of the Strathmore farmhouse his parents had passed along to Matt after their 50ᵗʰ wedding anniversary, when they'd packed up and moved to Phoenix.

"It's your turn now, son." Matt's dad had hugged his son and handed him the keys. Then he and Matt's mom, who didn't look much older than the flower child she'd been when Matt's dad had fallen head over heals in love with her during an extended holiday in San Francisco, had driven off to warmer climes.

Now, without mom or dad to turn to for advice and not sure how to dig himself out of the hole he'd buried himself in with the only woman he'd ever cared about, Matt paced and worried and paced and worried some more. How in blazes was he ever going to convince Irene that she mattered more to him than the Calgary stampede or any rodeo on earth after throwing down with her the way he had?

What in hell could have gotten into me telling Irene if she didn't show up at the rodeo I'd be rethinking the wedding. Even a moron with half a brain would know what a spitfire like Irene would do with an ultimatum like that.

"Well, me lad. Sounds like you've got that part figured out just fine. The question is, how are you planning to dig out of the hole ye've plopped yerself into?"

Matt jumped like he'd been struck by a bolt of lightening.

"What? Who are you? Where'd you come from?" Matt rubbed his eyes to make sure he hadn't conjured up the vision stretched out in his porch swing, looking for all the world like she'd always belonged there. One who had, moreover, apparently read his mind.

Mother Shipton stood up from the swing, shook out her long black skirt and wrapped the purple shawl closer around her shoulders. "Let's just say I have a vested interest in taking care of the Shipton family. Seeing as how they're all my direct descendants. Surely you've enough brains to figure out that little lassie of yours isn't just one of those cookie cutter cuties that hangs around that there rodeo ye've gotten yerself into such a mess over, haven't ye?"

Matt shook his head. "Are you real?"

"Of course I'm real. The question me lad, is have you gathered up your wits enough to know what yer next move's going to be?"

"You're—I've seen your picture! I've heard Mimi's stories about the famous family ancestor! *You're* Mother Shipton? From—what was it? The 1500's?"

"I am. So let's stop wasting time and you tell me. Are your wits all together again?"

"Oh I've gathered them up again, all right. In fact, there's only one possible move to make in this situation and that's complete and absolute groveling. I've only been pacing for the past hour trying to decide whether or not getting down on my knees and begging would do the trick or if I should just lie down on the ground in front of her and not get up till she forgives me. To be honest, ma'am, I don't mind at all what century you hopped in here from, I'd just be grateful for any advice you think might work."

Mother choked back laughter. Lillian and Irene had both sworn he was bright. Now all she had to do was give him a bit of instruction, coupled with a few threats to life and limb if he ever pulled a stupid stunt like this again, and things ought to work out just fine.

Following a very serious heart-to-heart between the two, Matt finally stopped Mother with one more question.

"I don't want to make you mad, ma'am"

"Well then, ye better fix that tongue in your head. You can call me Mother or Grandmother if you must, but I don't cotton to ma'am one little bit. I ain't yer local school teacher."

"Yes ma'am, I mean Mother. I understand."

"Now what was your question?"

"It's about the wedding. Honest, Mother, I don't have a good feeling about that gathering at all. It seems to me the wedding ought to be something special between Irene and myself, and just a few of our closest friends and family. Neither Irene nor I are big crowd people, and I don't want to insult anyone by leaving them out, and the fact of the matter is, if we hold that wedding anywhere around these parts it's going to turn into nothing short of a gigantic circus performance. Or rather, rodeo show."

"Well, is that all that's worrying you? Smart young lad like you ought to have it all figured out. Once you get down on your knees again, and you do a real good job of convincing that lovely woman you're lucky enough to have wanting to marry you that the only thing you want is to escape the rest of the world and go make her your wife, she's going to fall into your arms. So the only thing you need to do is get your bag, put it in your truck, run her into the city to pick up her own bag, which Lillian will have already packed. Then you head for the airport, stop at the West Jet Information Desk, ask for an envelope left for you by Lillian Shipton and she'll hand you your tickets, your itinerary, and your instructions covering exactly what to do and where to go once you get to Las Vegas. Now write down your credit card number and don't forget that expiry date thingy and give it to me. I'll see that Lillian gets all the information she needs, and she'll call you as soon as she books the flight to tell you what time you need to be at the airport. And don't worry one bit about friends and relatives and all that nonsense. You just leave that to Lillian and me. We'll have it all worked out with no hurt feelings anywhere. You just get yourself on over to Vegas and you'll find everything you and Irene need waiting right there for you to tie the knot."

"Mother, you're an angel. Can I hug you? I mean, you won't evaporate will you?"

Mother burst into delighted laughter. "You come on over here and let me give you the biggest hug you've ever had." She grabbed hold of Matt and pulled him into her arms for an all-encompassing mother of the universe style hug.

"Now don't you worry about anything. You get on that phone of yours and convince the love of your life you need her to come out here right now. I'll whisk on back to town and see that Lillian gets Irene's bags packed."

Matt nodded and pulled the cell phone out of his pocket.

Matt put the cell phone up to his ear, pressed a button and started to wave at Mother. One minute she'd been there and the next, she was gone. *Damn, I hope I didn't dream all that up.*

"Irene? Listen, sweetheart, I'm the biggest fool in the world and I know it. I love you. I don't want you to do anything you don't want to do, and I will never again ever talk to you like I did the other day. Please, sweetheart, will you come out here and let me make it up to you and give me the chance to convince you that I love you more than anything else in the world?"

Matt held the phone to his ear, his grin growing wider with every second that passed. "Yes, please, come now. I love you. I'll be right here waiting for you. Oh, and if Mother arrives before you leave, tell her thanks."

Matt laughed into the phone. "I'll explain when you get here. Just hurry."

Chapter Twenty-One

Bewitched

"I've never in my life seen anything so spectacular." Irene looked up into the smiling face of her soon to be husband.

They stood on the balcony of their 110th floor suite and gazed out at millions of blinking lights while they sipped from the bottle of complimentary champagne the Stratosphere had left in their room. Irene figured they had to be the happiest couple that had ever stood wrapped in each other's arms while what seemed like the entire universe celebrated the night before their wedding.

"I know you're one talented guy," she wrapped her arms around Matt's neck and pulled his head down so she could brush her lips across his, "and nobody's questioning your determination, but how did all this happen?" She swept her arm out, encompassing Vegas and all its lights.

"I guess you can chalk it up to a wee bit of magic." Matt grinned and Irene pursed her lips.

"Matt Dillon. I've got more than just a sneaking suspicion you've been conspiring behind my back with a pair of witchy little women who know a heck of a lot more about magic than a certain good ol' cowboy currently trying to do a snow job on the soon to be Mrs. Matt Dillon."

Matt grinned and Irene burst out laughing. "Okay, boy. Out with it. Just exactly what have Lillian and Mimi and a certain century hopping grandmother been up to while we've been flying across the country?"

"Oh, nothing more than their normal amount of meddling."

Irene shook her head. "I should have known they were up to something when they told me to get on the plane and never mind the details. So where are they? If you think I'm going to believe those nosy little ladies are sitting at home knitting while we're getting ready to tie the knot in one of the most spectacular wedding chapels I've ever laid eyes on, you've definitely got me mixed up with some little ol' gal that fell off a turnip truck."

Matt threw back his head and burst out laughing. "Oh, never would I make that mistake."

Irene gave him a smug little smile and held up her glass for a refill of the bubbly.

"Don't get me wrong. I'm thrilled about all this. It's gorgeous and I couldn't have wished for a better wedding venue than the Chapel in the Clouds. The room, with the lace and lavender and all those gardenias and roses. They're beautiful, and exactly what those self-same nosy little women we've been talking about would consider perfect to decorate the chapel where I was preparing to marry the only man I'd ever consider spending the rest of my life with."

Matt topped off both their glasses, set the bottle down and grinned at his soon to be wife. "I gave Mother my credit card number for Lillian who called me and told me to pick up our tickets for the eight o'clock flight from the West Jet counter at the airport. When I got the tickets, the woman handed me an extra envelope with the reservation for the limo from the airport to the Stratosphere, the confirmation for the Suite number and instructions for me to take you to the Chapel where a lady by the name of Cora would have everything ready for you to inspect." Matt held his hands palms up in a gesture of surrender. "That's all I know. I swear. I just followed instructions and did what I was told. What else was I supposed to do, I mean, the orders were from Lillian!"

"That proves you're one very smart cowboy, not even bothering to argue with her." Irene pulled him closer and hugged him tighter.

"Whew. I've been kinda sweating about how you'd react to them planning everything out for us 'cause honestly, love, I don't have a clue what else they might have planned."

"Oh, don't worry about that. I'll make them suffer a bit just for the fun of it, but knowing them the way I do, there's nothing that I won't be expecting. Now, what about that super comfy chaise over there? Seems like we're wasting way too much of this magical night talking."

Matt grinned and picked her up, carrying her straight across the balcony to the chaise lounge, where they sunk into the soft cushions and settled down for some heart stopping kisses and spectacular snuggles under what seemed to be a billion artificial stars. Irene smiled happily in the arms of the man she loved and resolved to simply float along with all the magical surprises that she was now pretty sure were only just beginning.

* * *

Lillian's ringtone roused Irene the next morning.

"Hello," she mumbled into the phone.

"Good morning sunshine! Are you all set to enjoy some of this fabulous Vegas warmth?"

"What I should be doing is bawling the heck out of you for all the manipulation all of you have been doing behind the scenes here, but you are the best sister anyone could ever wish for. The wedding venue is gorgeous, the flowers, the decorations, this room, the champagne, it's magical, Lilli, just like you."

Lillian blinked back a few tears and snuffled into the phone. "You're my sister,

Reenie, I couldn't let your most special day go by without magic. Now, if you'll just send that young man of yours out the door and tell him to head down to Room 923, I'll bring Cora to you in fifteen minutes. She's the marriage angel who's pulled all this together for us. We've got some dresses for you to pick from and don't worry about Matt, he's in good hands too. Tell him there's a wizard named Alfred who'll be meeting him in Room 923, and he'll take care of everything."

"Wow, talk about a whirlwind." Irene joined Matt at the breakfast table on their patio and picked up the coffee he'd poured her.

"I take it that was sister Lillian with your marching orders for the day?"

"Nope, not mine, yours."

"Uh-oh. What's she got in store for me?"

"Don't have a clue. The only thing she told me was to send you down to Room 923 where a wizard named Alfred is going to transform you into a cover model from Gentleman's Quarterly."

"Oh my God. Guess there'll be some cussing and yelling going on down there if anybody thinks I'm marrying my best gal without my lucky cowboy boots and my best Calgary signature Stetson."

Irene laughed. "Best thing you can do is grin and bear it, darlin'. Besides, you know Lillian, she'd never set you up to be turned into anything but the handsomest cowboy in the universe, which is exactly what you already are."

"Yeah. I get you, especially since we both know she's going to get her way anyhow."

"Exactly. Might as well sit back and enjoy the process. So I guess I'd better take my marching orders and make my way on down to 923." He planted a kiss on the top of Irene's head, grabbed his cowboy hat off the hall table and headed for the door.

"Have fun," Irene called after him.

Minutes later a knock on the door brought Lillian and an older lady with an armful of packages, followed by two young Mexican girls arms loaded with billowing white gowns.

"What is all this?" Irene's eyes popped open as she watched while the girls spread the gowns out across the couch and on the table and over the back of the other chair in the room.

"I had her bring six of them." Lillian smiled and motioned towards the grey-haired lady who'd just deposited half a dozen large plastic bags on the floor in front of the couch. "This is Cora. She's the good witch of weddings."

"Of course she is," Irene murmured under her breath. "It's very nice to meet you Cora. I hope my sister hasn't been working you too hard this morning."

"My pleasure, Miss Shipton, I'm enchanted to work with such a beautiful bride."

"It's Irene, please, and thank you very much. I've known my sister since I was in my crib, which means if she tells me to turn myself over to you that's exactly what I'm going to do, so whatever you want, you'll find me putty in your hands."

Lillian clapped her hands together. "Wonderful. Let's get started."

"Okay, but where's Mother?"

"Oh don't you worry about her. She's flitting about here, there and everywhere, getting acquainted with this exciting new to her city.

Watch out Vegas. Irene could hardly wait to see what kind of mischief her century hopping ancestor could get herself into exploring the City of Sin.

* * *

Strobe lights flashed, bells jangled and an endless stream of silver coins dropped into plastic tubs as Mother entered the gaming floor of Caesar's Palace casino, where the architects had pulled out all stops in designing a multi-sensory panorama contrived to entice everyone into joining the rows and rows of sunburned, tanned and stark white bodies perched on stools and pushing buttons or pulling handles – depending upon their fancy. Mother, whose 15th Century experience with gaming leaned towards the "tubs of pleasure" found in British spas like Bath, Epson and Tunbridge Wells, stood and acclimated her eyes to the neon lit darkness.

By all the Gods and Goddesses. Caesar himself would have been impressed.

"That he would have." A short-statured, ginger haired man with a Rip Van Winkle beard appeared at Mother's elbow.

"Mike Lodestone. You old sinner. I figured I might hook up with you in this self-proclaimed City of Sin."

"My stompin' grounds, for sure. A bit out of your way though. If I recollect rightly our last meeting was the Pagan Cultural Festival one of your great, great grandgirl's was attending at Oxford."

"That's right, and wasn't one of the boys from your lineage an instructor with that group?"

"That would be my Thad. He's a professor at Oxford now." Mike's shoulders straightened and his chest pushed out a little farther when he talked about the boy."

"You've every right to be proud as punch." Mother smiled. "I'm actually here in town because one of mine's about to get hitched. Not sure if you'd remember, but the girls came to their sister and aunt's graduation."

"It wouldn't be that little red-headed spitfire you were riding herd on, now would it?"

"The very same. She'll be leading the cowboy she's marrying a right merry dance for the rest of his days, I'm thinking."

Mike threw back his head and laughed. "Seems to me I recall an incident with the magician's white rabbit and one of your very own descendant's cauldron pot."

"That's Irene. She's every bit as nosy and hard headed now as she was back then. Lovely girl. I'm actually here at Caesar's looking for a necklace that'll fit the occasion."

"Well then, fate's played her hand just fine. You'll recall I've been in your debt ever since you showed up in the middle of the Mojave with a jug of water and whisked me back to civilization. What were you doing out there anyhow? I never did get the story on how a witch from centuries old England ended up rescuing a dying prospector in the middle of an American desert."

Mother grinned. "A minor misunderstanding between sometime friends and sometime competitors."

Mike lifted an eyebrow and waited for her to continue.

"Sadie Simpson and I were enjoying a bit of high-flying sport. I'd acquired a new broom and I guess I was showing off more than just a mite. Anyway, Sadie got sick and tired of my loops and whirls, and in a fit of pique she whipped up a gust of wind that ended up being a whole lot more powerful than even she intended. It caught me skirts and whipped me butt over teakettle till the next thing I knew I was whirling around in the middle of a sandstorm. Tossed me clear across the ocean and dumped me right in the middle of the biggest sandpile I'd ever seen in my life. Of course, once I figured out she'd sent me clean into the Americas, I shook out my skirts and prepared to rev her up again, when a pile of what I'd taken to be bleached bones sat up not a dozen yards from where I stood, and there you were, as sorry looking a sight as I'd ever seen."

"Well now, considering the fact that I was damn near dead you couldn't exactly blame me for not looking my best."

"Ever the peacock." Mother laughed. "Anyways, it's glad I am to see you again."

"And I you as well, and I'll be pleased if you'll give your friend Sadie a big hug and my sincerest thanks. Now, how about the two of us amble around a bit so's I can introduce you to a few of the regulars. We call ourselves the Spirited Eights."

"Unusual."

"Yep. Like us. Kind of a take on the *Crazy Eights.*"

"Very clever. So I'm curious. Since quite obviously none of you can actually pull those levers how do you go about playing the slot machines."

"I thought you'd never ask. It was Madeline's idea. She's a former casino manager and while she was living, she used to amuse herself during the long hours of watching the floor by picking players and betting on them – just for fun of course. She called them her ponies."

"Blimey, What a terrific idea. Tell me more."

"Sure. We meet once a week on the day they have the Mega slot tournaments. Each of us picks a pony from the players on the carousel. We put up stakes depending on what we've picked for the theme of the night, and then we ride our ponies 'til one of us comes up a winner."

Mother clapped her hands. "Fan-damn-tastic. So, what's the theme tonight? Can someone like me join your group or is it exclusive?"

"Of course it's exclusive, but we're all permitted to bring guests and I'd be more than honored."

Mother beamed.

"As for the theme. Tonight we're doing glitter and gold. Let's go meet the gang."

Floating over the throng below Mike led the way across the gaming floor to a raised platform where a band played and a group of extraordinary spirits, each representing their era and their own unique personalities, gathered at a round table which was normally reserved for private meetings, and had quite obviously been co-opted by the Spirited Eights for their weekly get together.

"I hope nobody's claimed that pony with the big brimmed hat and the marvelous purple feather." Mother pointed to a full bodied, big skirted woman parked on an end spot with the air of someone who planned on being there a long, long time."

"I'm sure there'll be no problem. After all, custom demands that guests be honored."

Mother clapped her hands. "Splendid. Now, let's meet everyone."

* * *

Mike strode up to the table and clapped his hands.

"Hey everyone, meet a very good friend of mine. This here's Mother Shipton."

"Of Knaresborough fame?" A slender man with thinning hair combed over a baldspot, a nose that needed no apologies, and a British accent that Mother at once recognized as a citizen from home spoke up.

"The same," Mother replied with a smile.

"Percival's one of your countrymen," Matt nodded to the man, and proceeded to make introductions. "Mother, this is Percival Montgomery, better known by all of us as Percy. He spent a lifetime as a conductor on the famous Orient Express, the train that inspired one of the best mystery novels ever written, also by another of your countrymen – or I should say countrywomen."

"Dame Agatha Christie, of course."

"The Orient Express remains one of the finest passenger trains of all time. Of course now it's become a tourist attraction but she's still a beauty."

"Indeed she is." Percy agreed. "It's very good to make your acquaintance Mother Shipton, and I'd be pleased if we found time to have a bit of a chat while you're here."

"My pleasure."

"Hey what are we, chopped liver?" A gangly carrottop youngster with buck teeth and a dimple in each cheek enhanced by his big grin, waved a hand to indicate the rest of the gang and winked at Mother.

"Okay Gary, don't get your tail in a knot." Mike flung out his arm in an all-encompassing gesture. "Ladies and gentlemen, may I present Mother Shipton. An old friend and guest who'd be pleased to join us for tonight's festivities."

"Perfect." A little old lady with short white hair and big blue eyes smiled at Mother. "Now we'll still be eight. Mavis, one of our regulars has taken a little trip and tonight we were only going to be seven. Of course seven's a wonderful number, but it's still off, from what we're used to, you understand." Breathless she nodded her head and flashed gleaming white teeth to everyone at the table.

"Excellent analogy Lydia. I hope we're all in accord." Mike glanced around the table and satisfied with the nods that indicated unanimous agreement he turned to Mother.

"Look like you're in for a night of high stakes fun. Oh yes, before I forget. Mother spotted a rather flashy pony parked at the end of the carousel. She really fancies that one if no one objects." After another look around, polling the table, Mike turned to the two members who had yet to welcome Mother.

"Come on Mother, wait until you meet the other two in this motley crew."

Mother's eyes lit upon an incredible visage, and Mike, seeing the direction of her gaze, beckoned to the woman who rose from her seat and sashayed toward them. A golden gown of crushed velvet hugged her curves, dipping in front to expose impressive cleavage. Her strawberry blonde hair was drawn up into a tall creation of perfectly formed ringlets.

"This is Miss Lace Heart," Mike said by way of introduction. "She owned a saloon in Abilene during the 1870s."

Mother couldn't prevent a wicked grin, though she tried to cover it with her hand. She knew a lot about women who had owned saloons.

Lace threw her head back and guffawed. "I know what you're thinking, Sugar, but my establishment wasn't like any you ever saw."

"Really?" Mother examined her more closely. "You didn't have -- girls workin' there?"

"Why, sure, I had me a good crew. A dozen of the purtiest gals you've ever laid eyes on. But my gals were special." She leaned a hip against a slot machine and pulled paper and a little sack from the depths of her bosom, then took her time rolling a smoke. Mother watched, fascinated. "See, my ladies were just that, when it came to carnal behavior. Gentlemen were not allowed upstairs to frequent their boudoirs."

Mother gaped. "Then, how

"How did we make money, you mean?" Lace blew out a cloud of smoke. "All sorts of ways. The men bought 'em drinks, of course.

Thing is, the drinks our bartender made for the gals were colored water, so we pocketed the liquor money. And my sweeties knew more about playin' cards than anyone in this here casino does, I'll wager." She laughed, "That was a pun, wasn't it? And, too, the men shelled out a silver dollar every time they wanted a dance. Believe me, they always wanted a dance."

"But--" Mother had so many questions. "If the menfolk didn't get to, well, you know, weren't they peeved?"

"Only the newcomers to town. The ones who lived in Abilene knew the ropes. And --" She leaned closer and spoke into Mother's ear. "Each of my beauties carried a silver derringer and knew how to use it. In case any feller tried to push things too far." She stepped back and finished her smoke. "If you're wonderin', yeah, there was a real cathouse in town. Just down the street, in fact. But I made triple the money they did. Seems men want what they can't have."

Mother stuck out her hand and Lace shook it firmly. "You're what my girls would call . . . cool. It's my honor to meet you."

Mother's looked around the table. "You said eight, didn't you? I only count seven."

Mike's lips twisted into a wry grin. "I wanted to make sure you were ready for this one." He pointed toward a slot machine which was hung with an "out of order" sign. A slender figure occupied the seat. Raven hair, so black it seemed shot through with blue highlights, cascaded down the back in waist-length waves.

Aha. Yet another pretty woman, Mother surmised.

Then the figure turned and stood.

Mother was surprised at her own reaction. Had her heart still beat, its pace would have quickened. If her lungs still functioned, breath would have caught in her throat. Her insides seemed to turn inside out, and her mouth hung open.

The young man approached with a slightly rolling gait, as if he were traversing an uneven surface. Or a moving deck.

Mike snickered. "Don't worry about it, Mother. I've never seen a woman, alive or dead, who could resist Jamie Snow. Jamie, this is . . ."

"A lovely lady, to be sure," the vision proclaimed, taking Mother's hand in his own and raising to his lips.

Mike was chattering on, but Mother only heard every other word. Something about "1728" and "the seas."

The seas, yes. Jamie Snow even smelled like the sea, a tang of salt wafting from a breeze he seemed to carry along with him. Mike didn't need to say the word "pirate." What else could this fellow be? He reminded her of someone, yet she knew she'd never met him during all the years she'd drifted through time.

He was, indeed, the most perfect human creature she'd ever beheld. A black and white bandana, wrapped around his forehead, held the glistening hair in place, preventing it from tumbling forward across his shoulders. His smile, slow and lazy, drew her attention to his full lips. A white, gauzy shirt, open to the waist, exposed perfectly tanned skin and molded muscles. Embarrassed, she snapped her gaze back to his face. A fish hook, glinting with the unmistakable gleam of genuine gold, dangled from his left ear. Jamie's eyes met hers, and his smile widened.

Oh, those eyes! Fringed with incredibly thick black lashes, giving the impression of mascara and eyeliner. Mint green eyes. Green as the newest leaves of Spring. The clear, deep green of Caribbean waters. Caribbean . . . Pirate . . .

"Johnnie Depp!" she shouted. A movie she had loved, much to the Sister Witches' amusement. "Captain Jack Sparrow!"

Jamie's smile disappeared and those beautiful eyes rolled heavenward.

"Now you've done it," Mike chided. "He's seen the movies, too, and he hates being compared to --"

"Blasted Johnny blasted Depp!" Jamie roared, and stalked away.

* * *

Matt made his way down the elevator to the 9th floor, strode along the hall and stopped in front of 923. A quick knock brought the muffled invitation to come on in. Matt turned the handle, pushed the door open and stepped inside.

A dapper little man wearing a navy suit and sporting a finely trimmed mustache, stepped forward and held out his hand.

"Greetings, Mr. Dillon. It's a pleasure to meet you. My name is Alfred and I'll be taking care of everything you need for the wedding."

Matt took the man's offered hand shook it and followed him into the sitting room of what was obviously an executive suite.

"Good to meet you. I don't know much about this wedding stuff," Matt settled into one of the chairs and accepted a cup of coffee. " I'm just hoping you understand that I'm kind of set in my ways about a couple of things."

"*Ah*, you mean your hat and boots." Alfred smiled his beaming smile again and nodded his head. "Don't you worry lad, we get lots of cowboys here in Las Vegas. As you know from your own experience, we host the national rodeo finals every year. I've been told you're last year's world champion saddle bronc rider." Alfred flashed that smile again, and Matt smiled back.

"Thanks," he acknowledged, "just my lucky year I guess."

"Well, put all your worries away. Your charming sister-in-law-to-be was very specific that we were planning a full-on cowboy wedding and I think you'll find everything I have laid out in the other room to your satisfaction. Please take your time, finish your coffee, and then I'll send you in there to take your pick. I doubt it'll take us long to have you all tucked out and ready for this afternoon's ceremony."

"Sounds like a deal." Matt drained his cup, set it down on the table and stood up. "Which room?" He motioned to the three closed doors, two on one side of the room and one on the other.

"That one on the left."

* * *

Back in Room 11006, Lillian and Cora each held a gown for Irene's inspection.

"I like the one you're holding, Cora. But not yours, Lillian."

Lillian replaced the rejected gown and picked up another. "This is my favorite." She held the gown up for Irene's inspection and watched her sister's mouth pop open.

Thought so. Lillian smiled when Irene's eyes lit up as she reached for the gown. She held it up in front of herself and walked across to the full-length mirror.

The lovely white linen sheath with scooped neck, snugged in at the waist and dropped in lacy ruffles to just above the knee, where it formed a cutaway with the sides and back of the dress, then dropped in even more ruffles to within an inch of the floor. The cutaway opening was perfect for displaying the fabulous pair of turquoise and silver cowboy boots that Irene had already picked from one of Cora's packages.

"Go try it on," Lillian urged, and without hesitation Irene lifted the dress in her arms and headed into the bedroom.

"You were absolutely right, Lillian." Cora smiled approval as she recalled their earlier conversation.

"She'll pick the linen and lace with the ruffles and the cutout front for showing off her cowboy boots," Lillian had said, "but let's take half a dozen of them, just in case I'm wrong."

"Oh, my word!" Cora gasped when Irene stepped out of the bedroom.

"You look like an angel," Lillian breathed.

Irene's face lit up in a mile-wide smile. "As if you didn't know just how devilish this particular angel can be." She walked across and wrapped her arms around her sister. "I love you, Lilli. Thank you for this, and for saving my engagement and for putting together this spectacular, perfect wedding. I don't have enough words to tell you how much it all means."

"Don't be silly. I didn't save anything. All you two needed was a little gentle meddling, and you know how good I am at that, little sister." Lillian hugged Irene back.

* * *

Cora and her girls had departed with arms full of dresses and packages, leaving Irene with a matching lace bra and panties to go under the dress, the prized pair of turquoise boots and of course, the crown jewel in the collection, the gorgeous linen and lace concoction. Lillian knew the combination would transform Irene into a cowboy princess, the perfect match for the handsome cowboy who would be waiting for her at the altar. The two women sat down at the table to enjoy the pot of tea and one of the scones that room service had just delivered.

"It's all so amazing." Irene buttered her scone, took a generous bite and smiled at her sister. "You really are a good witch, you know."

"Of course."

"And just exactly what does that make me?" Mother materialized in the other chair and reached across the table for one of the cups.

"I knew it," Lillian laughed. "I figured if this pot of tea and the smell of those yummy scones didn't bring you back here, nothing would. So let's hear it. What kind of mischief have you been up to out alone on the streets of Sin City?"

"Okay, Miss Smarty Pants, wait until you see what I've been up to this morning and I reckon you'll be singing another tune."

Both Lillian and Irene fixed eager eyes on the small package Mother produced from the multi-colored gypsy bag she'd obviously acquired during her morning jaunts.

"What—what is that, Mother?" Irene eyed the package hesitantly. *I hope I'm not about to get a good luck potion of eye of newt or wart of toad.*

"*Pshaw.* Ye of little faith." Mother proved once again that reading minds was the same as hearing words insofar as she was concerned. "How about you humor an old lady and get dressed up in all that finery? I betcha Lillian's got one of those fancy new phone cameras so I can take a picture of the two of you getting ready for the big event."

Irene grinned. "Okay, change the subject. But I agree, we do need a picture of me and Lillian. I don't suppose you—" She looked expectantly at her centuries old ancestor, but Mother shook her head and smiled.

"I'm afraid you'll have to keep pictures of me in your mind's eye. Seems there's something about the incorporeal body that doesn't show up too well in those new-fangled talking cameras you all seem to love."

Lillian smiled and nodded to Irene. "It's too bad, but Katherine has promised each of us a copy of her portrait so whenever Mother decides to whisk herself off to some other century, at least we'll have her likeness around to keep us company."

Irene grinned. "Oh, don't worry, Lillian. I know how to get her back anytime we need her. I'll just get myself into trouble. Or better yet, I'll have me a little Dillon girl and she can help me get into the kind of mischief that'll bring Grandmother flying back in a heartbeat."

"Get off with you." The subject of their banter clapped her hands. "Now go put on your finery while Lillian shows me how to operate that contraption of hers.

* * *

While Lillian and Mother were finishing their tea, Irene slipped into her dress and pulled the cowboy boots over her slender feet.

"Okay, what do you think?" She spoke from the doorway of the bedroom.

"*Ohhh!*" Lillian breathed the sound.

"I'd say that's just about perfect." Mother appeared behind Irene without seeming to have moved a step.

"It's spooky how you do that." Irene twisted her head to see Mother standing behind her.

"Stay still just a minute and let me get this catch closed."

Irene felt the weight of a cold metal object slide around her neck and settle in the crevice between her breasts.

"What in the world?" She walked towards the mirror and gasped at the beautifully wrought silver and gold necklace. It was studded with sparkling diamonds and set off with a turquoise eye the size of a quail egg that lay nestled between her breasts.

"*Wow.* Mother, wherever did you get this necklace? I swear I've never seen anything so beautiful in my life."

Lillian joined the two women and mimicked Irene's awestruck *wow*. Then she turned to Mother. "Where exactly did you get this? It must have cost a fortune." Lillian's suspiciously raised brows triggered a laughing fit on Mother's part.

"Don't be silly, Lillian. As if I'd pilfer anything that I'd be giving to the most beautiful daughter in the world. You'll perhaps be remembering that I've a bit more knowledge about the what and whereabouts of some of the world's treasures than most of the mortals who drive themselves batty trying to find 'em. It just so happens I took advantage of my free time this morning to whisk back into the 1920's and have a little chat with a fellow named Lodestone Mike. He sent his good wishes for the wedding, by the way." She smiled at Irene, who could only shake her head and smile back.

"Anyway, to continue, Mike was out in the desert dying of thirst when I happened along and whisked him over to an oasis I knew about and saved his life. That happened right before he discovered the biggest vein of silver that's ever been found in the State of Nevada."

Lillian and Irene listened in fascination as Mother told them about hopping back into another century, visiting with the man who'd discovered and kept hidden the secret of the Lost Vegas Silver Mine, the mine hundreds had searched for after Lodestone Mike had gone to that big silver mine in the sky but never found.

"Well, to make a long story short," Mother continued, "Mike was only too happy to repay me for saving his life by directing me to the location of a chest of baubles he'd hidden away before he passed on, and this one struck my fancy. It seems I wasn't far off either, seeing that it fits exactly where it is like it was made for it and just held for a century waiting to grace the bosom of the most beautiful bride in any century I've ever visited.

"Oh, Mother!"

"It's happier than a toad on a lily pad I be, me girl. Now, I'll leave you two to finish up your preparation while I go take a wee bit of a nap. It's old I must be getting cause century hopping didn't used to fag me near this much."

Lillian shook her head, and hugged Irene as they stood together and gazed at the exquisite necklace that did indeed look like it had been crafted in another century.

"We'll be giving that back to Mother to carry home to Calgary for us once the wedding is over, I'm thinking." Lillian unfastened the necklace and balanced the heavy metal in her hand. "We'd have one heck of a time making up a story that'd satisfy those customs guys."

"You bet your boots we'll have Grandmother take it back." Irene shuddered at the thought of explaining where she'd acquired what was obviously a museum piece. "Getting locked up in an American jail is definitely not on my honeymoon itinerary."

"Speaking of honeymoons, have you and Matt given the matter any thought?"

"Actually, you'll probably laugh, but we're planning on tossing a tent and our camping gear into the back of our Supercab, loading up our horses, hooking onto Matt's double horse trailer and heading out to the Brazeau Lake area for a few days and then on up the Rockies to Jasper. We both figure that after all the glitz and glitter of Las Vegas, we'll be needing to spend some time with Mother Nature."

"That sounds like the perfect honeymoon for the two of you and a great way to start off your marriage. So, let's have one more cup and finish off this pot and then we've got to get busy. Three o'clock will be here before we know it, and once we finish getting you ready, I've got to slip down to my room and make myself presentable. It's not every day I'm lucky enough to watch my little sister marry the man of her dreams."

"Are you standing up for us? We didn't even think of that. Matt doesn't have a best man here either, but I guess Cora's got that all figured out."

"That's right. You just don't worry your little head about details. Others are taking care of that for you today. The only thing you need to worry about is getting into the shower and being ready for the hairdresser. Who's going to be showing up here in exactly thirty minutes, in fact.

"My gosh, Lillian. You think of everything." Irene's smile lit up the room and after she'd drained the last of her tea and headed for the shower, Lillian watched her leave and lovingly wrapped her arms around herself and squeezed with happiness.

* * *

Downstairs in 903 Matt stepped out of the bedroom and stopped for Alfred's inspection. "You're going to have all the ladies swooning," the older man said, and Matt smiled.

"Only one little lady I hope to have that effect on. Thank you, Alfred, this is exactly what I would have wanted but would never in the world have known where to find on my own."

"Hubba, hubba!" A woman's voice spoke from the doorway of one of the other rooms in the suite and Matt whirled to face his audience.

"Katherine! Lillian didn't tell us you were coming."

"It's a surprise for Irene." Katherine moved aside and Parker stood in the doorway. "Darling, I'd like you to meet your future brother-in-law slash uncle-in-law. It gets really confusing so let's just go with the brother thing. Parker, this is Matt Dillon."

Parker grinned and stepped forward with his hand outstretched. "I promise not to make any of those jokes about your name I'm sure you've heard a thousand times."

Matt grinned and shook the offered hand. "I've heard 'em a few times all right, though truth to tell, being a bronc rider, it's not that big a deal. Most folks figure I picked it up as a stage name."

"Well, whatever the name, I'm pleased to meet you and I sure hope it's okay I've been drafted as your best man for this occasion."

"Don't mind one bit, and thanks for accepting. I've had a bit of experience with Lillian's kind of drafting, so I'm just glad to hear that her recruiting process was peaceful."

Katherine beamed. She knew her husband and her brother-in-law to be were going to get along like they'd known each other all their lives.

"You two look mighty fine yourselves." Matt admired Katherine's turquoise and silver sheath, set off by the sparkling diamond showcased by the deep V-neckline. "That's quite the rock you've got there."

Katherine beamed. "Thanks. Parker gave it to me at our honeymoon dinner in Maui. I can hardly wait to see Irene. Lillian showed me the boots we both knew she'd choose, so I made it a point to choose a dress to match."

"Well, my compliments." Matt turned to Parker. "And thanks for wearing cowboy duds for the occasion, I'm honored. I hope the ladies didn't twist your arm too hard."

Parker laughed at Matt's reference to his western cut white shirt and black string tie fitted with a turquoise rock, and black pants."

"Matt, my family's *Texan*. Complete with Apache ancestry from back in the day, something my Dad really takes to heart." Parker grinned. "You'd like him. And unless I'm in the middle of business that needs a suit, I'm in jeans, tees, and cowboy boots. These black dress boots are *mine,* right out of my own closet."

Matt grinned. "*Whew*! You don't know how much better that makes me feel."

"So where are you two off to for the honeymoon?" Katherine smiled approvingly when Matt told her about their plans for escaping the city and heading out into the country with a tent, their backpacks and their horses.

"Sounds absolutely perfect for Irene."

Parker couldn't resist. He knew his own bride very well indeed. "I could have taken you camping, honey, why didn't you say something?"

"I said it was perfect for *Irene.* You couldn't pay me to go camping."

"I've got her a honeymoon gift." Matt pulled his cell phone out of his pocket and opened his camera to one of the pictures in his "Irene" album. "What do you think?" He handed the camera to Kat.

"*Oh my God!* Look Parker!" She held the phone up so Parker could see the screen. Both of them gazed in awe at the golden Arabian mare that stood calmly munching on a handful of grain being held out for her pleasure.

"She's the most beautiful horse I've ever seen. Irene's going to go insane when she sees her. I'll tell you what, Matt, you've scored a home run for sure with this gift. And Parker, feel free to follow suit with that. *Not* the camping trip, the mare."

"I'll see what I can do. She's really something. And from what I've gotten to know of Irene, she's going to fall head over heels in love with that little lady."

Matt grinned and put the phone back in his pocket. "Thanks. I think so too. The only challenge is going to be keeping her from sticking her nose in the trailer and checking on the horses before we leave the ranch."

Katherine nodded. "I'm sure you'll think of something."

* * *

The Chapel gleamed in the glow of a thousand fairy lights as Katherine, Parker and Matt followed Cora down the aisle and took their places at the altar.

"The bride is on her way, and she doesn't know that her parents will be here to escort her down the aisle."

"Great! That's perfect! Where are they?" Matt scanned the room looking for the Shiptons.

"Yes, I'm going to get them now, they're just in the back." Cora stepped back from the altar. "I'm afraid you'll have to wait until after the ceremony to say hello because we need to have everyone in their places within the next five minutes."

Candles flickered on either side of the podium. Matt stood on one side and Katherine and Parker on the other.

"Oh, there you are, Mr. Drayton." Cora raised her voice and called out to someone behind them.

"You mean me?" Parker gave her a puzzled look and turned his head. "Dad! What are you doing here?"

"Well, you didn't think I was going to miss out on the chance to spend some more time with my new family, did you? And I certainly wasn't going to miss the wedding of my new daughter's sister. You do recall your father is an ordained member of the Apache Nation, don't you, son?"

"You're going to perform the ceremony," Katherine squeaked. "That is so perfect."

"Quiet everyone," Cora interrupted the reunion. "The bride's about to enter."

Irene swept through the door and began the traditional measured pace down the aisle. She was so focused on Matt as he waited for her at the altar that she didn't notice the two figures, one on either side, moving close to her until they each hooked an arm through hers.

"Mimi! Poppy!" Tradition flew through the door as one very happy daughter threw her arms around her parents and pulled all three of them into a family circle. "I didn't think you could get here in time!"

"Baby. Ye of little faith." Bill Shipton smiled down at his youngest daughter. "We wouldn't have missed this."

"Not if we'd had to fly on brooms." Mina Shipton whispered into her ear and reached out a hand to stroke her daughter's cheek.

"You know I finally know you're not really joking when you say that, don't you?" Irene whispered back.

"My dear, you've known that all your life. You just didn't know you knew it. Now, let's finish this walk down the aisle. Matt's waiting for you."

* * *

Justin Drayton smiled at Matt and Irene as they faced him, then turned to the gathering of guests in the room, opening his arms in an enveloping gesture.

"We are gathered together in the presence of family and friends, and ancestors seen and unseen but present nonetheless, to join in marriage Irene Shipton and Matt Dillon. Irene and Matt, will you please face each other and join hands."

When the couple had done so, he continued.

"Matt Dillon, do you take Irene Shipton to be your lawfully wedded wife, to work together and play together and dwell together as long as you both shall live?"

Matt looked down into Irene's eyes and took both of her hands in his own.

"Irene Shipton, I give you my life and my eternity. All that I have, all that I am, and all that I will ever be is yours. For the years of my life and forevermore, I will always be yours."

Justin turned to Irene. "Irene Shipton, do you take Matt Dillon to be your lawfully wedded husband, to work together and play together and dwell together as long as you both shall live?"

Still holding Matt's hands and looking up into his eyes, Irene spoke her vows.

"Matt Dillon, from today through forever you will be my husband. My heart will beat because of you. My eyes will see because of you. And I will love you forever."

Justin turned to Parker. "May I have the rings?"

Parker pulled the box out of his pocket and opened the lid to reveal two shining gold bands with Matt's Circle D brand spelled out in tiny diamonds across the top of each.

Justin took the rings from his son and turned back to the couple.

"Irene and Matt, as a ring is a circle which has no beginning or end, neither will true love ever end. Please exchange your rings."

While everyone watched in anticipation, they placed the rings on each other's fingers and held up their joined hands for everyone to see.

Justin gave the final blessing.

"In the words of my Apache ancestors, I give you this blessing.

Now you will feel no rain, for each of you will be shelter for the other.

Now you will feel no cold, for each of you will be warmth to the other.

Now you are two persons, but there is only one life before you.

May happiness be your companion and your days together be good and long upon the earth.

It is my great pleasure to pronounce you husband and wife. You may seal your vows with a kiss."

Epilogue

That Ol' Black Magic

Calgary Herald, the morning after the Stampede

Reigning champion Matt Dillon failed to show up for the rodeo finals, and the favorite to take over Dillon's position as world champion saddle bronc rider, Chance Mayfair, claimed to have received a visitation from Epona, goddess of horses. Mayfair claims this apparition told him that if he ever rode a horse at the Calgary stampede again, he'd become infected with a mysterious flesh-eating disease and would never ride again.

Sources reveal that Mr. Mayfair is under the care of a local psychiatrist who suspects that stress and a recent emotional breakup with his long-term partner seem to have caused Mr. Mayfair to have hallucinations. No further information is being released. Texas cowboy Darcy Harkins took home top money in the saddle bronc riding.

The End.

Jude is the daughter of Lillian, granddaughter of William Shipton and according to legend and family folklore, both Lillian and William are direct descendants of {*Ursula} {reputedly the witch known as Mother Shipton}*. Jude loves all magic and is a proud follower of her magical ancestor.

As an author Jude has published the mystery/romantic suspense novels *Deadly Secrets, Deadly Betrayal, Deadly Consequences and Deadly Lights*. She's also published the paranormal mystery novella *Street Justice* with John Wisdomkeeper

Mother Shipton and the Sister Witches is a collaborative work with author Gail Roughton based on fictional accounts of the lives of descendants of Ursula Shipton.

Gail Roughton Books published by BWL Publishing

To purchase any of Gail Roughton's books visit her BWL Author Page or request them in your local bookstore. Gail's books are available in eBook and Print at major retailers

https://bookswelove.net/roughton-gail/

The War-N-Wit, Inc. Series

The Witch – Book 1
Resurrection – Book 2
The Coven – Book 3
MeanStreet, LLC – Book 4

Stand Alone Novels

The Color of Seven
Vanished
Country Justice

Gail Roughton is a native of small-town Georgia whose Deep South heritage features prominently in much of her work. She's a retired paralegal who lived in a law office for over forty years, during which time she raised three children and quite a few attorneys. She kept herself more or less sane by writing novels and tossing the completed manuscripts into her closet, most of which have now emerged in published form. A cross-genre writer, her books range from humor to romance to thriller to horror and she's never quite sure what to expect when she sits down at the keyboard. She usually has a project or two burning on the back burner but never talks about them for fear of jinxing herself. This should come as no surprise to anyone who knows her.

Bibliography

http://www.crystalinks.com/mother_shipton.html Ursula Southeil (c. 1488 - 1561), better known as Mother Shipton, was an English soothsayer and prophetess. The first publication of her prophecies, which did not appear until 1641, eighty years after her death... Mother Shipton lived in the time of Henry VIII of England and predicted his victory over France in 1513 in the Battle of the Spurs. She also predicted the Dissolution of the Monasteries. This led to the redistribution of the wealth and land held by the monasteries to the emerging middle class and the existing noble families.

https://www.bibliotecapleyades.net/esp_shipton01.htm Ursula Sontheil reputedly was born in 1488 in Norfolk, England. From an early age she exhibited stunning psychic gifts of foresight and prophecy. She was a contemporary of Nostradamus, but, being a woman, was not allowed his level of education and lacked his medical and astrological training and the forbearance of royal friends at court to nurture and protect her. At the ripe old age of 24 she entered a difficult marriage to Toby Shipton.

Ursula Southeil (c. 1488–1561) (also variously spelt as Ursula Southill, Ursula Soothtell[1] or Ursula Sontheil[2][3]), better known as Mother Shipton, is said to have been an English soothsayer and prophetess. The first publication of her prophecies, which did not appear until 1641, eighty years after her reported death, contained a number of mainly regional predictions, but only two prophetic verses – neither of which foretold the End of the World, despite widespread assumptions to that effect.[4]

The following purportedly comes from the original script of Mother Shipton's Prophecies is from a photocopy passed down through generations of the Shipton family, author unknown, originating with Mina Fetterley Shipton circa. 1800 .

Mother Shipton's Prophecies
[Archaic spelling has been modernized]

A carriage without horse shall go.
Disasters fill the world with woe.
In London, Primrose Hill shall be,
Its centre hold a Bishop's See.
Around the world men's thoughts shall fly
Quick as the twinkling of an eye
And waters shall great wonders do,

How strange, and yet it shall come true.

Then upside down the world shall be,
And gold found at the root of tree.
Through towering hill proud men shall ride,
No horse nor ass move at his side.
Beneath the waters men shall walk;
Shall ride, shall sleep and even talk.
And in the air men shall be seen,
In white and black and even green.
A great man then shall come and go,
For prophecy declares it so.

In water iron then shall float
As easy as a wooden boat,
Gold shall be found in stream or stone,
In land that is as yet unknown.
Water and fire shall wonders do,
And England shall admit a Jew.

The Jew that once was held in scorn,
Shall of a Christian then be born. [borne?]
A house of glass shall come to pass
In ENGLAND - but alas!
A war will follow with the work,
Where dwells the pagan and the Turk.
The states will lock in fiercest strife
And seek to take each other's life.
When North shall thus divide South
The eagle build in lion's mouth.
Then tax and blood and cruel war
Shall come to every humble door.

Three times shall lovely sunny France
Be led to play a lovely dance,
Before the people shall be free.
The tyrant rulers shall she see.
Three rulers in succession be,
Each sprang from different dynasty.

Then, when fiercest fight is done
England and France shall be as one.
The British olive next shall twine
In marriage with the German vine.
Men walk beneath and over streams
Fulfilled shall be our strangest dreams.

All England's sons that plough the land -
Shall oft be seen with Book in hand.
The poor shall then True Wisdom know
And waters, wind, where corn did grow.
Great houses stand in far flung vale,
All covered o'er with snow and hail.

And now a word in uncouth rhyme
Of what shall be in future time,
For in the wondrous far off days,
The women shall adopt a craze
To dress like men and trousers wear
And cut off their lovely locks of hair.
They'll ride astride with brazen brow
As witches on a broomstick now

Then love shall die and marriage cease,
And nations wane as births decrease.

The wives shall fondle cats and dogs
And men live much the same as hogs.

In nineteen-hundred twenty-six
Build houses light of straw and sticks,

And roaring monsters with man atop
Do seem to eat the verdant crop.
And men shall fly as birds do now,
And give away the horse and plough.
When pictures live with movements free,
When boats like fishes swim the sea,
When men like birds shall scour the sky
Then half the world, blood drenched shall
die.

For then shall mighty war be planned
And fire and sword sweep the land.
But those who live the century through
In fear and trembling this will do;
Flee to the mountains and the dens
To bog and forest and wild fens
For storms shall rage and oceans roar,
When Gabriel stands on sea and shore
And when he blows his horn
Old worlds shall die and new be born.